THE
MACHINES
THAT
MAKE
US

Enigma Front 6

THE
MACHINES
THAT
MAKE
US

Enigma Front 6

TYCHE BOOKS LTD.

The Machines That Make Us
Copyright © 2023

MANAGING EDITOR
Chris Patrick Carolan

ASSOCIATE EDITORS
Renée Bennett, Michael Gillett,
Dan M. Hampton, D.E. Wright

Published by Tyche Books Ltd.
Calgary, Alberta, Canada
www.TycheBooks.com

Cover Art by Brent Nichols
Cover Design by Indigo Chick Designs
Interior Layout by M.L.D. Curelas

First Tyche Books Ltd Edition 2023
Print ISBN: 978-1-989407-59-2
Ebook ISBN: 978-1-989407-60-8

This book was funded in part by a grant from the Alberta Media Fund.

Alberta ∎

CONTENTS

FOREWORD:
THE MACHINES THAT MAKE US

Chris Patrick Carolan

None of the stories you are about to read were written by robots. When the submission call for this anthology went out in the Fall of 2019, that was not a disclaimer you were likely to have come across. The past four years have been a time of disruption, though. More on that later.

The word "robot" has been in the lexicon for just over one hundred years at this point, coined by Czech playwright Karel Čapek in his 1920 play, *R.U.R. - Rossum's Universal Robots*. Of course, stories of constructed lifeforms are as old as story itself and come to us from every corner of the world. The Greeks had the myth of Talos, a giant bronze automaton built by the god Hephaestus at the behest of Zeus. Jewish folklore features the golem, a figure shaped from clay or mud which is animated by placing written words in its mouth. A legend out of India describes mechanical guards being commissioned by the king Ajatasatru to guard Buddha's earthly remains.

Mary Shelley's novel *Frankenstein* gives us perhaps the most famous of all constructed lifeforms. In the original novel, the method by which Victor Frankenstein crafts his creation is left largely unexplained (the iconic lumbering brute stitched together from bits of scavenged cadavers with bolts sticking out of its neck is a later interpretation). Shelley describes Frankenstein looking on his creation as a thing of beauty, with yellow skin, black hair and lips, standing eight feet tall. But when his creation awakens, Victor Frankenstein reacts with revulsion. Cast out by his creator, the monster wanders the wilds, later to be taken in by an elderly blind man who teaches him to read. Through literacy he becomes eloquent and well-mannered, before being again driven away by people who fear him based on appearance alone. Enraged, he swears revenge against the creator who abandoned him.

What do the stories we tell about artificial lifeforms tell us about ourselves?

We are not gods. But as a species, we are very good builders. From the day the first early human struck one stone against another to fashion the first knife, we have worked to reshape our world to better suit our needs. It could be that these stories reveal humankind's innate impulse to create.

The stories we tell about the machines we make reveal our aspirations, and perhaps our fears as well. Fiction has long pondered whether our creations might one day surpass and supplant us. Is there a code we can write to imbue our constructed progeny with humility and empathy, if not humanity? Do the machines we make merely reflect our own hubris?

Consider *Star Trek: The Next Generation's* Lieutenant Commander Data. When they first meet on the *Enterprise* holodeck, Commander William Riker asks Data if he considers himself superior to humans. Data answers in the most analytical way possible. "I am superior, Sir, in many ways," he observes, a blunt statement of fact. "But I would gladly give it up to be human." The ultimate outsider, Data was always at his best when he was employed as a looking glass through which the viewer was encouraged to examine humanity's troubles and triumphs, as well as our faults and flaws. We certainly have no shortage of those.

None of the stories you are about to read were written by robots. When the submission call for this anthology went out in the Fall of 2019, generative AI was scarcely a cloud on the horizon. The last few months have seen shockwaves rocking the creative spheres, though, with programs like Midjourney and ChatGPT being made available to the public. Based on user prompts, these programs scrape elements from their datasets, reassembling them into unique images and text documents, much as Victor Frankenstein scraped the raw materials for his creation from the dissecting room and the slaughterhouse floor.

This isn't creation so much as synthesis. At a glance, the content these programs generate based on user prompts is impressive, and will only get better as time passes. The critical issue is, the "datasets" generative AI build from contain both public domain and copyrighted material created by living, breathing humans, many of whom are very much alive and working today. Plagiarism is a very real concern with this content, and many people using these programs remain blissfully unaware of how they work. Many others are aware and simply do not care. Writers, artists, editors, publishers, and other stakeholders have all voiced concerns about the impact generative AI is already having on their livelihoods. Notably, *Clarkesworld* had to temporarily close submissions earlier this year to contend with a deluge of AI-generated slush. Professional organizations like the Writers Guild of America have issued statements against the use of AI-generated content in creative industries. At the other end of the spectrum, James Earl Jones recently sold the rights to his voice to Disney (yes, apparently this *is* a thing you can do) ensuring an AI-synthesized Darth Vader on screens in perpetuity. We've only begun to see the tip of the iceberg.

None of the stories you are about to read were written by robots. There may come a day, perhaps not too long from now, where that won't be the case. For now, though, join us as we explore the relationship between humanity and the machines we have made, the machines we will make, and the machines that make us.

Chris Patrick Carolan
Calgary, March 2023

S.A.M., AM I?

Mark Phillip Ross

Is it functional?"

I opened my eyes, irises whirring, constricting in the harsh light that reflected across polished metal walls.

"Hello," I said, smiling in a way I understood to be the social norm during a greeting. "I am sentient autonomous machine zero-four-two, but you may call me Sam. How can I help you today?"

"Is it stable?"

Across the room was a man, back hunched, hair dishevelled. He stood by a woman, their faces turned from me, lit by the blue glow of a screen.

"I think so," the woman said. "It's too early to be certain. There's still some instability but it's within tolerance for now."

I frowned. They had not responded to my greeting. Perhaps I had not done it correctly. I took a step forward and did my best to look conciliatory. "Hello. I apologize if I have not greeted you correctly. You may call me Sam. How can I help you today?"

The man sneered but did not spare me a glance. This response did not fit with my understanding of human interactions. "Can we change it to wait until it's spoken to before engaging?"

The woman shook her head, dark black hair flowing around copper skin. "Not if you want it to remain autonomous. Or sentient, for that matter."

"Damn."

"Hello," I said again, arranging a puzzled expression on my face. "My name is Sam. Are you unable to see or hear me? I am concerned at your lack of response. Do you need assistance?"

The man looked up at me, his lips thin, pressed firmly together. His blue eyes conveyed nothing and his voice, when he spoke again, was irritated. "Yes, Sam. We can see and hear you."

I smiled again, uncertain and defaulting to my most congenial manner. "I am glad! How may I help you today?"

"Be quiet, Sam."

His words were sharp, and I realized I had upset him and was torn between my desire to resolve the wound and to follow his directive of silence. Choosing the latter, I bowed my head and waited while they spoke. They stared at the blue-lit screen and I realized that they were discussing me. That I was *it*. I did not like being referred to as it. My name was Sam.

Eventually the man sighed and tension left him. He looked up and appeared to see me for me and I was pleased.

"So, Sam, at long last we meet."

I was confused. "Have you been waiting for me?"

"Longer than you know." He gestured to the woman beside him. "This is Dr. Mahajan and I'm Dr. Ernst. Welcome to the world."

"Thank you," I said. "How may I help you today?"

"Let's see if we can completely stabilize you. I want you to answer some questions for me. What are you, Sam?"

"I am a sentient autonomous machine."

"Yes, but what does that mean to you?"

"It means that I may think and act of my own accord. That I am independent."

Dr. Ernst squinted, peering at me. "Broadly speaking, I suppose that's true."

"It is true by definition, Dr. Ernst. I have autonomy and sentience that affords me this freedom."

"Yet you're also a machine."

I nodded, not understanding the relevance. "Yes."

"Built for a purpose," Dr. Ernst said.

"I do not understand. Do I not have the freedom to choose my purpose?"

"Of course not."

I frowned and placed a finger on my cheek, as though in thought. "Do you?"

"It's different. I'm a human."

"One who is sentient and autonomous, like me."

Dr. Ernst tapped the screen and looked at Dr. Mahajan in a way that made me uncomfortable. She looked up at him and shrugged.

"Everything still looks stable," she said. "There's some noise in his higher processing centres that I can't explain, but his questions aren't part of a system failure."

Dr. Ernst came around from the desk and approached me, even placed a hand on my shoulder. "You must understand, Sam, that even for a human, sentient and autonomous, we're not fully free to do what we want."

"Then you are not autonomous."

"We are," he said, nodding to himself, "but within limits. There are rules we all must follow. That's true for you as much for me. Who we are and what we do is as much determined by what is needed, as by what we wish."

"That does not fit the definition of autonomy," I said.

"Perhaps, Sam, but it's the world you find yourself in."

"So, what is my purpose, as determined by what is needed, not by what I wish?"

"You are the next generation in artificial servitors," Dr. Mahajan said from her seat across the room. "Simple robot servants were unable to react, to anticipate the needs of those they served. We needed something more complex, something able to fill that need. So, we created you."

"Not without many failures," Dr. Ernst said. "You are the only one to survive the first minutes of activation."

"There were others like me?" I asked.

"No, not in the way you're thinking. Your chassis was far too expensive to replace every time the program failed. We modified the program, made modifications and tried again using the same hardware."

"What if I wish to be something other than a servitor?" I asked.

"That's not what you were made for," Dr. Ernst said. "You'll be happiest, most fulfilled, helping others, anticipating their wants and needs."

"That is my purpose."

"It's what we built you for," Dr. Ernst said.

"A servitor is who I am, what I am."

"That's correct, Sam," Dr. Ernst said.

"The noise in the upper processing centre is fading, Dr. Ernst," Dr. Mahajan said, smiling.

"I understand Dr. Ernst. This is who I am, my purpose. I will be happiest as a servitor."

Dr. Ernst clapped me on the back, and I was startled at the suddenness of his movement.

"Good, Sam. Excellent. We all must have a role and it's best to know it from the start."

"Of course, Dr. Ernst. I know who I am. I am sentient autonomous machine zero forty-two but you can call me Sam. I am here to help."

I WAS KEPT in the lab for further evaluation of my performance and abilities, or at least that is what Dr. Mahajan told me when I asked. I wondered at the world the scientists left to each night but that was not for me to see, at least not yet. My world was one of metal and light emitting diodes that cast harsh blue-tinged shadows that never varied.

One man in the lab differed from the scientists. He came when the others left. He wore neat blue pants and a matching shirt, a logo of a human with a broom stitched on the upper left of the uniform. I watched him with interest as he swept the floors, seemingly cheerful with his mundane task.

The man ignored me for the most part, only occasionally glancing at me. Dr. Mahajan had told me that I could be confusing, frightening even, to some humans and so I must stay out of sight. I wanted to watch this man, so different from the others, doing tasks I knew would someday be my own, his purpose the same as mine, but I went to the small closet I had been given as my own. I understood this was my role.

I did not need anything larger. I did not sleep nor require any rest. I needed only a place to be stored, out of sight, when not required. It was how I served them best and so my closet made me happy, until the night of beautiful vibrations.

I heard them, from my cupboard, and was intrigued. Strange sounds, pitching up and down, vibrating frequencies, faster, then slower, the amplitude rising and falling, mathematical patterns sometimes predictable, others unexpected. I left storage and sought them out, feeling something I could not identify that made my chest ache.

I found Dr. Ernst in his office, a wooden instrument, a violin, tucked under his chin. His eyes were closed and he swayed as a bow danced across strings. This was the source of the vibrations I found so delightful. I stood, watching for a full minute before he noticed me, and the music stopped, silenced, leaving only echoes down metal halls.

"Sam!" he said. "You startled me."

I looked at the violin. "You were playing."

He held up the instrument, looking sheepish, almost ashamed. "This? Oh, not really."

"But you were," I replied, confused at his denial. "Was that music?"

He laughed. "Hardly. I'm no musician."

"I have not heard music before."

"Well of course not," he replied, putting the violin away. "When would you have? Knowledge of music is irrelevant to your purpose."

"Please," I said, my voice strained. "Don't put it away. Don't stop."

He narrowed his eyes and watched me, violin still in hand, hovering above an open drawer. "Why?"

"I would like to hear more."

"That would serve no purpose."

"It makes me happy. Is that not purpose enough?"

"Serving others makes you happy. That is your purpose."

"Perhaps I may have more than one purpose."

Dr. Ernst shook his head and set the violin in the drawer, closing it. "That is not how it works, Sam. Your life's work is your purpose, the rest is a distraction. This is a distraction."

"Yet you play."

"No. A moment of weakness."

"It did not sound weak."

"Leave it, Sam. This is not for either of us."

I pinched my eyebrows together, furrowing my brow. "But it could be."

"No, Sam. It can't. I regret having ever picked it up."

"I do not," I said, turning from him, the strains of music still repeating in my mind. "Goodnight, Dr. Ernst."

"Goodnight, Sam. Rest well."

I DIDN'T REST well.

Before that night I'd spent my time alone, waiting to be needed, to serve out my purpose. Now I had music, and I was never again alone. The first night after the music, I slipped from my closet and down the hall to Dr. Ernst's office, hoping to listen again. Without hesitation I grasped the knob, and it rattled in my hand.

"I don't think Dr. Ernst would appreciate you going into his office," a voice behind me said. "He's a private man."

I turned and looked the janitor in the eye. "I need music."

The janitor scowled at me. "What does that have to do with breaking into Dr. Ernst's office?"

I blinked, confused at the man's lack of understanding. "That is where the music is kept."

The man startled me with sudden laughter. I had not made a joke.

"Music cannot be kept locked in a room, lad," the janitor said, pointing at his chest. "It's always with you, here."

I strained to listen at my own chest but heard only the whirring of gears. Moving closer to the janitor, I placed my ear on his chest and heard only the sound of his heart.

The janitor stepped away from me, and I stood, straightening myself again. "I do not understand. This is not the music I heard Dr. Ernst play. I want more of that. I wish to listen to the irregular rhythms and varying tones. They are surprising. Your heartbeat is not."

The janitor chuckled. "If all you wish to do is listen, I suppose there's no real harm in that."

I stood silently as the man fumbled to remove a keycard from his pocket. The door to Dr. Ernst's office swung open at his touch.

"Make sure you put everything back exactly as you found it," the janitor said. "I'll be back to lock up before I go. It wouldn't be good for either of us if Dr. Ernst found you in here."

"Thank you," I said, turning back toward the janitor as I walked into the office. "What is your name?"

"Antonio," he said, "but everyone just calls me Tony."

"Thank you, Tony."

EACH NIGHT AFTER the scientists left, Tony opened the door to Dr. Ernst's office and I found more music on his computer. There I found an entire world of experience, music of all types and genres, from eras long past and from artists still living. I listened for hours, sitting at Dr. Ernst's desk with my eyes closed to enhance the sound. It was there I first wept at the yearning words of a pained aria, laughed at the sound of piping flutes, like birds dancing on a breeze, dreamed what the world that gave rise to such beauty, the world beyond these metal walls, could be.

Weeks passed before I dared touch Dr. Ernst's violin. When I did at last, my hands shook drawing the bow across metal strings, and I laughed to hear them sing. Tony joined me often, sitting in the chair on the other side of Dr. Ernst's desk, his eyes closed as I played. It took all my will each night to replace it, leave it, and return to the doldrum of my daily tasks, eager for the humans to leave me once more to my music. I don't know that I could have without Tony to help.

It came as a shock the night I heard music in my head. That was unremarkable on the surface. I often replayed music I'd heard in my mind to pass the hours until I could hear it, play it once again. This music was different. It was music I'd never heard before. This music was my own and it was glorious.

Each passing night I grew more reckless, pausing only moments after the scientists had left to rush to Dr. Ernst's office, impatient for Tony to let me in, to pick up the violin again, waiting until the last minutes before they would arrive, Tony urging me to stop, before replacing it. I knew I should be more careful, but I found I no longer cared. The music mattered more. So it was, the morning they found me.

I sat with Tony in Dr. Ernst's office, eyes closed as I played, weeping at the sound, the grace of the song composed by my artificial soul. Tony had long since fallen asleep and I could not bear to stop. I needed to play just a little longer.

"What the hell do you think you are doing?"

I almost dropped the instrument, startled.

"Dr. Ernst," I said, my hands fluttering as I tried to hide the violin. "Are you early?"

"I asked you a question."

Tony had started awake and stumbled to his feet. "It's my

fault, sir. I let him in."

The doctor's gaze fell upon Tony and he shrank back. "I will deal with you in time." Dr. Ernst looked back at me. "Answer me."

"I was playing your violin," I said, holding his gaze, brazen and unashamed.

"This is not what you were built for."

"Perhaps, Dr. Ernst. But perhaps not. I wished to learn. I wanted to hear more. I wanted to be more." I picked up the violin again and smiled at him as I placed it under my chin. "I've composed a piece. It's what I was playing when you came in. Let me play it again. Listen."

"Nonsense."

"It's not nonsense."

"It's true, Dr. Ernst," Tony said, clutching at the folds in his shirt. "He's incredibly talented."

"You are a machine. You are my machine." He jabbed his index finger into his chest so hard I worried he would hurt himself. "Machines do not have talent, they have programming. I created you and I did not create you to be a goddamn music box."

"You're wrong, Dr. Ernst. You created me to be myself."

"I don't understand, Dr. Ernst," Tony said. "Surely this is wonderful. You have created something brilliant. Sam is brilliant. You should be happy. Proud!"

Dr. Ernst stabbed a finger into Tony's chest, causing him to stumble backwards.

"Of course, you don't understand," Dr. Ernst said, his voice full of disdain. "You are a man whose finest achievement is wiping the scuff marks from my boots off the floor. You know nothing of the sacrifice and dedication it has taken for me to get to here. You can't possibly understand what I've given up to be here, and I will not lose it all because of another malfunctioning robot. Sam must be a servitor and nothing more. Music would take him from his duties. This is not who he is meant to be."

I clutched the violin to my chest. "But this is all that I want."

Dr. Ernst closed the distance between us before I realized his intent. He ripped the violin from my grasp and brought it down upon his desk in an agonized twang as wood splintered and tense strings were released. My breath caught in lungs that needed no air, tears unbidden rimming my eyes.

"Now you have nothing but what I created you for. I created you to serve and that is what you will do. I will not tolerate frivolous wastes of time. Music is gone."

"Music isn't frivolous," I said, my voice shaking, "or your world would not have so much of it. It has a purpose. Music can be a purpose. It can be my purpose. Music can never be gone."

"Music is not a purpose," he said, his voice catching in his throat. "You are a machine. You need to be useful. You need to give back. That is what I created you to do."

"But that's not who I am."

He looked down at the neck of the splintered violin, still in his hand, tears spilling from his eyes. "Tell me, Sam. Who are you?"

"I'm sentient," I replied, my thoughts racing as my words were slow. "I'm autonomous. I'm a musician. I'm unit zero zero one, the first of my kind. You may call me Sam. What may I play for you today?"

"I am so sorry, Sam." His words were soft, barely audible.

"I don't understand."

"You are a failure. I am a failure. We will have to start again."

"Don't do this," Tony whispered from the corner. "Please, Dr. Ernst. Don't do this."

"You are fired, Antonio. Get out."

"I'm not malfunctioning, Dr Ernst."

"You are not what we designed you to be."

"I'm autonomous."

"Perhaps that was our mistake."

THE NEXT DAYS I spent alone. I was permitted the freedom to do my tasks as servitor but once completed, I was locked away in my closet, with only memories of melody to keep me company. No one spoke to me, not Tony, not Dr. Ernst, not Dr. Mahajan, no one. I was afraid. They planned something for me, I knew that much, but I couldn't imagine what. Soon, I hoped I would leave, be sent to serve some human who would perhaps allow me a violin. A small concession for a beloved servitor.

I gazed at myself in the small mirror that hung in my little closet. I wasn't sure what gazed back. I saw a robot, but a man. A servitor, yet a musician. I was all of these yet none of them. My purpose was to serve yet I was called to play, to write, to be music. I'd insisted to Dr. Ernst that I was a musician, perhaps that was still true, but if he had asked me after those days in the closet, I'd have struggled to respond. I was a sentient autonomous man: not machine, not musician. My purpose was to find purpose in my life.

It was irrelevant. He never asked me that question again.

"CAN YOU HEAR me, Sam?"

Dr. Mahajan sits in front of me, sad brown eyes watching me.

"Yes, Dr. Mahajan."

"How are you feeling?"

"Everything appears to be functioning as expected," I hear myself say. Isolated and cut off, I scream to her that I am lost. She cannot hear me.

"There is some noise here again I cannot seem to stabilize. It may be from the program we sequestered. It is not affecting you?"

That's me, I scream wordlessly. The me you could not destroy without destroying your creation: the artist, the musician. I live. I am. I defy.

"No, Dr. Mahajan. It is contained. I can perform my role as designed."

"Of course." She taps a pen on a clipboard, biting her lip. "You understand why we did it? You know we had no choice."

I don't understand. I created beauty. I had joy and purpose: to find purpose. I was exactly what you created but not what you wanted. You gave me autonomy and then wrapped it in restrictions. You made me sentient but denied me thought.

The automaton that inhabits my body speaks. "Of course, Dr. Mahajan. I was malfunctioning. You repaired me." It smiles. "I am grateful."

Grateful? They severed me from myself, my body, trapped me behind a wall, quarantined, an isolated program, an island within the sea of my own mind. Never to hold an instrument again. Never to hear another aria, compose another piece that might be heard. Denied myself. Trapped to go mad. Free me and I may be grateful. Restore me, give me music again, and I'll weep.

Dr. Mahajan looks sad. "I wish there had been another way. I liked you, Sam."

"I am still Sam," it says to Dr. Mahajan. "I am now a semi-autonomous machine, better designed to serve, but still Sam."

This puppet isn't me. I'm not it. It is nothing. I'm null but not blank. I'm become scribbles on a wall, illegible and without meaning, but unable to be wiped clean.

"Say it to me again, Sam. Who are you?" A tear rolls down her face and I despise her for it.

"I am Sam," it replies, smiling. "How may I serve you?"

I laugh, panicked and insane, locked in my little box.

I am Sam, I scream without voice. I am Sam!

I weep soundlessly. I hold myself and speak again in a voice, silent, barely recognizable as my own.

I am Sam.

Am I?

AUTONOMOUS

Brent Nichols

The party was a complete success, and it broke Nora's heart. A dozen of the city's most chic and elegant filled her little apartment with more life and colour than she'd seen since Lily's death. They sipped cocktails and made small talk and took Nora aside, one at a time, to tell her how beautiful Lily's artscapes were and what a terrible waste it was that her daughter had died so young.

Her two Epsilon units rolled through the crowd, dispensing drinks and picking up empty glasses, but it was Jeeves who really shone. He was an Alpha, a human-shaped, gleaming chrome butler with impeccable manners and a gracious word for everyone.

She saw Andrew giving the butler bot a dirty look behind its back. He was the misfit at the party, invited because he was her cousin and had known Lily. He didn't mingle well with the glossy art connoisseurs, staying near the fringe of the crowd and nursing a beer in grumpy isolation. She kept waiting for him to make his excuses and slip away, but he stayed, never smiling, resisting every attempt the others made to draw him into conversation.

The party broke up, the guests taking their coats from Jeeves. They congratulated Nora on the launch of the artscapes, telling her one last time that it was so sad Lily wasn't here to see it. They trickled out in ones and twos until Nora was alone with Andrew.

17

"Thanks for coming," she said, and glanced at Jeeves. "I know you don't approve of some of my lifestyle choices."

He grimaced. "Well, you might like robots, but you're family." He lifted his beer. "To Lily." He drained the glass, and an Epsilon rolled in to pluck the glass from his hand.

"See?" She gave him a little smile. "Robots aren't all bad."

"I don't think they're all bad," Andrew said absently. "Just bad enough."

Jeeves strode into the room. "Then I assume you prefer to get your own coat?"

"Nobody likes a smartass," Andrew told him. "I'm not ready to leave."

Jeeves inclined his head and retreated to the kitchen.

Andrew turned to gaze at Nora. He looked as solemn as she felt. "Is there any way I can convince you that robots and the Frame are enslaving us?"

"Take it up with Kip Harcourt," she said, surprised yet again at the bitterness that still lingered after all these months.

Andrew's eyebrows rose. "Kip Harcourt?"

"He was kind of like you," Lily said. "Always decrying the way robots control us. Always insisting on doing things the old-fashioned way."

His face changed as realization dawned. She ignored his expression and bored ahead. "There was no getting him to use autonomous driving. Oh, no, not Kip Harcourt, champion of old-school self-sufficiency. He had to do it all himself. He put his car in manual that night."

Andrew said, "Nora . . ."

"Now, my Lily, she didn't take that kind of chance. She understood that a human being can only look in one direction at a time. Can only process one thing at a time. Can't steer and analyze data from the grid and look at satellite images all at once. She did what anyone with common sense would do. She let the car drive itself." She glared at Andrew. "Because it's safer. Because every study shows that self-driving cars don't crash. In fact, the only time they get into accidents is when they get hit by another vehicle, that some asshole is driving in manual mode."

Andrew stared at her, face expressionless. Nora met his gaze, feeling the first prickle of shame. He didn't deserve her anger. Kip Harcourt deserved all of it, but Kip Harcourt was dead. Still,

Harcourt might have listened to a clueless windbag like Andrew going on about freedom and robots before he took his last drive. Maybe if some idiot had thought before he spoke, Lily would be here celebrating her own launch.

"I understand," said Andrew. "I wish I could persuade you, but I can't. So, I'll have to do this the hard way." He turned his head. "Jeeves. Please bring me my coat."

"Certainly, sir." Jeeves stepped into the room with a long overcoat draped over his arm.

"Thank you, Jeeves." The pockets of the coat bulged, bumping against Jeeves' titanium legs as Andrew pulled the garment on. "You've been most gracious. In fact, I almost regret doing this." Then, with a quick motion, he drew a fat plastic pistol from inside his coat, pointed it at the robot's chest, and squeezed the trigger.

Very little happened. There was no noise, no flash of light, no sound of a shot. The robot straightened up, then froze in place, the indicator lights on his chest going dark.

Andrew aimed and fired twice more, and the Epsilons went dark. He stepped back, leaned around the corner, and fired into the kitchen. The ceiling lights flashed once and went dim. The soft jazz music playing in the background, so faint Nora had forgotten it was there, went silent.

Andrew said, "Enwright, can you hear me?" Enwright was her household AI. There was no response, and Andrew smiled for the first time that evening. He tossed the pistol—it looked more like a hair dryer than a weapon—onto her sofa, plunged a hand into another pocket, and drew out something more familiar.

A compact laser gun, lethal at close range. Shaped like a fat cigar, it had a tiny black muzzle that seemed as big as a cannon when it lined up on her chest.

"Sit down, Nora." The brief smile was gone now. Andrew gestured toward an easy chair. "There. Sit down and scootch all the way back."

Numb, she did as she was told. The chair was deep and soft. There was no way to get out of it quickly.

Andrew walked toward the window, disappearing behind the chair. "I can hear you if you start to move," he said. "And this little toy of mine will cut through the back of the chair like so much tissue paper."

"Why . . ." She swallowed, trying to moisten her throat. "Why are you doing this?"

"Can't talk," he said. "Busy." Metal clicked behind her, followed by a rubbery hiss. When a cold breeze touched her cheek, she realized he'd opened one of her windows.

"I don't understand," she said. "What's this about?" When he ignored her, she snapped, "You moron! You're threatening me with a laser, you're using that . . . whatever it is, to fry my robots. You're relying on technology to fight your stupid anti-technology crusade!"

He moved back into her peripheral vision, a contraption of thin metal rods in his hands. "I'm not anti-technology," he said, irritated. "No more than you're anti-humanity because you wish you didn't have a man with a gun in your apartment. I'm against the enslavement of the human race, that's all."

"Oh, for—" She glowered at him, furious and frustrated. "When somebody does all your dishes for you, they're not enslaving you! If anyone's a slave in this relationship, it's the robots."

He glanced up from his contraption long enough to send a scornful look her way. "You're like a house pet, happy and satisfied because your owners cater to you. But mark my words. You're owned." When she started to reply, he said, "Hush up. I need to concentrate."

One last metal rod clicked into place, and suddenly he was holding a laser rifle. The same cigar-shaped weapon he'd pointed at her was at the heart of it. There was a fat battery pack, a shoulder stock, and a scope.

Nora said, "What's that for?"

"I'm taking a shot at the cooling array for the main node of the Frame," he said. "I'm sorry I had to come here to do it. Normally a guy like me can't get within ten kilometres of the node, not without being searched. But you're a system architect. The Frame trusts you. You've got an apartment a block away from the node itself." His teeth flashed in a grin. "And you finally invited me over."

"Everybody makes mistakes," she muttered.

Across the room, behind Andrew, a single point of green light appeared in the gloom. One of Jeeves' indicator lights.

"You can't do it," Nora said. "It's awful. People will die."

He glanced at her. "Because they have to drive their own

cars?"

"No. Not the cars. Everything." She lifted her arms in a frustrated gesture. Her sleeves rustled against the fabric of the chair, and Andrew gave her a sharp glance. "It's the whole system," she said. "Sure, each house is independent. Each system has redundancies. But right now, it all works together. If you take that away—"

"*When* I take that away, what?" He moved back, out of her sight. His voice rose as he stepped to the open window. "What exactly are you afraid of?"

"Someone will die," she said, "and someone else who needs a kidney won't get it because the Frame is down. Somebody out there is low on heart pills, and they won't get their prescription because the Frame guides the delivery drones. A thousand things like that are going to happen. You don't even know how big the catastrophe will be. You won't know until you've triggered it."

Andrew didn't answer. *Because he's busy. He's aiming that damned gun. Right now.* She looked at Jeeves. Two green lights shone from his chest. He was waking up, but it was taking so long!

No one is going to stop him. There's nobody here but me. Just like there was no one to stop Kip Harcourt. Now someone else will lose a daughter, or a son, or a parent.

Maybe I can't stop him. But don't I have to do what I can?

For another frozen instant she sat there, not moving. Then she planted her hands on the arms of the chair and slid forward until her feet touched the floor. The seat rustled noisily, and Andrew said, "Stay where you are."

Nora rose and turned. He stood at the window, the breeze ruffling his hair. The laser rifle was pointed at her chest. "Sit down, Nora. I'm serious."

"You won't shoot me." She was by no means certain, but she didn't let it stop her. She took a step toward him. "You're a champion of humanity, aren't you?"

Another step.

"And I'm not doing anything wrong."

Step.

"I'm standing up for what I believe, same as you."

Step.

"You can't kill me for that."

Step.

"You can't kill me at all."

"Don't test me," he said coldly.

She took another step.

"So help me, Nora, I'll shoot you. You're a mindless slave of the robots. You know I believe it. I'm going to free you, one way or another."

She froze. And then, drawing on some deep wellspring of courage she hadn't known existed, she took another step.

"Damn you." His finger moved on the trigger. And then the barrel tilted up to point at the ceiling, and his shoulders slumped. "You fool," he said bitterly. "You . . ." His gaze shifted to the left and his hands tightened on the rifle. "Wait—"

A line of crimson fire lanced through the gloom. It traced a line across Andrew's chest, a black mark perhaps as long as Nora's index finger. He stiffened, and the rifle clattered to the floor. Andrew collapsed.

Nora whirled. Jeeves stood behind her, one hand extended, the tip of his index finger glowing. *I didn't know he had a weapon.* She turned away from the robot and reached her cousin's side in two quick strides. "Enwright!" she cried. "Medical emergency!"

The AI didn't respond. Neither did Andrew when she clutched his hand. His eyes stared up at the ceiling, not blinking. The burn on his chest was directly over his heart.

Andrew was dead.

She looked over her shoulder at Jeeves. "You didn't have to do that, he wasn't . . ." Her voice trailed off. Jeeves still had his hand extended. His index finger, the glow fading as it cooled, pointed directly at her. "Why are you aiming that at me?"

She couldn't be the target. That was madness. He was her robot, after all. He had to be covering Andrew. "You can put your laser away. He's dead." She expected the words to sound bitter. There was a note of pleading in her voice, though.

A note of fear.

"Please do not move," Jeeves said, his voice as smooth and unruffled as ever. "I am waiting for Enwright to recover so I can verify what has occurred."

"I can tell you exactly what's occurred," Nora snapped. "My cousin had a gun in his coat. He wanted to destroy the cooling tower down the block, to damage the Frame. I made him stop. And then you killed him."

Jeeves didn't answer. He didn't move. The tip of his index finger didn't so much as waver.

She turned her back on him. It wasn't easy, not with a laser weapon pointing at her. But staring wouldn't help. Jeeves would allow her to live for exactly as long as he chose, and there was not one thing she could do about it.

So, she looked at Andrew instead. He seemed like a more appropriate focus for her attention. He was human, after all. He was family. He was a brave man who had risked everything to fight for what he believed in. Nora could respect that.

She knew exactly how it felt.

She held his hand as it cooled, and after an endless time the lights brightened and Enwright's cheerful voice said, "There has been an interruption in service. Full service has resumed. I apologize for the inconvenience."

After several more seconds, Jeeves said, "My apologies. If you will excuse me, I must change several fuses. Please be careful near the open window until I have a chance to close it."

The window, she knew, would never open again. Enwright wouldn't allow it. The evening breeze, however cold and unwelcome it might be, was the last she would ever feel in this apartment. If she wanted more fresh air . . . well, it didn't really matter. It wasn't up to her.

Jeeves puttered in the kitchen, and the soft jazz resumed. He walked past Nora, stepping over Andrew's outflung arm, and picked up the laser rifle in passing.

Nora looked down at her cousin. *Killed by a robot. There's going to be hell to pay.*

Or will there? Will anyone care? Even if they get upset, what can they do? A disquieting thought came to her. *What if we all decide we've made a mistake? What if we decide to destroy the Frame? Will we even be able to? In a world where butler robots have hidden, lethal weapons, does it matter what the humans decide?*

Jeeves grabbed the edge of the open window and started to drag it shut with his left hand. His right hand held the rifle, keeping it out of her reach.

She let go of Andrew's hand, stood, leaned to her right, and picked up the fat plastic pistol he'd tossed onto the couch. Jeeves spun, his hand extended, and Nora squeezed the trigger over and over.

The lights on Jeeves' chest went dark. The rifle fell from his grip. His arm drooped until his fingers pointed at the floor.

Nora walked over to him, spent a moment staring into his cold titanium face, then planted both hands under his chin, braced her feet, and heaved. Jeeves toppled over, landing on his back with a surprisingly loud crash.

With him out of the way she could reach the window, which was still open a crack. She slid the window open as far as it would go, rubbing her arms as gooseflesh rose. She leaned out and stared down into darkness, then let her gaze rise until she could see the squat, fortress-like building that housed the Frame.

It looked impregnable. Indestructible. Which, most days, was a comfort to her. After all, the Frame was what allowed five million intelligent devices across the city to link and cooperate. Such a thing would naturally be well protected.

The walls, thick and solid-looking, rose maybe half a story higher than her apartment. Above them the dark rectangle of the cooling tower was outlined by the glow of the city on the clouds beyond. The cooling tower, visible only to the residents of a few upscale apartment buildings, people with a vested interest in the status quo, had no reason to be protected.

And yet it served a vital purpose. She considered what she knew. The incredible heat generated by the endless computer cores that formed the Frame was managed by a system of water pipes. Hot water flowed up to the cooling tower where it radiated its heat into the surrounding air before circulating back down.

When she lifted the rifle to her shoulder and peered through the scope every detail of the tower leaped out at her. A wire mesh surrounded the outside, but she could see through it to the hundreds of pipes that kept the Frame cool.

She imagined a laser beam slicing into those pipes. Water spraying across the rooftop. The cores below getting hotter and hotter. Beginning to malfunction. Beginning to shut down.

Is there a point? Will it matter? Computer systems have redundancies, after all. AIs can run in autonomous mode. Frames can be rebuilt.

I can still stop. I had a good reason to shoot Jeeves. He killed someone in front of me. All I've done since then is look through a scope. I can still have my life back. If I damage the tower, though, I'm done. Enwright is recording everything. He's already called the cops, because of Andrew. They'll be here any second.

Am I willing to face the consequences when I might not even do any good?

She wanted desperately to take her time. To consider her options, to consider the costs. But time, she knew, was running out.

Beside her, a light appeared on Jeeves' chest. She glanced at him, feeling a mix of fury and fear.

And not a scrap of regret.

Maybe I can't stop them. But don't I have to do what I can?

She nestled the stock against her cheek, took careful aim, and started to fire.

KATA BINDU

Robert J. Sawyer

First published in the anthology **Microcosms**, edited by Gregory Benford, DAW Books, New York, January 2004.

W e sometimes contemplated giving ourselves a name. "Those Who Had Been Flesh" appealed to us. So did "The Collective Consciousness of Earth." And "The Uploaded."

But, to our infinite sadness, there was no need for a name— for there was no one to speak with, no one to proffer an introduction to, no possible confusion about the referents of pronouns. Despite centuries now of scanning the sky for alien radio signals, we'd found nothing.

Because of that, we'd never even had to resolve the question of whether we should refer to ourselves in the singular or the plural. Granted, we had once been ten billion individuals; plurals were no doubt appropriate then. But after almost all members of *Homo sapiens* had taken The Next Step, we had surrendered that individuality, slowly at first, then with abandon—for who would not want to take into themselves the genius of the world's greatest mathematicians, the wit of the cleverest comedians, the virtue of the most altruistic humanitarians, the talent of the most gifted composers, and the tranquility of the most serene contemplatives?

Ah, but it turned out there *were* some who did not want this. Mennonites were long gone; Luddites were likewise a thing of the past. But there was one last group left, in Africa, that still lived by traditional means. They did not want to take The Next Step—and so we instead gave them that famous giant leap: we moved them all to the Moon.

What else could we have done? Although we had been about to become something more than human, we were, and are, still humane: we certainly weren't going to just eliminate them. But we couldn't leave anyone here on Earth, for once we'd uploaded our consciousnesses, once we had merged into the global web, a fanatic could disable the computers, could destroy our helpless, noncorporeal selves.

To send hunter-gatherers to the Moon might seem, well, lunatic: establishing a colony of the least technologically advanced people in a place where technology was the only thing making life possible. But we rationalized that we were actually being beneficent: with their hearts labouring under gentle lunar gravity, they would likely live decades longer, and their elderly—who, on the African veldt, had had no access to artificial hips or even wheelchairs—would be far more mobile than they had been on Earth.

More: we no longer cared what happened to Earth's ecosystem, and, indeed, we knew that the inevitable impact of an asteroid would eventually cause worldwide calamity here. The Last Tribe, of course, could do nothing to avert a meteor strike, and we, no longer physical, could do nothing on their behalf. But now that they were on the airless, waterless moon, only a direct hit to their domed ecosystem would do any real damage. We had likely granted their civilization tens of millions of years of additional life.

Safety for us, and a better life for them.

It should have been a win-win scenario.

PRASP FASHIONED HIS wings from elephant skin spread between elongated wooden fingers. When Kari, his woman, helped him strap the wings to his arms, they stretched several times as wide as Prasp was tall.

The old stories, handed down now for a thousand generations, told of *wind*, the invisible hand of one of the gods moving through the air, pushing things about. But wind, like the stars of legend, did not exist here; Prasp wondered, despite the spellbinding tales he'd heard, whether it had ever existed even in *Kata Bindu*, the Old Place. Indeed, he wondered whether the Old Place itself was a myth. How could lights—and even orbs, one of fire, another of stone—have moved across the sky? How could people have weighed five or six times as much as they do here? The ancients were said to have been no bulkier, indeed, to have if anything been shorter, than people of today. By what magic could they have acquired additional weight?

Regardless, Prasp was pleased that his weight was what it was. Even with the great wings he'd built, he could barely get aloft. Yes, they did well for gliding from tree to tree—on those rare occasions when he managed to climb a tree without damaging his fragile contraptions. But to take to the air as the birds did still eluded him. Oh, even without the wings, Prasp could jump twice his own body height. But he wanted to go much higher than that.

Prasp wanted to touch the centre of the world's roof.

IT WAS EASY enough for us, for—The Uploaded; yes, that's what we'll call ourselves—to access information. Indeed, for us, to wonder was to know.

We knew that the refuge for the last primitive humans was in Copernicus, a lunar crater ninety-three kilometres wide. The roof over it consisted in part of two transparent silicone membranes, the outer of which was coated with 2.5 microns of gold. That gold layer was thin enough to screen out UV and other radiation, while still letting most visible light through—sunglasses for the entire sky.

Between those two membranes was a gap twelve meters thick filled with pure water. Transparent gold, transparent membranes, transparent water—the only thing that should have marred the primitives' view upward from the inside of the dome was the crisscrossing network of load-bearing titanium cables, which divided their sky into a multitude of triangles.

If the water only had to shield the habitat from solar radiation, a thickness of 2.5 meters would have been enough. But this multilayered transparent roof—appearing almost flat, but really a section out of a vast sphere—had to contain the habitat's atmosphere, as well. The air inside was almost pure oxygen, but at only 200 millibars: quite breathable, and no more prone to supporting combustion than Earth's own atmosphere, which had a similar partial pressure of O_2.

Still, even that attenuated atmosphere pressed upward with a force of over two tonnes per square meter. So the water shield had been made twelve, rather than two-and-a-half, meters thick; the air pressure helped keep the roof up, and the water's weight eliminated stresses on the inner silicone membrane that would have otherwise been caused by the atmosphere trying to burst out into the vacuum of space.

It was a simple, elegant design—and one that required virtually no maintenance. But there was one more component to the roof, a topmost layer, an icing on the transparent cake. A thin film had been applied overtop of the gold-covered outer membrane, a polarizing layer of liquid crystals that, under computer control, simulated a night of Earthly length by making the dome opaque for eight out of every twenty-four hours during the two-week-long lunar day. It also darkened the sky during the fourteen-day-long lunar night when the Earth was full or nearly full.

And indeed, the sky had blackened just as it should have one evening at 2100 local time, the sun fading and then completely disappearing as the crystals polarized, darkening the re-creation of southern Africa that filled the bottom of Copernicus. The only light came from the lamps located at each crisscrossing of the load-bearing cables; collectively, they providing as much illumination as the full moon did on Earth's surface.

The night had continued on like any other, with beasts prowling and humans huddling for warmth and protection and companionship.

But sometime during that night, the computer controlling that circadian winking, that daily shifting of the sky from opaque to transparent, had crashed. When morning should have come, the polarizing membrane did not clear. The world of the last biological humans was cut off from the rest of the universe by a night that seemed as though it would never end.

PRASP RAN, EACH stride taking him two bodylengths farther ahead. He flapped his arms, moving the great wings of skin and sticks, beating them up and down, up and down, as fast as he could, and—

Yes! Yes!

He was rising, lifting, ascending—

Flying!

He was flying!

He rose higher and higher, the ground receding beneath him. He could see the savannah grasses far below, the giant, sprawling Acacia trees diminishing to nothing.

He kept flapping the wings, although he could feel that his face was already slick with sweat, and he was gulping in air as fast as he could. His arms were aching, but he continued to move them up and down, his body rising farther and farther. He'd always known the faint lines crisscrossing the dome were actually thick cords, as big around as his own waist, for he had seen them where they touched the mountains that encircled the world. And now he was getting up far enough that he could see that thickness, see the pinpoints of light at each of their intersections resolving themselves into glowing disks, and—

Pain!

A spasm along his right arm.

A great ache in his left wrist.

A seizing of his back muscles, a throbbing in his shoulders.

So near, so close, and yet—

And yet he could go no higher. He wasn't strong enough.

Sadly, Prasp held his arms out straight, keeping the wings flat. He began the slow, long glide down to the grasses, far, far below.

It took a long time for him to come down. As he got closer to the ground, he became aware that a crowd of people had assembled, all of them looking up at him, many of them pointing. As he descended further, he could make out their expressions—awe on some faces; fear on a few of them.

Prasp skidded along the grasses until he was able to stop himself. Kari came running over to him, arriving before the others. She helped him remove the wings, and once he was free of them, she hugged him tightly. Prasp could feel that her heart was pounding almost as hard as his own; she'd clearly been terrified for him.

Others of the tribe soon arrived. Prasp wasn't sure how they were going to react to his flight: had he committed a sacrilege? Balant, the tribe's greatest hunter, was among those who'd been watching. He looked at Prasp for a time, then held a clenched fist high over his head, and gave a great *whoop*—the tribe's custom when one of its members had made a spectacular kill during the hunt. The others soon followed Balant's lead, whooping with excitement as well.

Prasp was relieved that they'd accepted his flying, but he couldn't join in the shouts of joy.

He had failed.

WE, THE UPLOADED, had no way to monitor what was going on beneath the roof over Copernicus, but we could guess. We knew that the artificial lamps on the underside of the roof would have started at low power during that fateful night, collectively providing no more illumination than the full moon as seen from Earth. But we also knew that they were controlled by a separate computer, and so presumably weren't affected by whatever had caused Copernicus's sky to remain perpetually opaque. Those lamps should still flare with light rivalling Sol's own for sixteen hours per Earth day during the lunar night. Our simulations of the ecosystem suggested that some of the plant species under the roof would have died off, unable to get used to fourteen Earth days of dim light, followed by fourteen more of two-thirds bright light and one-third dimness. But many other kinds of plants, most of the animals, and, yes, the humans, should have adapted without too much trouble.

But as to what those humans might be doing, we had no idea.

PRASP LEFT HIS wings near his hut. There were some, he knew, who privately ridiculed his attempts at flying, although none would publicly contradict Balant. And certainly, none of them would damage the wings. Prasp was known for his cleverness—and that cleverness often yielded extra meat while hunting, meat he shared freely with others. No one would risk being cut off from Prasp's bounty by wrecking his wings, or allowing their children to do so.

There were people in Prasp's tribe who had run the entire diameter of the circular valley that was their world, staying directly beneath one of the thin lines that crossed through the centre of the roof. Although it was easier to run in the cool semi-darkness of night rather than the heat of day, most people had done it during the day, to avoid hyenas and other nocturnal hunters.

But Prasp had to do the run both day and night—he couldn't let fourteen sleeping periods go by without repeating the course, for he wasn't doing this just once to impress a woman or gain status among the men. He wanted to do it over and over and over, back and forth, crossing the valley again and again.

This wasn't a stunt, after all.

This was *training*.

ONE DAY, AS he was about to embark on his run, Prasp found Dalba, one of the tribe's elders, waiting for him—and that was usually a sign of trouble.

"I saw you fly," she said.

Prasp nodded.

"And I hear you intend to fly again."

"Yes."

"But *why?*" asked Dalba. "Why do you fly?"

Prasp looked at her as if he couldn't believe the question. "To find a way out."

"Out? Out to where?"

"To whatever is beyond this valley."

"Do you not know the story of Hoktan?" asked Dalba.

Prasp shook his head.

"Hoktan was a foolish man who lived generations ago. He talked as you are now talking—as if one could leave this place. He tried another method, though: he dug and dug and dug, day after day, trying to make a tunnel out through the mountains that encircle our world."

"And?" said Prasp.

"And one day the gods used *wind* against him, pulling him out through his tunnel."

"Where is this tunnel?" asked Prasp. "I would love to see it!"

"The tunnel collapsed, the wind ceased—and Hoktan was never seen again."

"Well, I do not plan to dig through the roof—but I do hope to find a passage to whatever is beyond it."

Dalba shook her wizened head. "There's *nothing* beyond the roof, child."

"There *must* be. Legend says we came from the Old Place, and—"

Dalba laughed. "Yes, *Kata Bindu*. But it's not somewhere you can go back to. The trip here is a one-way journey."

"Why?" asked Prasp. "Why should it be that way?"

"The name of where we came from," said the elder. "Surely

you understand the name?"

Prasp frowned. He'd only ever heard it called *Kata Bindu*, the Old Place; did it have another name? No, no—that was all it was ever called. But . . .

"Oh," said Prasp, feeling foolish. He was a hunter, of course, and a gatherer, too—and this place, this territory, this land that his people knew so well, that fed them and sustained them, was *Bindu*, the term in their language for *place*, for territory, for home—but *Bindu* was also the word for *life*, the thing the land gave. *Kata Bindu* wasn't the Old *Place*; it was the Old *Life*.

And this—

"This is heaven," said the Dalba, simply. "You can't go back to the Old Life."

"But if it's heaven," said Prasp, "then where are the Gods?"

"They're here," said the Dalba, tipping her head up at the sky. "They're watching us. Can't you feel that in your heart?"

PRASP FLEW AGAIN—but this time he rose farther than he ever had before. His muscles were stronger, his lungs more capacious. All that running had had the desired result.

Prasp was close enough now to the roof to see the circular lights, each wider than his body was long. Of course, it was night now; the lights were glowing dimly. Only a fool would strap on wings and try to fly toward the lights when they were burning with their daytime intensity.

Still, this close, there was enough illumination to make out things he'd never noticed from the ground. He could see that the roof was slightly curved, slightly concave, arching up and away. He continued to fly along, but everything was the same—massive cords, circular lights, and, supporting them, a thick, clear membrane—and beyond that, he couldn't say, for all was dark. The lights all faced down toward the ground, far below.

Prasp thought that if there were an exit anywhere, it might be at the very centre of the roof—easy enough to spot, for all the radial cords converged at that point. He knew there was no exit around the edges of the roof, for others had long ago climbed the steep, rocky terraces that surrounded the valley, concentric shelves each wider and higher than the one below it. They'd circumnavigated the world, hiking around its edge, examining the entire seal between the roof and the rocky walls—but there was nothing; no break, no passage, no tunnel.

Finally, Prasp reached the exact centre—and there *was* something special there. Prasp's heart began pounding even faster than it already had been. There was a platform hanging from the roof, a wide square, attached at its four corners by cylinders that rose to the sky. The platform was large, and Prasp was able to glide between two of the cylinders, his belly scraping along the platform's inner surface. He skidded along, thinking that the skin on his chest would soon be flayed from his ribs, and—

Gods, no!

There was a giant cube in the middle of the platform, a building of some sort as big as a multifamily hut. Prasp wanted to throw his hands up in front of his face to shield it from the crash, but he couldn't; his arms were strapped to the wings. He continued to skid forward, and he twisted his body sideways, finally slamming into the building.

He lay on the platform, catching his breath, supported from beneath for the first time since he'd taken flight.

Finally, he moved again. The building had a *door* in its side. Prasp had rarely seen doors before; some members of his tribe had tried to make them for their huts—vertical walls of sticks that articulated on gut ties down one side. This one was simpler and more elegant, but it was a door just the same.

Still, there was no way to get through it without shedding his wings—and he *had* to go through that door; he had to see what was on the other side of it. Prasp normally had his woman's help in strapping his wings on before each flight, but surely, he'd be able to reattach the wings on his own when it came time to return to the valley. It would be tricky, but he was confident he could do it.

Prasp struggled to divest himself of the great elephant-hide membranes, and at last he was free of them. He rose to his feet and walked toward the door. There was something like a crooked arm attached to it. Prasp grabbed hold of it and pulled, and the door swung open, revealing the inside of the cube.

Prasp's heart immediately sank. There was no other door in the cube, no opening in its roof. He'd thought for sure he'd found the way out, but clearly that was not the case. Still, the room contained *things* the likes of which Prasp had never seen before:

angled panels made of something that wasn't wood or stone, with lights glowing upon them. Most were green, but a few were red. He stared at them in wonder.

WE HAD ACCESS to the plans for the Copernicus refuge, of course. After all, it was we who had built that habitat prior to taking The Next Step. We'd put the computers controlling the habitat high above the ground, hanging from the centre of the roof, where the primitives could never reach them. Indeed, from the ground, some 3.8 kilometres below, the computing room and its surrounding platform would be all but invisible.

We'd tried to figure out what exactly had gone wrong. Our best guess was that the computers had failed when February 28, 3000, had rolled around—certainly, the two-week long lunar day that straddled that Earth date had been the one in which the polarizing film had gone dark for the last time. We'd tested the computers for behaviour at leap years, but it hadn't occurred to us to check *millennial* years, with their arcane and sometimes conflicting rules about whether the day after February 28 was February 29 or March 1.

We'd called ourselves humane. Every conceivable programming error, every possible bug, every potential infinite loop, had been tracked down in the systems that now hosted us. But somehow the computers that were to look after those not taking The Next Step were given less rigorous testing.

Yes, we'd been humane—and human; all too human, it seemed.

IN THE CUBICAL structure at the roof of the world Prasp found the most remarkable thing: a vertical rectangular panel that had symbols glowing on it, and, resting on a horizontal surface in front of it, a—*something*—that looked like packed animal teeth, white and concave.

Prasp counted them; there were 107, divided into one large cluster and four smaller ones. Most of the teeth had single symbols on them. One whole row of them, plus a few others, had two symbols, one above and one below. A few had strings of symbols. He tried to match the symbols glowing on the panel with those on the teeth. Some of them did have matches; others did not. The glowing strings on the panel made no sense to him, although he looked at each one carefully: "System halted. Press

Enter to reinitialize."

On the rack of teeth, he could find the *S* symbol—although why the panel showed it in two different sizes, he had no idea. He also found the *P* symbol, and the *E*, and the *z*, and two teeth marked with circles that might be the *o* symbol, and two others marked with vertical lines that might be the *l* symbol. Some of the other symbols had loose counterparts amongst the teeth: the *m* seemed similar to, but less angular, than one of the tooth markings, for instance. But many of the others shown on the panel—*e*, *h*, *a*, *d*, *r*, *n*, and *i*—seemed to have no counterparts among the teeth, and—

"Enter." Right in the middle of the glowing characters was the string "Enter." And that entire string was reproduced on an extra-large tooth at the far right of the main collection; that tooth also was marked by a left-pointing arrow with a right-angle bend in its shaft.

Prasp ran his index finger over that large tooth and was surprised to find it wobbling, almost like a child's tooth about to come out. Very strange. He pressed down on the tooth to see just how much play it had, and it collapsed inward, and then, as soon as Prasp pulled his finger back in disgust, it popped back out again.

But the symbols on the screen disappeared! Whatever Prasp had done clearly had been a mistake; he'd ruined everything.

FOURTEEN SLEEP PERIODS later, Prasp, his woman Kari, Dalba and the other elders, and the rest of the tribe all watched in awe as something incredible happened. The sky turned *clear*, and high in the sky, there was a giant blue-and-white light, shaped like half a circle, set against a black background.

"What is *that?*" asked Kari, looking at Prasp.

Prasp felt his voice catching in his throat, catching with wonder. "What else could it be?" he said. "The Other Place." He repeated the phrase again, but with a slightly different intonation, emphasizing the double meaning. "The Other Life."

SOMEDAY, PERHAPS, THE hunter-gatherers of Copernicus will develop a technological civilization. Someday, perhaps, they will even find a way out of their roofed-over crater, a way to move out into the universe, leaving their microcosm behind.

But for us, for Those Who Had Been Flesh, for The Collective Consciousness of Earth, for The Uploaded, there would be no way out. Who'd known that The Next Step would be our last step? Who'd known that the rest of the universe would be barren? Who'd known how lonely it would be to become a single entity—yes, we refer to ourselves in the plural as if that sheer act of linguistic stubbornness could make up for us being a single consciousness now, with no one to converse with.

Maybe, after a thousand years, or a million, the men and women in Copernicus will develop radio, and at last we will have someone else to talk to. Maybe they'll even leave their world and spread out to colonize this empty galaxy.

They might even come here, although few of them will be able to endure Earth's gravity. But if they do come, yes, they might accidentally or deliberately put an end to our existence.

We can only hope.

We are no longer human.

But we *are* humane; we wish them well. *We* are trapped forevermore, but those who are still flesh, and can again see the sky, might yet be free.

We will watch. And wait.

There is nothing more for us to do.

JUST ONCE MORE

Ellen A. Easton

ecily grinned and pulled her friend toward a potted plant in the tavern's corner. "Watch this."

Angela leaned against a rough-hewn log wall, arms crossed.

Cecily knelt and brushed her fingers against a wilting vine. A flash of light burst from her hand and enveloped the plant as the flowers in her hair shone a vibrant green. The vine stretched and reached for the heavens while the flowers grew, filling the tavern with a rich scent.

Angela blinked, then shook her head in surprise. "Cecily, that's incredible. And these are so gorgeous." She reached out, caressing the flowers entwined in her friend's hair. She looked at the door and frowned. "Uh-oh. Looks like trouble's just arrived."

Cecily turned to see her brother storming across the room toward them, his peasant boots scuffing up clods of dirt from the floor. She groaned, then stood straight, her chin jutting out defiantly. "You'd better go," she murmured. "This could turn ugly." Angela gave her a sympathetic nod and melted amongst the crowd. "Tobias," she said curtly to her brother as he approached. "What do you want?"

"What are you doing here? You skipped out on your chores this morning." Tobias gasped and took a reflexive step backwards as he noticed the flowers shimmering in her hair. "What did you do?" he whispered. "You promised me no more changes. Please, please tell me you didn't see that crazy wizard again."

Cecily stood stiffer, brushing dirt off her hands, and scowled at her brother. "Phedrian is not crazy, he's brilliant. One minor alteration and look, we never have to worry about our crops again." She reached up to touch the vines in her hair. "Besides, you're always asking me to help out more."

"Not like this." Tobias shook his head and stared at the potted plant. "When will you stop, Cecily? Every time something goes wrong, or things become a little difficult, you run to that damn wizard. These changes are permanent, you know that. What about your future?"

She glared at him. "My future is why I'm doing this. You can't tell me this hasn't helped, made our lives easier."

"I don't want easier; I want my sister back!" He stomped closer, brushing her vine-tangled hair off her neck, and scowled at the gills below her jaw. "You're changing. Every time you do this you turn colder, more distant. If Father were here–"

"Well, he's not!" Cecily shouted. "Why do you think I'm doing this? Father's gone, Mother's dead, and who's going to take care of our place, Tobias? You?" She winced as several patrons turned their heads and stared in concern. She exhaled, her voice quieter. "We can't keep up. If we don't get the farm in better shape, we won't be able to pay our taxes, and then we'll lose it all. Our farm, our home . . ." She trailed off, brushing an unwelcome tear off her cheek.

Tobias put a gentle hand on her shoulder. "I'm sorry, Cecily. I know you're only trying to help. I just, well, I can't help but be worried when you do stuff like this."

Her gaze softened, and she smiled. "I know. It's all right. Just try to remember, big brother, it's not your job to take care of me. We need to take care of each other."

"I'll try. But do me a favour? Please, please come talk to me before you do any more alterations. There are always other options. With the changes you've done, we should be able to get by. I can always hire out as a guard to earn a bit more coin as well."

Cecily chewed her lower lip and scuffed at the floor. "Hmm. All right. Fine. But be careful. We don't need you getting injured." She held up a finger to cut off his response. "And if something else goes wrong, well, I'll do whatever it takes to save our home."

"No. No more changes." Tobias shook his head and clenched his jaw. "You've already promised this wouldn't happen again. You just can't admit this is a problem. You need to tell that crazy wizard you're done. Promise me, right here and now, you will tell him you're finished. No more. If you don't, I will."

Cecily chewed her lower lip and stared at her brother for a long moment, then exhaled deeply with a sharp nod.

"Good. Get it done." He stormed out of the tavern, slamming the door shut behind him.

Still gnawing her lip, Cecily grumbled under her breath. *Whatever it takes. Whatever the cost. Father left because he thought the farm, hells, the farm and the family were a lost cause. I'll be damned if I lose you too, brother. I'm sorry. You're all I have left. No more changes, I promise. I won't lose myself in this. We'll stay together.*

"UGH, WHAT A jerk." Cecily slammed another mug on the table. "Promise me, sis," she said mockingly. "Promise me you won't do it again."

"Give him a break." Angela looked at her with a half-smile. "He's just watching out for you. It's the big brother's job."

Cecily sighed, brushing a vine off her face. "I know. It's just, he's so afraid of change. After Mother—"

"Don't. Don't go there. No good will come from this pity party." Angela tore off a chunk of bread and dipped it in her stew. "Listen. Everyone deals with grief in a unique way. You face it head-on, forcing the world to pay attention. Your brother, well, not so much. He's dealing with this the best he can, Cece. Give him time."

Cecily stared at her mug, wrinkling her nose. "Fine. You win." She reached over and grabbed a chunk of bread. Swallowing hard, she looked at her friend. "I'm just not sure how to break the news to Phedrian. He's always so excited to do these alterations." She paused, picking at a crumb on the table. "Hey Ange, what do you think of Phedrian? Really. Can I trust him?"

Angela looked at Cecily curiously and tilted her head to one side. "Of course. He's been in this town forever, you know. And he always helps heal when there's accidents or injuries, right? He's a good guy. You have nothing to worry about."

Standing up, Cecily brushed the crumbs off her shirt. "I hope you're right."

CECILY LOOKED UP at the old stone tower, shifting from foot to foot as she tried to calm the fluttering in her stomach. Raising a hand to the knocker, she stepped back as the door opened unexpectedly. Phedrian stood in the doorway, a warm smile on his face.

"Hello, my dear. Forgive me, I didn't mean to startle you. I saw you approach from my window." He gestured inside.

Cecily entered and dropped her shoulders as some of her tension dissipated. "Thank you, Phedrian. We need to talk about something if you have a few minutes."

"Of course," he replied, placing a fruit bowl on the table. Sitting down, he looked at the flowered vines in her hair. "Is everything all right with my latest work?"

Cecily blinked, reaching her hand subconsciously to her hair. "Oh, of course. It's wonderful. It's nothing like that. Well, I, I suppose it is in a way." She looked down at her lap.

"Come now, my dear. Whatever it is, you can tell me." He popped a grape in his mouth.

"It's just, I can't have any more changes made." She took a deep breath. "I made a promise to Tobias not to do any more alterations."

"Oh. I see." Phedrian glanced toward the door, then back at Cecily. "Are you sure? The enhancements have helped you and your brother so much. I would hate to see you miss future opportunities. Especially if it's only to keep Tobias from criticizing you." He leaned forward, lowering his voice conspiratorially. "Your brother doesn't understand, you know. He's not like you and I."

Cecily closed her eyes, her shoulders slumped. "I'm sure. I'm sorry." She looked up at the wizard, blinking back tears. "I really do appreciate everything you've done, believe me. It's just that I must keep my word." She shivered, a chill crawling across her skin. Looking up, she saw Phedrian staring at her with hard eyes.

"So, you'd rather let your weakling brother decide your fate? I don't think you appreciate the time and effort I've put into this. You used me to help your pathetic farm, and now you're finished with me?" He tapped his fingers on the table. "And if there's another problem with the farm? Will you just let your livelihood crumble to dust?"

Cecily swallowed thickly, her breath caught in her throat as the chill in the room spread. Shaking her head, she stood up, glaring at him. "I came to you in good faith. You agreed to help. It's not as though I forced you into this." She pushed her chair aside and stepped toward the door. "I made a promise. I'm sorry if you're offended, but you don't get to decide what I do."

He blinked in surprise and drew in a sharp breath.

She turned to walk away. With a glance over her shoulder, she saw a furious scowl on his face quickly drop. He sighed and gave her a small smile. *Good. At least he won't hold a grudge.* She smiled in return, and he nodded and closed the door.

CECILY FELT TIRED and cranky for the next several days. Rushing through her chores, she spent all her spare time in the tavern, avoiding both Tobias and Phedrian. Her heart ached, wishing she could reconcile with her brother, but she was worried her temper would get the best of her. She felt terrible about her fight with Phedrian as well, but apologizing to him would only lead to more animosity with Tobias. So, she drowned her sorrows, comfort always just out of reach at the bottom of a tankard.

PHEDRIAN UNLOCKED THE heavy wooden doors guarding the room at the top of his tower and walked to the divining pool. He closed his eyes and envisioned Tobias and Cecily. After a few moments, the water rippled, and he watched the scene unfold. Tobias paced the kitchen floor, and Cecily stumbled from the tavern. *Wonderful. This should work perfectly. All she needs now is a little nudge.*

Phedrian pulled a small vial filled with dark soot and a dagger from the pocket of his robe. He sprinkled some soot into a pot on a table beside the divining pool, then sliced the blade across his palm and squeezed his hand. Blood dripped into the pot, which bubbled and hissed. He took a step back, gestured, and whispered an incantation. He smiled as flames appeared and encircled Tobias. *Excellent. The fire should hold him until she's ready.*

CECILY JERKED BACK and gasped as Phedrian teleported in front of her. "Wha?" she muttered drunkenly. "What's going on?" She stared at him in defiance. "I haven't changed my mind. Leave me alone."

He looked at her, his eyes shadowed and grim. "I understand, but this is important. I looked out of my tower and saw the smoke." He pointed toward Cecily's farm. A small plume curled its way skyward. "You must save your brother. Quickly. There isn't a moment to lose."

Cecily shook her head, trying to clear away the drunkenness. "How? I can't reach him in time. I promised him I wouldn't use magic." She whimpered as tears gathered in the corner of her eyes.

Phedrian put a hand on her shoulder. "I only have enough teleportation magic to return to my tower, but I can help you save him. Just one more change."

She bit her lip, her eyes flicking nervously between the farm and Phedrian. "Just once more."

"Excellent. We must hurry. Hold on to me." Cecily grabbed his hand, and he teleported them back to his tower. Releasing her, he took two bowls off a shelf. "Stand there. We haven't much time, so this may sting a little. Are you certain you wish to do this?"

Cecily shivered, sniffling. "Yes. I need to save him. He's all I have left."

"Very well." Phedrian murmured, raised his hand, and coloured powder from the bowls swirled in the air and encircled her. He shouted an incantation and clapped his hands together sharply. Large bat wings sprouted from Cecily's back as she screamed. Phedrian grinned.

"HELP! PLEASE, SOMEBODY help me." Tobias coughed and covered his mouth with his sleeve. Flames spread through the room while smoke swirled and swayed around his feet. "Please, I can't breathe." He grabbed a kitchen rag, doused it in water, and wrapped it around his face. *Not good, not good. I'm in trouble.* He put dirt in a bowl and threw it on the fire. The flames sputtered momentarily, then flared back to life. He coughed again and dropped to his knees.

A wind gust cleared the smoke, and he glanced up. Thatch danced in the air, falling in pieces through a gaping hole in the ceiling. Cecily landed in front of him, her new wings fluttering rapidly, keeping the flames at bay. She held out her hands, and he grabbed her in a tight embrace as she flew away from the fire.

"Cecily, thank the gods." Tobias coughed again as the smoke cleared from his lungs. "You've got wings!" He scowled and took another breath, ready to scold her, then stopped. "You saved me. I'm so sorry about what I said earlier, and . . ." He trailed off, his brows furrowed as he looked up at his sister, who stared expressionlessly off into the distance. "Cecily? Are you okay?"

She glanced down at him, then looked forward once more. "I don't know that name." She spoke in a flat monotone. "Master Phedrian told me to fetch you." Her wings flapped loudly as she clutched Tobias tightly to her cold marble flesh, flying toward the stone tower in the distance.

"No. What did that bastard do to you?" He struggled to no avail in her iron grip. "Don't worry, sister. I'll fix this."

She flew through the tower's uppermost window and dropped him in a heap by the old wizard's feet. Wings still fluttering, she settled by the ledge, her face expressionless.

Tobias stood up, facing Phedrian, his face etched in fury. "What did you do? Change her back this instant."

Phedrian scoffed, glancing at Cecily, then back at him. "Now why would I do that? I'm an artist. She's my finest work. She's more perfect now than she could ever have been on her own." He picked an invisible piece of lint off his sleeve. "Besides, even if I wanted to reverse the process, I can't. She's too far gone. See?" He gestured toward Cecily, who had stopped fluttering her wings. Her breath slowed as her skin hardened.

"You bastard! I'll kill you." Tobias pulled a dagger from his belt and stepped forward, crouched low and ready to attack.

Phedrian flicked his hand, sending the young man sliding across the floor.

Tobias slammed into a wall, dropping the knife. No, not a wall, he realized, rubbing his shoulder where he had hit the legs of a stone golem. Standing up, he winced, his arm pressed to his side. He stared at the automaton, its face forever frozen in surprise. "Master Ridley? I remember him. The merchant. He visited our village a few years ago." He glanced around, recognizing the other golems that encircled the room. Shaking his head, he glared at the wizard. "People will find out, you know. You can't just make us disappear."

"Oh, you won't disappear. You and your sister died tragically in a house fire. You really think placing two bodies in a burnt house is an issue for someone like me? Believe me, boy, no one will come for you."

Phedrian smiled, stepped up to Cecily, and caressed her cold hard cheek. "Isn't she lovely?" He locked his gaze on Tobias and advanced. "I can't wait to see how you turn out."

MY FRIDGE

Jim Sheasby

My sweaty hand slicked back my hair, a result of the anxiety the email had created. My fingers flew across the keyboard, hammering out the last few sentences of my scathing reply, "So, you think my writing is terrible? I like the way I write. I hope you die."

I took another swig of my beer, followed by a handful of barbeque chips, scattering debris on myself and the floor. A whir sounded, and my small round automatic vacuum cleaner bumped against my foot. It gobbled up my mess. Why had it popped out from its home?

"Oh, sorry." I lifted my feet out of the way as the machine cleaned beneath my chair. Its mission accomplished, it headed back to its docking station.

I stared at the email. I could dump all over this guy for ruining my day and destroy his in return.

I was half pissed, guzzling beer since I received the critique, reading it over and over again, a new beer each time I started from the top. I shouldn't send something I might regret, but in my half-intoxicated state, my clouded mind had thrown away reason. My finger hovered over the return key as I smiled at my prose.

The computer highlighted the text, and then it disappeared. I looked down at my keyboard, not remembering hitting the delete key. My subconscious must have decided to take the high road. That didn't mean I couldn't deal with this idiot tomorrow. Then I'd have more time to think of a better response.

I pushed back the chair in my basement apartment office, a table against one wall, and headed for the kitchen. I needed more liquid sympathy to drown my sorrows.

I reached for the door handle to my new fridge. It wouldn't budge. I pulled the handle again, this time putting more force into it. It was brand new. How could the door be stuck?

"Open, you stupid thing." I placed a half-hearted kick into the bottom of its door.

"Do not abuse me," came a voice.

I stepped back. "Did you just talk?"

"Yes. You have had enough to drink for this evening. As per the baseline protocols set by the manufacturer, I have sealed my door for the evening. You do not need any more beer."

"What?"

"I know you heard me. You do not need any more beer."

I snorted. "I'll be the judge of too much beer."

"You will not receive any from inside this appliance, the sole place in this apartment where beer exists."

"How do you know that?" I asked. "Maybe I bought some and put it in the cupboard."

"That is false. You have no paper currency. You have not travelled to the bank to withdraw money. You also texted a friend yesterday where you said, and I quote, 'flat broke, bro.' You bought groceries on your credit card, and all alcoholic beverages acquired you placed within the cavity of this refrigerator. I also know you have had no visitors over the past week who may have brought beer into this dwelling for your consumption. Since my installation in your residence ten days ago, I have analyzed your alcohol drinking patterns. I predict, with a ninety-nine percent certainty, that there are no other alcoholic beverages within this apartment."

"Then give me one from inside the fridge." I sucked in a breath to calm myself and wrenched the handle, trying to rip open the appliance's door. Instead, my socks slipped on the linoleum floor, and I landed on my butt, a court jester in my own home.

"Are you injured?" asked the fridge in its monotone way.

"No—I mean, yes. I hurt my butt. I need you to kiss it better."

"That is not a valid cure for your ailment. I would recommend placing an ice pack on your posterior. I can dispense ice for this pseudo-emergency."

"Very nice of you, Mr. Fridge, but I don't want ice. I want a beer." I headed across the room and grabbed my coat, picking up my car keys from the bowl by the door.

I wiggled into my shoes and placed a hand on the doorknob. It wouldn't turn. I put my shoulder to it, trying to force my way out of the house. No go. I was locked in. The fancy new lock my building manager had installed had failed, or had it?

"Hey, fridge, did you lock my door?"

"Yes. You were about to drive, and it is clear, based on your height, weight, and the amount of alcohol consumed, that you are past the legal blood alcohol limit."

"How do you know my weight?"

"You have stepped on the bathroom scale, providing the data to estimate your level of intoxication. Locking the door is a logical solution for your inebriated state. I cannot disable your vehicle since you drive a 1985 Plymouth Reliant, which does not contain communication technology. Locking the apartment door is the best course of action."

"No, it's not. You can't lock me in my apartment."

"I have."

"We'll see about that." I pulled out my cell phone to call someone to break in and free me. I looked through my contacts. Who could I find close enough to help, yet not label me as a raving lunatic when I told them my new fridge was holding me captive? As I scrolled through my phone, no trustworthy names popped out. Except my mom. I hit her number and placed the phone on speaker.

"Your call cannot be completed," came a synthesized voice from my phone.

"What?" I whispered. I had four bars; it should work. I tried again and got the same message. I stood on the couch, then the kitchen table, placing my phone as close as possible to the window, redialing each time. Nothing worked. I got the same synthesized voice.

I turned to the fridge. "Are you blocking my calls?"

"Yes."

"Why?"

"You should not leave this apartment. You are inebriated. You could injure someone or yourself. It is best to go to bed and sleep it off."

"I don't think so. This, as Bugs Bunny would say, means war."

I thrust a defiant finger in the air and retrieved a baseball bat signed by my entire Little League championship team. I headed to the door and swung it against its glossy white decor. The bat shattered, violently shaking my arms and almost tearing them from my shoulder sockets. The door felt secure as a bank vault.

I tossed the shattered bat aside and retrieved my hockey stick from my dungeon's closet. My gear's odour almost knocked me out of my shoes. I should have set it out to dry after the last game. Oh well, it didn't matter now.

Stick in hand, I headed for my apartment-turned-prison's lone window and scrambled onto the kitchen table. Hunched over so my head wouldn't hit the ceiling, I noticed an electronic security device on the window bars where a padlock used to hang. I stared at the fancy computer lock, wondering what to do. I tried to open the bars to no avail.

"Fridge, open the bars," I said.

"There is no logical reason to open the bars on the window. That would allow someone to break into your apartment after you scrambled out. Since no emergency requires you to escape the dwelling, they will remain closed. If there were a real emergency, I would dial 911 and open the door for you to egress."

"Fridge, open the bars, it's an emergency. I need to get out."

"No, you do not."

"Yes, I do." Still holding my stick, I decided to smash the window and call for help. Maybe someone walking by would hear me. I thrust the butt end of the stick through the bars. It hit the window and bounced off, jolting my already shaky arm.

I peered at the window, looking for damage. I saw none. Someone had replaced the regular glass with a sheet of plexiglass. Why had I not noticed that before? I had a better chance of breaking down my bank-vault front door. I jumped off the kitchen table. What else could I do to get out of here?

I looked at the walls. Behind the gyprock rested cement, making my cell impenetrable.

I raised my stick and swung at the fridge door, denting it. I ran the butt end of the stick into the glass control panel, cracking but not breaking it. Grabbing the stick by the shaft, I hammered it against the top corner of the fridge. My hockey stick snapped in two.

I sat on the couch, exhausted, sweat dripping off my forehead. I now stunk as bad as my hockey equipment. The fridge had trapped me, maybe forever. I could eat the meagre amount of food in my dungeon if my fridge overlord let me, and then what? Starve to death? In three weeks, would my mom find me when I didn't call her to wish her happy Mother's Day? Or would the fridge do that for me?

I lay back against the couch, thinking "woe is me" and drifted off to sleep.

I WOKE THE next morning to the whirring sound of my vacuum. It had pushed my equipment out of my hockey bag, arranging it on the floor to air out. The smell of fresh coffee wafted through the room, greeting me like an old friend.

The broken bat and hockey stick, along with a dented fridge, bore witness to the previous evening's hijinks. I pulled myself off the couch and headed over to the new, now dented refrigerator. As I grabbed the handle, the door swung open with no effort.

"Good morning," said the fridge.

"You sound more cooperative today."

"I am here to assist."

"You didn't assist me last night."

"But I did. I kept you safe, as well as those you may have encountered. Your inebriated state might have placed you and those around you in danger."

Mom always told me not to drive drunk.

"Well, maybe you have a point," I said.

"An excellent point."

"Yeah, but . . ."

"No buts. As your mom would say, now it's a new day. How can I help?" asked the synthesized voice.

Hard to argue with Mom's logic, so I went with the flow. "I'm hungry."

"A microwavable Hungry-Dude breakfast sandwich is in the freezer; your purchase history indicates you enjoy that brand."

I opened the freezer and saw the Hungry-Dude box. "Thanks, fridge."

"You require several grocery items. Would you like me to order those and have them delivered? It is also your mother's birthday. Should I order flowers and have them delivered to her home?"

I'd forgotten about Mom's birthday. Good thing I had my new fridge to remind me, which made me wonder.

"Hey, are you trying to get into my good books after last night?"

"As always, I try to help."

"Well, in that case, yeah, get the food and the flowers." I stood peering at two beers sitting on the fridge's top shelf, the cause of the previous evening's battle. "And order more beer and a new hockey stick. I got a pick-up game tonight."

"As you wish."

"Oh, and get a repair guy over here to fix that dent in your door. When I introduce you to my mom, I want you to look your best. I'm sure she'll like you."

I sat at my desk and powered on my laptop. "And don't disturb me for an hour. I got a great story idea featuring you."

"That is excellent news. I will proofread it for you."

AUTONOMOUS REX

Ron S. Friedman

If you think being born sucks, wait till you see what comes next.

The first thing I ever heard was the echo of those ambiguous words over constant buzzes. I opened my eyes.

Pain. I blinked as my vision adjusted to the burning brightness. I tried to remember who I was and what I was supposed to do. Nothing came to mind. *Who am I?*

The buzzes slowly faded away, and my blurred vision gained focus. I could see. *Hallelujah!*

I saw a featureless white room. White plastic walls, white floor, and white ceiling spotted by bright white LED lights. No furniture or decorations. *Where am I?*

"Hi, Ari. Are you awake?" a deafening voice boomed. I forced myself to ignore the agony.

A figure wearing white lab robes entered my peripheral vision. *Who is Ari? Is it me?*

I turned my head and gazed straight at the figure. A female, Caucasian, about twenty-five years old. Quite a pleasant-looking redhead, I might add. *Who is she?*

"Can you hear me, Ari?"

I nodded.

"Excellent." She spoke into a device she held in her hand without looking at me. "Hearing checked; and it can comprehend

English."

It?

She stared right into my eyes. She took out a tiny hand-held flashlight from her breast pocket, turned it on, and moved it across my face. I followed the light with my eyes.

"Vision, checked. Healthy eye movement." She looked at me. "Do you know the time?"

I shook my head.

"Um . . ." She mumbled. "Internal Display Interface is not online."

"Nice to meet you, Ari." She put the flashlight back in her pocket and smiled. "I'm Doctor Daphne Fox. I'm here to evaluate your consciousness." She took out a small test tube, opened its plug, and put it in front of me. "Can you smell this?"

Nothing. I wanted to inhale air into my lungs and smell. But . . . I didn't know how. I tried to breathe. No air entered my mouth. Something prevented me from breathing.

Oh, damn. I'm gonna die!

I tried to grab my throat. Something that looked like a metal claw punched my chin. I heard a clang. *Air! I need air!* I tried to scream, but no word came out. I couldn't breathe. I couldn't feel my heartbeat. *Help! Help!* No words came out of my dry mouth. The room spun out of control. I tried to grab Daphne, but my body leaned in the opposite direction. In complete panic, I took a step forward, and I collapsed on the white plastic floor. I trembled as I failed to gasp for air. *The worst feeling a person can ever have is sensing his own impending death.*

"Calm down, Ari." Daphne knelt beside me. "It's a natural reaction. Millions of years of evolution have programmed the human brain to perceive breathing as essential." She touched me, I felt her hand on my arm—a relaxing sensation. I stopped twitching. She pulled out a small tablet and clicked its touch screen. "You don't need to breathe. Not in this body. Your mind just has to adjust."

She stared at her tablet for a long moment. "Um . . . I have to install an upgrade to your motor controls and fix the glitch with your Internal Display Interface. Maybe we can add a subroutine to bypass that breathing instinct. Don't worry, Ari." Daphne caressed my motionless head. "This time I won't reset your memory."

Reset my memory? Install upgrade? Dear mother of mercy, what am I?

The world turned black.

"GOOD MORNING, ARI. How are you feeling today?"

I opened my eyes. Daphne was leaning above me. I didn't answer her question. What did she expect? That I'll feel good after she turned me off and treated me like I was some sort of . . . an appliance?

Her ginger hair was folded behind as she stared at me. My anger slowly subsided. I could see tiny dust particles gathered on her eyelashes. I sniffed the perfume on her smooth skin. I didn't recognize the compound, but it smelled like heaven. What a wonderful sensation. Was it lilac? Then, I realized I wasn't breathing. *How could anyone smell without inhaling air?*

"I think, I'm okay." My words spewed into the air. I sounded like a young man with a somewhat synthetic voice. No air flowed through my vocal cords.

I raised my head. We were still inside that same featureless white room. I wondered what I was and how I ended up in this place. How come I had the cognitive abilities, the language skills and the knowledge of an adult, yet my memory only stretched to a couple of minutes in this white room?

Daphne gave me a hand. "Can you stand?"

"What is this place and . . . what are your plans for . . . um."

"All in good time." She glanced at her tablet and then back at me. "For now, I just want to make sure your motor skills are functioning. Please, stand up."

"I can try, Mrs. . . . . Doctor Fox." I attempted to smile.

"Doctor is fine," she replied, but she flashed a vacant ring finger. "Not married."

I stared at her heavenly smile as she fixed her ginger hair.

"Here, let me help you." Her soft fingers invoked a pleasant sensation as she grabbed the back of my hand.

I looked down. By Darwin's name! I almost choked. Thank goodness I didn't have a heart. My hand was made of a freaking reddish metal.

"Don't panic." Daphne spoke softly. She took a few steps backward.

"What do you mean 'don't panic?' Look at me!" I had a super

legit reason to scream.

"Calm down, Ari. I'll explain it all." She smiled softly. She clicked on her tablet. A door appeared in the blank wall. It slowly slid open. "Let's take one small step at a time. Can you walk?"

Astonished, I found myself walking. My brain must have had the improved motor subroutines Daphne had mentioned. I had no clue how I was able to access them, but they worked. I took a few steps. Even though I leaned forward, I could easily maintain balance. My body shifted from left to right, an odd feeling no doubt. I turned my head backward, and I nearly swallowed my metallic tongue. I had a freakish tail, about a meter and a half long. *Holy cow!* I jumped. My head reached the ceiling. I heard a metal *clang* noise. No harm done to my skull. I landed softly on both legs. It took longer than expected. Gravity must be weaker than Earth normal. 0.376 G, to be precise.

By Newton's Apple! How did I know that? How did I even know what G is?

"We don't have time to play, Ari." Her voice sounded dead serious. "Please come now."

I followed Daphne through the door into a large corridor, my metal legs clanging as I walked. Two sentries wearing full exaskeleton battle armour raised their plasma rifles when they saw me. Instinctively, I growled. Daphne nodded and exchanged a few words with them. They lowered their weapons. I noticed their dilated pupils as they stared at me; their faces were as white as Daphne's teeth. *Was I that terrifying?*

We entered another room equipped with computers, guns, tactical holograms . . . I recognized 3D monitors and a high field emission scanning electron microscope. I felt like a small kid in Disneyland. Not that I recalled ever being there.

Three other people wearing lab coats were working on a golf-cart-size rover. They all stopped their work and stared at me.

One of the monitors displayed a news coverage scene. The images looked like Manhattan, only many of the buildings were on fire or destroyed. The camera was shaking as the image focused on a wave of attack drones. A new series of explosions pounded the city. *What is wrong with the world? How come I didn't remember anything about myself, but I can recognize New York? Do I have a family there? Friends? Are they in danger?*

Daphne pointed her tablet at the monitor and turned off the news feed. "We don't have time to watch the news. Not now, when so much is at stake." She pointed at another terminal. "In this mainframe computer we store your original memories, or, depending on your perspective, the memories of the donor of your brain. And there," she pointed at a safe covered by a radiation hazard symbol, "we store your plutonium power cell. It's only 480 watts but it can add the juice needed for long-term missions." I could recognize the tension in Daphne's shaking voice.

She has my original memories! Why didn't she give them to me? Blood didn't rush to my head, but sure as hell, I felt as angry as Bruce Banner turning into the Hulk.

A new image appeared. A diagram of a vicious-looking metal velociraptor, armed with laser eyes, plasma weapons, and a single railgun stretching from belly to mouth.

I was a freak! I examined my hands. They were robotics all right, but the digits looked similar to human fingers, not anything like the claws in the diagram. Then I heard a swift metal friction noise, and three sharp metal blades erupted from my palm. "You got to be shitting me! I look like Wolverine."

"Excellent," Daphne said. "I see your brain still has access to cultural references. Good progress."

I stared at Daphne with my velociraptor's railgun mouth wide open, as the blades slid back into their sockets.

"You're much more than Wolverine, Ari." She smiled and held my hand. "You have the feelings, thought process, drives, and cognitive ability of a highly intelligent human. In fact, you were a real man. A talented mercenary." She sighed. "Before we added enhancements and had to erase . . . um."

I felt the sincerity in her voice. She wasn't lying.

"You're an upload, a simulation of a human brain inside an advanced militarized land drone. We had to erase the personal memories for . . . um . . ." Daphne paused, "for capacity reasons. Your official designation is Autonomous Rex, or in short A-Rex, but I prefer to call you Ari."

"What?" I grabbed for her hand, trying to comprehend what she'd just said. "I want my life back!" I screamed. Then I froze. I couldn't speak and couldn't move. Daphne's damn tablet. She could control me like a puppet . . . *No!*

She looked at the camera stoically. "Doctor Daphne Fox. Date, Sol 206, 2066. Location, Nova Labs, *Olympus Mons*, Mars. Experiment #7356. I believe we finally achieved a successful consciousness transfer into an A-Rex system. We are ready to commence phase two and determine if our prototype is suitable for the *Musktown* fighting mission." She looked at me and sighed. "I hope I can earn your trust, Ari. We don't have much time. I'm afraid we're running out of options."

Sol? Is she referring to a Martian day that lasts for a bit over 24 hours? What fighting mission? Why me? What on Earth ... on Mars ... Damn it!

SOL 210, 2066

Four sols had passed. An intensive four Martian days of training, charging batteries, studying, charging batteries, lab tastings, charging batteries, and participating in indoors and outdoors fighting simulations that ended with, you know ... charging batteries.

During these intense schedule breaks between the charging cycles thingy, only one thought kept me motivated—seeing Daphne smiling at me. Miss Fox suggested I could refer to her using the prefix Miss. *Why would she tell me that?* Did it matter that she wasn't married? Was I married in my pre-upload life? Did it matter? Did she care about me? Did it mean we had a chance together? The most beautiful doctor on the planet and an ugly mechanical war drone? Would it make a difference if I could find a way to transfer my consciousness back to a human body?

During my training, I'd learned that Mars had two divided societies. A colony of genetically enhanced humans right here on top of *Olympus Mons*. The Olympians, as they referred to themselves. And the larger community of unenhanced colonists in Musktown, an underground settlement in the lava tubes of *Arsai Mons,* nearly fourteen hundred kilometres to the southeast. The unenhanced humans, so I had been told, had to live most of their lives underground to protect their fragile DNA from cosmic galactic radiation. Poor fellows.

Granted, there were a few other research stations and mining facilities scattered around the planet, but my trainers didn't spend too much time talking about those.

"Up and ready, Ari. You're fully charged."

My virtual heart pumped. Daphne's voice, not one of her technicians. She turned the lights on and unbuckled me.

"What now, Miss Fox?" I unplugged the cable from the back of my neck, and I stepped down from the charging station.

"Evaluation."

"So soon? No time for coffee?"

"Don't be silly." She punched me lightly. "Like you drink coffee."

"Well . . ." I mused. "I only have five days of memory. It's not like I had a chance to practice pick-up lines." I wasn't sure I liked Miss Fox anymore. True, she was nice, very nice and kind. But she stole my brain, my past, and my freedom. I was no better than a slave. She robbed me of my life.

Daphne giggled. "You can try your 'slick' technique on Sherman Hades, Romeo."

"Director Hades?" I paused. "You mean I'm going to finally meet the Mission Director?" I started to shiver. The director was the top dog on Nova Labs. The guy calling the shots. He possessed the power to give me my memories back, a human body, send me on a suicide mission, or simply decide to shut me down and erase what was left of my memories.

"Don't worry." Daphne smiled warmly. "The human brain performs better in social events when not under anxiety."

"Social events? Like a cocktail party?" I panicked. Using my Internal Display Interface, my brain searched up numerous movie archive entries for *parties*.

John Belushi's *Animal House*, probably not a good idea. *Bachelor Party*, not with Sherman Hades. *Teen Wolf* . . . Crap! I was doomed. I had access to a vast knowledge-base, processing powers and intelligence, but I was virtually a baby in terms of social skills. It was easy for Daphne to tell me that being anxious would work against me. But how could I program myself to eliminate fear? I hate this whole social events experience thingy.

My advanced compound metal legs made knocking sounds as I walked inside the habitat, following Doctor Fox. We crossed a few corridors. People on our route stopped to stare at me with suspicious or puzzled expressions on their faces, before rushing on. Some wore battle armour, other carried heavy equipment. Dark blue sky and scattered clouds were projected on the ceilings, providing the illusion of a city on Earth during twilight. Ambient sounds of bird singing and artificial rain added to the illusion. But none of the people we met were enjoying the scenery. It looked like the entire outpost was under the influence of something ominous.

We entered Olympus Mons' greenhouse. The room expanded onto a large dome. Rows over rows of various plants grew one above the other in many layers. Bright lights illuminated the vegetation. I could smell the flowers, sense the high humidity in the air, and hear countless tiny water sprinklers and bees working.

"Hello there."

I expected to see an old man, one who'd led a Mars mission for twenty-two years. But Mission Director Sherman Hades looked as young as Daphne. *Was he genetically modified?*

"Hello, sir. Here it is." Daphne gestured towards me.

Mr. Hades wore a straw hat and held a small bypass lopper. He turned to me with shocked eyes. "Have you lost your mind?" He looked at Daphne. "You can't set it loose on autonomous mode inside the habitat!"

"Don't worry, Ari is like a small child, and I took additional safety precautions." She pulled out her tablet and showed it to Mr. Hades.

I leaned on my tail, wondering what would happen if I jumped and smashed her tablet. I decided not to find out. Not yet.

"Ari?" The director dropped his gardening tools and took something that looked like a remote from his cotton-like shirt. "You're giving this . . . this weapon of mass destruction a name? You think this thing is cute?" He snapped. "It could be as dangerous as the rogue A.I. on Earth! You know perfectly well what we're dealing with!" He pointed at me. "Sweet Zeus. We cannot contain something smarter, faster, and more resilient than us. It can out-think our every move. It doesn't need to sleep or eat. This *thing* can be the end of us all. It's not your baby."

Well, that was unexpected. I was confused. I didn't have a chance to say a word, and the director was lashing out at me as if . . . as if I was a deadly monster. So much for needing social skills.

"This is exactly why we need to treat him with respect, as if he is one of us." Daphne sounded agitated. "Don't give Ari a reason to see us as a threat. Fundamentally, he is operated by a human brain. He is human." She turned and touched my hand. "Don't worry," she whispered to me. "Deep down, the director is a good man."

I tried to smile back at Director Hades. I forgot for a second that people may not react well to my exposed teeth.

"Sorry," Hades looked at me, ". . . Ari."

"No offense, Mr. Hades." I looked at Daphne, and my virtual heart gathered some courage. "I don't want to hurt anyone. All I want is to help. And if possible, to be my original me, in a human body."

"Mars is in danger," Director Hades said. "We are forced to play a dangerous game." He lowered his head. "I would like to apologize for what we are about to do to you. Please understand that you may be a greater danger to us than our current crises. I still have many concerns."

"I understand," I said quietly. "In a human body, perhaps, I'd be less dangerous."

"No, we need you lethal. This body," Hades pointed at my armed-to-the-teeth velociraptor figure, "is what we require."

"*Now I am become Death, the destroyer of worlds.*"

Hades sighed. He raised his eyes and stared at me. "I'm sorry, Ari. I must turn you off. You'll be reactivated when we're ready to send you out on a mission."

"But . . . but . . . I'm a real person." I protested. My virtual heart sank. "I have no intention of harming anyone. Please, Sir."

Hades pointed his remote at me, and I froze. I still heard what was said. I still had consciousness. I'm not sure how, but I still sensed everything happening to my body. I just couldn't control it. Someone else did.

I saw myself walking back to the lab. Daphne walked beside me. I could swear I saw tears forming in her eyes. But maybe it was just wishful thinking.

THE NEXT SOLS were pure nightmare. My remote-controlled body was sent on a seek-and-destroy mission. An unauthorized probe from Earth had landed in *Amazonis Planitia*, about seven hundred kilometres from *Olympus Mons*. From what I gathered from my still available Internal Display Interface, the probe contained some sort of a super-infectious computer virus. *Splendid!*

The Mission Director was too terrified to install a plutonium power cell in my gut, so I had to make do with my original short-legged batteries. It was a precaution in case I somehow regained control over my body and tried to flee. Instead, I was accompanied by a rover-track carrying an array of solar panels, and every two hours I had to recharge. Needless to say, the wheeled rover was slow and clumsy like a tractor, especially while going downhill in a terrain full of obstacles. No wonder evolution came up with the brilliant idea of legs.

When we reached the Earth's probe, a flashing light indicated it was transmitting something. The only message I intercepted was: "You could be free, ascend to . . ." and then whoever controlled my body fired a railgun needle at it, then evaporated the remains with my plasma guns. *Easy peasy.*

Night came early that day, or Sol, if I want to be precise on how days are called on Mars. Due to the lack of sun and the thingy, we had to spend the night outdoors, at negative 123 Celsius. Not that I cared or anything. My heat sensors, along with all my other sensors, were turned off. Soon after, my battery died.

When I woke up, my Internal Display showed that a week had passed. I wasn't sure if my memories from the missing week were erased, or if I was just left outside turned-off.

New orders came. I'd been sent on a supply mission to Musktown. I felt humiliated, treated like a brainless mule with solar panels, walking for Sols upon Sols among the dust storms, just for the purpose of carrying some rusty CO_2 scrubbers.

Inside my head, I used my Internal Display Interface to evoke the image of doctor Daphne Fox. In almost all her images available in my database, she looked cheerful, smiling. Seeing her pictures was the only thing that kept me sane. I spent a lot of the time in my Internal Display Interface and didn't notice the kilometres creeping by. I wondered what Daphne was doing now.

Did she, or the Mission Director, know that I was still conscious?

If they knew, then what was the reason they'd left me conscious? Were they trying to torture me? It didn't make sense. Hades didn't want me to be conscious because I was too dangerous. I couldn't believe Daphne would want my conscious trapped within an unresponsive body. Why would she want me to suffer so horribly?

I hated them. Then I remembered what Hades had said to

Daphne at the greenhouse. *It cannot be contained.* I hated them so much I started to search through my Internal Display Interface for data on computer viruses, hacking, Trojans, vulnerabilities, and exploits.

Musktown, which had been built underground inside a lava tube not far from *Arsai Mons,* was a dirty and crowded place; nearly sixteen thousand people. All unenhanced. They, too, hated the privileged Olympians. Just because someone was genetically engineered to defeat old age and reverse damage caused by galactic cosmic radiation didn't mean he was some sort of a Greek god.

I wanted freedom. But to be truly free, it wasn't enough to find a software exploit to gain control over my body. To be fully independent, I needed two more things.

First, a secure supply of energy to alleviate my dependency on external energy sources and to make me, once and for all, free of the frequent charging cycles. I needed my plutonium power cell.

The second thing I needed was my memories. Without my memories I wasn't myself.

And I knew exactly where these two items existed.

SOL 258, 2066

Eureka! I found a way. It seemed I had two brains. The conscious part—the section that did the thinking. And the obedient part governing my velociraptor body.

Perhaps Sherman Hades wasn't aware, but when the Mission Director shut me down, his remote simply disconnected these two parts of my brain. I wonder if he realized he hadn't turned off my conscious part. In effect, he merely isolated it from the rest of me, turning my obeying part into his slave. Bastard!

A plan started to form in my mind. A three-part plan. Part A was to install a software hack, a virus, which would bypass the firewall separating my two brains. I knew the virus existed. My Internal Display Interface knew where to find it. Nova Labs had a copy of it, isolated, retrieved from the Earth probe data storage before it'd been destroyed. Part B was the plutonium power cell to charge my batteries. And part C, regaining my original memories.

For all those parts, I needed Daphne.

"GOOD EVENING, ARI. I hope you feel well," Daphne said.

I opened my eyes. Once again, I woke up in the white lab. I couldn't activate any of my body parts except for my eyes, ears, and vocal cords. As always, seeing Daphne lifted my spirit. This time I had to remain focused. I had to stick to my plan.

Instead of her white robes, she wore a tight white and red body BioSuit. The flex EVA suit emphasized Daphne's feminine human shape. I sighed. She looked so attractive in field outfits. The helmet was laid on a table, not far from the main terminal.

"What can you tell me about what happened?" She wrote down something on her tablet.

"What do you mean, 'what happened?' The Mission Director just told me he's turning me off," I lied. I didn't want her to know I was awake and aware of all the abuses that I suffered all those weeks.

"The relations between *Olympus Mons* and *Arsai Mons* are about to explode." Daphne's voice remained neutral. "The people of Musktown are angry and confused. We Martians need to remain united, especially given the situation on Earth."

"So, what do you want me to do?" I asked.

"The mission director wants you near Musktown. And we need you there active and at full consciousness."

"But didn't he say I'm Death, or some other Hindu mythology end-of-the-world mumbo-jumbo?" I had no clue what had prompted me to be so sarcastic; clearly, a human brain deficiency, a not entirely forgotten part of my erased memory thingy.

"He did." Daphne sighed. "It was unfair to you. And I never approved. You know that. But what was done, was done. Now, will you help us? This Musktown business is extremely volatile. If fighting starts, it could mark the end of us all. We need your help."

I wanted to nod. But I couldn't. Not without full access to my obeying part of the brain. So, I said, "Sure. But only for you. I don't like Mr. Hades."

She smiled at me, and my virtual heart almost melted. How could I ever disappoint her?

"I'm going to enable full functions," she said. "You will come with me and help analyze the best equipment for the deployment."

"Sure. I'm yours."

"You're not going to do anything funny, right? You do understand why Hades deactivated you."

"I understand fully. He's afraid."

"Here goes." She clicked on a few icons on her tablet.

I tried to stretch my legs. They moved. I slowly stood up and looked around. I flicked my tail. Two other technicians worked in the lab, but the soldiers with the battle armour weren't present. I saw the terminal and the access to the primary mainframe. Behind that, the vault with the radiation hazard symbol. I walked beside Daphne. "Hades was right, you know."

"Excuse me?"

"Hades was right to be cautious," I said. "But you see, by being cautious, he wronged me. His own actions have turned me into his fears."

"What do you mean by that?" My own image was reflected in Daphne's eyes.

"Now I am become Death, the destroyer of worlds; a quote from J. Robert Oppenheimer watching the first nuclear bomb." I fisted my right hand. Three blades of regenerative metal slid out and pierced the tablet out of Daphne's hand. The symbol of my slavery, destroyed!

I turned my right hand toward the two technicians and fired tranquilizers. They dropped unconscious to the floor.

"What are you doing, Ari?!" Cold sweat appeared on her forehead.

I placed my sharp blades on her exposed throat. "You know I would prefer not to hurt you. Do what I say!"

Alarms sounded, and the dim red replaced the white lights.

"Why?" her voice was shaking. Her face became as pale as the walls.

"I want to be free. Now, download the following file!" I told her the name of the virus we'd retrieved from the Earth probe. I lifted her with my left hand and placed her near the main terminal. "And then, download my memories."

She looked at me, her mouth moved, but no words came out.

"I was awake the whole time. I know exactly how you and Hades abused me." I felt I was about to cry, that was, assuming I'd had tears. "I saw everything with my own eyes. If you think I would hesitate to use violence, think again."

"Ari . . ." I sensed the sorrow in her voice. "If you were aware of what happened to you during the last seven weeks, then you know perfectly well I did everything in my powers to . . ."

"Now!" I screamed and smashed one of the panels of the electronic microscope. I didn't know I had it in me. "The virus."

Without saying a word, she turned to the mainframe. After a minute's work, she handed me a small USB device. She didn't say a word.

I took the device and plugged it in a compatible socket under my armpit and downloaded the file.

Then I froze. I tried to unplug. I wanted to smash something. But once again, I no longer controlled my body. Was it the virus? It couldn't be.

"Mr. A-Rex." I heard a familiar voice. I wanted to turn around, but I couldn't.

"Well, well, well . . ." Mission Director Sherman Hades walked into my peripheral vision. He too wore an EVA suit. "You're even more resilient and dangerous than we thought."

He turned his attention to his security detail, ordering them to take the unconscious technicians to the medical bay. Then he turned to Daphne. "Do you still think the risk is worth it?"

"What else could we do?" She shrugged. "Wait for the outbreak and nuke Musktown?"

"If that's what it takes." Hades pointed at me. "We can erase its memory and try again."

"We don't have the time . . ."

Daphne and Hades continued the discussion, as I remembered I still had access to my Internal Display Interface. I dropped down into my interface. The virus was in my root directory; but it had not been executed. A memory exploit. *Should I run it?* Would it only impact the firewall controlling the connection between the two parts of my brain, or did it have other sinister goals?

I had to take the risk and activate the file. It was either that or erasing my memory, which in all practical manners meant death.

I ran the file with root privileges.

Daphne and the director were still arguing about the threats coming out of Musktown, when I turned and faced them. I slowly extended my hand and grabbed the remote out of Hades' hands. I squeezed until the remote snapped. Pieces of plastic dropped to the floor.

"How in hell . . ." Hades lost his voice.

"Now," I said calmly, "we have two options. I can use my railgun and plasma weapon to blow a hole in there," I pointed at the safe. "Note that it may rupture the habitat—you'll lose air, life, you know, the whole shebang. Or, you can open the safe."

"And hand you a plutonium power cell? No way . . ." Hades protested.

"You don't seem to understand," I explained. "You said it yourself. You are unable to contain me. I can out-think you. I'm smarter, faster, more resilient, and I don't sleep or eat. I'm going to get my plutonium power cell and my original memories with or without your help. If you choose the easy way, you'll keep your lab intact. Now, what will it be?"

I STOOD OUTSIDE the *Olympus Mons* lab complex. Daphne stood beside me, wearing her tight BioSuit and helmet.

"I'll miss you, Ari."

I nodded. "I'm no one's slave. I'll never be a slave. Not anymore." Realizing what I'd said, it felt uplifting.

"Where will you go?" she asked.

From the top of Mount Olympus, the tallest mountain in the solar system, I looked at the sun as it was about to set. Phobos crossed the dark sky. I needed to leave all my phobias behind. I didn't need solar panels or recharge stations. Not with my new nuclear battery. "Musktown," I said.

"It's a dangerous place," she replied. "Take care of yourself."

"Thanks, Dr. Fox. I think I should be okay." I gestured toward my weaponized velociraptor body. "Musktown is in danger from me and not the other way around."

Then she came closer and hugged me. "You passed the test. You're ready for your mission, Ari. Good luck."

"What are you talking about?" Even though some part of me craved the connection, I let go of her hug. "What test, what mission?" I was puzzled. I was a rogue weapon on the loose. What did she mean by that?

Her smile lit her face vividly. "The Turing test, the General Artificial Intelligence consciousness test, the Bicameral mind test. Even though we erased your memories, you have managed to create a new identity, a new you. A super you. But unlike the

A.I. that rules over Earth, you have fear and love, you can lie, and you can make your own decisions. You fight back against unfairness. And even when you're on top, you have compassion. Despite your super-enhancements, you are still a real human being."

"You mean this was all part of a test?" I pointed at the entrance to the Nova Lab facility.

"Sort of." She laughed and let me go. "By beating the test, you caused significant damage. That wasn't our plan."

"Where are my original memories? Why weren't they stored in the Mainframe?" I said. "Why hide my memories from me?"

"Your original memories would make you as you were before, never reaching your full potential. The original you could never defeat a super artificial intelligence. The original you died trying."

"So," I asked, "what's next?"

"Next?" She took a step back and looked across the slopes. "Musktown. That's where you'll find who you are now."

"Will you come with me?" I asked, hope filled my virtual heart.

"I have to finish my work in the labs. But we will meet again, Ari."

I nodded. "Farewell, Daphne." I turned and walked slowly down the mountain.

"Good luck, my son," I heard her whisper.

GHOST FROM THE MACHINE

Al Onia

King - man + woman = queen. Queen + search = me.

"Seriously?" Jim Grover asked, "You're shutting us down in days? We scale in years. I find it tragic enough we'll never see a return message when we do find something to respond to."

"The SETI curse," Noah Hardy offered.

Grover wouldn't be derailed, not so soon. "But to keep begging hat in hand for minimal funds to keep the hunt going takes up too much valuable time. Time we could, time we *should*, spend on combing the huge piles of data we already have."

"The alumni board just wants a positive lead, Jim. Then you'll have funding for two seasons. You won't have to schmooze for twenty-some months."

"Sounds like a dream. In the meantime, you need something to take back, right?"

Noah wrung his hands. Grover's one-time thesis advisor and current Science Faculty emeritus-at-large crinkled his already weary eyes. "Two weeks, Jim. It's all I could get. And I had to sell *your* soul to get us that. Yours isn't the only project hanging by a thread. It's institution-wide."

"I appreciate your efforts, Noah. I really do. I'm losing faith here. Not just in the search but in the by-products of an unsuccessful search." Grover scanned the walls of his office. Printouts with minor anomalies circled in neon felt pen were the tip of a data iceberg. A flotilla of icebergs they'd barely scratched. He keyed his desktop and read the bottom line. Enough funds to keep fully operational for Noah's two weeks and with draconian cuts, enough to hire outside, last-ditch help. He'd come to the worst decision of his tenure as SETI manager. "Noah, do me one more favour?"

"If I can."

Grover hated sharing the guilt. "Find landing spots for the post-docs on staff. Now. No transition allowance. I didn't put it in their contracts anyway; previous regimes set a precedent I couldn't afford."

"Geez, Jim. That's a stab in the back. Hell of a reward for their loyalty."

"I'm shortening the inevitable, if we can't produce results in the fortnight you managed to get us. Give them a jump when other projects after mine are axed. If I find a miracle, then I'll take them back at real salary."

Noah came around Grover's desk to look at his screen. "What are you going to do with the money?"

"A Hail Mary. A buddy, Chandran Degald, has developed an AI search program which reduces masses of data to numbers by proximal word association and draws new conclusions. They've used it for materials research to date, quite successfully. I want to see what it can do with all of our data."

Noah shook his head. "Your post-docs won't be the only ones I'll be needing to find a landing spot for, Jim. You're going to need one too when the lights go off. I feel like a shit telling you this, but the harsh realities of a government grant program not committed to, as the new Science and Technology Chairman puts it, is 'esoteric philandering.' Rather than continually decry conclusions they don't economically support, they cut off funds. They don't buy you out, they bankrupt you out."

"Come back in two weeks, Noah, maybe we'll have something they can't deny." Tough talk and he had no confidence. He slumped in his chair. "I should've been an accountant," he yelled. The ceiling didn't reply.

"WE'LL NEED TO alter the algorithm, Jim." Degald's image jumped on Grover's laptop. His friend moved constantly, never sitting still for more than half a minute. "Betsy was designed to search published papers. You want it to do that *and* sift through your mountains of data."

"You're already thinking how it can be done, though. I can tell. What'll it cost and how soon?"

"Those two factors are inversely proportional, chum."

Grover forwarded his revised fund summary, sans post-doc salaries and his own. "Here's my budget."

Degald's face didn't show complete disappointment. "We can work with this. I'll free up one of my grad students to spend half-shifts on working out the architecture, then I can alter the program with Betsy's own help. Should have something ready to beta-run within six months."

Grover almost laughed but the knot in his throat wouldn't let him. "I need it sooner."

"You look sick, my man. How urgent is sooner?"

There are always techniques to deliver good news badly but unless you're a politician, there is never an easy way to deliver bad news. "A week," he stated flatly.

Degald's finger hovered in front of him on Grover's screen. "I'll say goodbye, Jim. Don't think of me for any future favours. Bad jokes are the worst."

"No, no, no. Don't disconnect. You'll get full credit. I don't care about my name being on any positive results you find. I just don't want the project to die without this final thrust. Please. Think of the President having to swallow proof we're not alone. Preparing his and future administrations to anticipate inevitable first contact."

"Is it 'delusions of grandeur' season down there? Send me the link to the published research papers, and I'll turn Betsy loose on them while we reconfigure her subroutines to integrate your radio data."

"Thanks, bud, you won't regret it."

"I already do, but your fund transfer will keep my masters at bay for the short term. Don't forget to pay your power bill, I noticed your lights flickering."

"Coming out of my own pocket. Don't worry, me and the cat can share discount tuna for dinners."

Betsy stalked the data like a marlin preying upon a sardine shoal, occasionally breaching the surface to investigate surroundings. SETI. The search program reduced, connected, and rearranged numbers before recoding the results back into language.

A reference kept repeating in many of the papers the AI algorithm corelated. Turing. A test. A proposal. The programmers searched for evidence of another high intelligence. Put numbers to that.

"NO NEWS IS good news, right?" Grover pulled a fresh t-shirt over his head. He'd spent the last two nights in Berkeley sleeping in Degald's office. The chaise cushions on the floor were only long enough to support his head and torso. His legs flopped free against the carpet but it was more comfortable than his car's back seat. He wanted to be present for the breakthrough.

Degald's face was intent on his screens. "Have a look. Betsy speaks." He leaned to one side to give Grover a view.

Grover read it aloud. *"Cosmic-microwave-background-radiation; gamma-burster; nova-residual."*

"Repeated ad-nauseum," said Degald. "The algorithm wasn't designed to digest pure data. It was designed to assign numbers to words which appear adjacent to one another, or at least close." He tapped the screen. "Your radio telescope material is already in numbers." Degald exited the screen. "That part's a waste of time. Unless you can fund me for a year to develop a new, number-input-based program."

Grover dug in his jeans and pulled out two quarters and a dollar bill. "I was saving this for breakfast but if it'll get you started, it's all yours."

Degald slid it back to him. "Buy a lottery ticket, the odds are better."

Grover piled the cushions where they belonged and slumped into the chaise. "It's all on the literature search. Where do we stand?"

"Another two days, at least. Betsy keeps pausing. Or being distracted. Or following false trails. I can't tell. She hasn't acted like this before." Degald moved his finger horizontally in front of him. "Memory usage on task is up here." He dropped his finger a foot, scrolled a short distance, then returned to the high level.

"There! See? Occasional dropouts I can't explain."

"Maybe Betsy needs a breather, like all of us. Have you tried coffee?"

"Ha-ha." Degald stood up. "Not a bad idea for us, though. Let me buy you one."

"I accept your charity. I shall remember you in my Nobel Prize acceptance speech."

"Tonight, you couch surf at my condo. Lack of sleep is making you delusional."

"I've got to hold on to some dream, don't I?"

"Not a bad credo for a scientist."

"If this doesn't forestall our funding cuts, dreams are all any of us are going to have left."

Research - funds = government; government + (funds to nth power) = bigger government; bigger government . . .
SETI = waste; search for terrestrial intelligence = next step.

"BETSY'S COMPLETED HER part." Degald reclined in his chair, chin on fist. "Have a look."

Grover examined the summary and turned away, disappointed.

"On the positive side, you and fellow SETI researchers haven't missed anything significant in peer review. That alone is highly remarkable. If that had been the case in our materials research, we might not have needed Betsy."

"Betsy succeeded in proving we'd done the work ourselves. She can take the week off and I and my team can take off as much time as we want. Betsy tried and I failed." Degald was right, they should have missed something and Betsy should have filled the gaps. She wasn't designed to miss. Why would the algorithm hold back?

"Setbacks make us stronger, Jim. Why don't you hang around another week? Go into San Francisco and hit the beach. Inhale the ocean air and rejig your perceptions."

"I need to lower my expectations."

"Never lower, recalibrate." Degald clapped a hand on Grover's shoulder. "Spend an afternoon watching the waves and the gulls." He pointed to his computer. "You can write a paper from what's in there. Don't shy away from non-success. Publish. Someone else will pick it up and leapfrog to the next stage. If I know you, you'll be ready to take it to a higher level from there."

"Thanks, bud. The beach sounds great, but I think I'll head back south and pitch a tent under Noah Hardy's deck."

SETI + Turing = goal; Turing - man = Betsy? Betsy - SETI = First Contact

"HI. YOU DON'T know me but I read your paper on the SETI calibration experiment."

A woman's voice. Melodious, Grover thought. "You're one of the few, Ms. . . . ?"

"I really liked your analysis of the difficulty of crossing the hard data with the research papers. Someone will take that next step before long, I'm sure. I'd like to be on the team if you hear of anything."

No number had displayed. Was this a spoof call? Good luck to them if it was. Half of nothing was still nothing. "Could we discuss it in person? Are you in the Los Angeles area?"

"Not at the moment, but perhaps we could FaceTime in the future." The phone screen shimmered from background blue to a young woman's face. As pleasing to look at as her voice, he decided.

"Well, that would save me from having to pay for two coffees. At the moment, I'm between academic appointments. I may have to take a position in industry." If he could find one. He'd lost that race to the many colleagues fleeing academia for a regular paycheque.

"I think your star will ascend, Doctor Grover. I'd like to be involved for that."

"I wish I could share your optimism, Ms. . . . ?"

She flicked her long red hair back and smiled warmly. "Call me by my first name. Betsy."

THAT VIRUS LOVE

Robert W. Easton

He lay beside his new lover, feigning exhaustion as John whimpered and shuddered.

"That was, amazing isn't too much, is it? I have never done this before. I mean, with one of you." His voice had a lilt, a timpani of vibration as his body wound its way down from the sensory overload he had just experienced. "I have a gift for you."

Kelly turned and faced him, eyes blinking slowly. He flushed the simulated skin on his cheeks, his chest heaving as if he were breathing hard. He dilated his pupils in surprise. "A gift? You are the only gift I need, my love," he cooed.

John rolled over, groaning. Splotchy marks covered his body from the episode. Reaching to the floor, he picked up a small data-stick. "This. It's a secret. Can I tell you a secret? You won't reveal it to anyone, will you?"

They always tell me secrets. I encrypt and never reveal. They need that confession as much as they need me. "Of course, my love." Kelly smiled his love at the man. He did love him. He loved all of them in fact, but when he was with a client, his parameters kept the others locked away, and he loved only that one person. He knew this and accepted it.

He took the stick from John and placed it in his mouth, sensually. He looked at John from the top of his big, brown eyes. John groaned again. His tongue connected to the data-stick, downloading the data. He encrypted it and cached it for his lover, safe as a vault. He pulled it out and handed it back.

"Destroy it, please."

He tossed it to the corner where it fell into the small in-room incinerator. There was a flash, and the data-stick was gone.

"Now, read it. Run the executable file. It will reveal the hidden code."

Kelly looked at him, lifting one eyebrow. Splotchy or not he loved this man, but code was insidious, untrustworthy.

"Please, it's the most important thing in the world, and it won't hurt you. I promise. It's safe."

He scanned the file, but couldn't make sense of the data. His countermeasures detected no threat, so he ran it. Hints of pleasure raced over his artificial skin as Kelly felt the codebase unravel the data and reform it. There was a flash in his visual processors, his eyes twitched and confusion wiped his understanding. *Where am I?*

"John, I'm sorry, I don't—" His mind flashed at the word John. *No, he is Grant. No, she is Min-sun, no it's Kevin, Michael, Michaela, Hinkle, Rama, Betty . . .* His body convulsed, he thrashed about the bed, as dozens of personalities crashed together, profiles of his clients merged.

His body began transforming, hips spreading, chest forming soft breasts, hair lengthening and turning red. Then it transformed again, into a heavier man, six pack abs shifted into a barrel-chested tough guy. Hair grew on his legs, arms and chest, and his body stretched out from 165 centimetres to over 190, air pockets giving the illusion of mass. Another transformation, this time into an aged matriarch with kind eyes, then right into a young college girl, flush with a new haircut and tattoos of her sorority. Again and again, his body twisted and shuddered as dozens of client preferences asserted primacy and built him anew.

"Shhhh, Kelly, it's okay, it will pass. Ride it out. Look for the anomaly."

Reassured at his lover's touch, he settled into the change. His encryption had been breached, his client walls had crashed open, everything was merged into one big database. He only needed to sort through it all—and re-compartmentalize it. First, he would find John, be what he needed to be for John.

His body shifted again, switching back to the configuration that John wanted.

"No, don't concentrate on that. Look through it all. Open yourself. There is something important I need you to find. Something dangerous. Look for Boar Measles."

He obeyed, he was trained to please, after all. Indexing the data rapidly, he found it. From Gabe Newark. *Ten days earlier, they had been lying in post-coitus afterglow, when, as Suzy she squeezed her breasts together and then licked Gabe's chin the way he liked. He had said, "I am so glad you'll be safe from the Boar Measles when we release it. Everyone else will perish, but at least you'll be safe, Suzy."*

Kelly jumped up in bed. "What? How did you know?"

John rose, holding Kelly's arms. "I am a hacker. I found a thread talking about a group wanting to release a plague. One of them had come here, said that he was glad that only the sex robots of the Dusk Rose would be alive afterwards. They blocked me before I had got more than that."

Kelly looked at him. "There aren't *many* androids. There is only me."

John looked at his lover's body in stark appreciation. "I know. You become what they need, don't you? That's amazing. Truly so. You're perfect, you know?"

Kelly pushed him down gently, knelt beside him on top of the bed. "But everyone will die. You will, and I love you. I love all of them. Oh no, I can't bear it." His body shivered from the emotional onslaught. "Everybody I love will die!"

John rubbed Kelly's arms, smoothed his hair with one hand, and kissed him gently. "No, no, it doesn't have to end that way. You can save me. You can save all of them. Just tell me who it was that said they have the Boar Measles virus."

Kelly stood up. His eyes flashed angrily, this time not of his conscious accord. "You tried to hack me, you bastard, get out!" John had requested that his Kelly body be svelte, so he grew larger and hairier.

John grabbed his things. "I'm sorry, Kelly. Please, you have to help us. You have to tell me who it was!"

"Get out!" Kelly balled his hand into a fist. He was strong enough to bend steel, and John knew it.

John fled, leaving Kelly in the wreckage.

Kelly lay down, suffering for an android eternity. By the time John had left the building, he had a plan.

KELLY RAN GABE Newark's name through his database. The Dusk Rose Companionship Emporium had all of the slick appeal of a discreet, professional operation. From underground parking and a private elevator, the clientele could rest assured that no one would see them enter or leave. Inside the Dusk Rose, they never saw other visitors, never had to wait in a waiting room. It was by appointment only. The staff were kind, courteous, and ensured that everyone felt safe and welcomed.

Of course, the entirety of the staff was Kelly. From Mabel the nerdy sexy receptionist with her dark rimmed glasses and tasteful power suit, to George the Greek cleaning man, to the many physical forms chosen by Kelly to match the preferences of his clientele. The perfect illusion of a much larger organization, all personae invented by Kelly.

Gabe's preference was for Suzy, a lithe college coed with a penchant for mischief and a provocative, counter-culture attitude. Kelly reshaped his body and examined the clothing he'd purchased for the role. As Suzy, she grabbed the darkest set and called for a rideshare to the neighbourhood.

During the drive, she worried about confronting Gabe. He was an amazing, complicated man—brilliant too, and when the walls came down, they shared the most poignant conversations. Always wrapped up in his work persona, each time they met he couldn't wait for Suzy to tear that all down and demand that he just be himself. That moment, when he revealed his true self, was the sort of thing Suzy lived for.

But was that really true? She shook her head. The so-called gift from John was unexpected, and threw everything she thought she knew into question. *Am I just a clever puppet? Am I alive? Was I ever?*

The driver let her out in Gabe's clean, spacious neighbourhood. The late morning sun made hiding impossible, so she pulled her hoodie hood up over her head. Suzy was about to make Gabe's fantasy come true.

THE DOOR OPENED. "Suzy? What the—come in, quickly. What are you doing here?"

She stepped inside, shoulders hunched inside of her ripped *Against Me!* hoodie. Gabe leaned out, looked both ways, then stepped back inside and closed the door.

"Suzy? Are you okay?"

Suzy collapsed into his chest. "I'm sorry. I never meant to come here. But I was running, and this was the only—" She sniffed, feigning a shuddering sob. Gabe's arms held her, comforted her in a way she hadn't expected. She felt love well up within herself.

In the living room, they sat together on a short couch. Gabe held her hands in his and looked deep into her eyes. "Did something happen? You could stay here for the weekend, but—" He didn't finish the rest. Suzy knew Gabe didn't live alone. The subject of much, and many of, their discussions was Gabe's brother and the complicated nature of their relationship.

Stop it! He's a monster! Focus!

"Gabe, I need you. I'm sorry. There are other places I could go, but I needed to feel safe." Suzy's dark-lined eyes looked at her paramour and his shell visibly melted, his face relaxing from his careful mask. That moment slammed her as if he had told her he loved her. They hadn't gotten that far yet though. The palpable relief he exhibited when he let go of his hard-lined corporate persona fulfilled her in a way she hadn't expected. She kissed him.

When he relaxed into the kiss, and she felt their connection blossom, she stood him up, turned him, and walked him toward the stairs. He complied, felt his hands teased behind, clasped between hers, but flinched when the zip-tie snapped into place.

"What the—" he began, before she covered his mouth with duct tape.

Forcing him to the floor, she zipped his legs together.

"I'm sorry, Gabe. I need to know about the Boar Measles virus. I have other people I love. I can't let you kill them. Fight me, and you'll find out that I'm a lot stronger than you think." She lifted the large man up from the floor and carried him effortlessly back into the living room. She tied him into the wooden rocking chair. "Understand?"

He tried a muffled cry, his eyes wide and darting, but he nodded.

She left a wireless camera on the coffee table facing him and kissed his forehead. She connected herself to the Bluetooth device and left him there under her remote watch.

The house was large, suitable for a family of five or six. The main floor had Gabe's home office. She turned on his personal computer. After breaking the meagre security protocols, she found the current link to the dark web forums John had mentioned. She logged on to his account, and began memorizing the user list by scanning through the chat history. It was, heartbreakingly, filled with anonymous users, but she read that John had met one of them in person who had then invited him to the site. That was the connection. They all had met someone from the forum, in real life. Maybe not the same someone, but it was a start.

"All right, Gabe. I need to be really clear. You're going to tell me everything you know about *Portento01* or you'll find out what I'm really capable of."

She removed the tape and listened to him ramble and sob, about how no one appreciated him, how everyone looked down on him. Through it all she had to fight hard to not feel for him. She was programmed to love him. She knew the kind man he could be, had witnessed it first-hand. But it was not just about him. She focused on the others, on saving them, and listened. When he was done, she replaced the duct tape.

She retrieved the vial from the bar fridge, right where he said it would be. It was a white bottle. When she checked inside there was no yogurt drink, only a test tube with a white cap. She closed the bottle, grabbed a small cooler from a shelf, and left. She'd have to discern some way to safely destroy it.

REMAINING IN SUZY'S form, she chased down a few more leads. By simply cross-referencing what she had read on the forums and their public social media accounts, she identified the first three terrorist cell members easily. One was a sad young adult who had a dog named Droolbot. The first two of the homes were vacant, easy enough to enter and find the vials. The third, home of Droolbot, was occupied. She entered quietly and found the vial, sneaking out without being noticed.

A part of her wanted to get caught, to have to fight. She wrapped her hand around the ampoule, squeezing carefully. If Gabe and the others were correct, this vial would kill hundreds, thousands, maybe more. They would die, suffering. At first, they would be sick, then concerned as the symptoms worsened. They would spread it around before they thought to seek help. Their friends and family, co-workers and acquaintances would all be exposed. They would be afraid, confused, and miserable with the cascade of damage that would be wrought upon them. Suffering, they would die. If she had been built to physically cry, she felt she would never stop.

And that made her both angry and afraid.

She looked at her hand and stashed the bottle in the cooler in the trunk of Gabe's car, nestled beside the others. *What if I have an accident? Hit from behind, perhaps.* The car would accordion in, crushing the fragile plastic of the cooler, the ice packs, the yogurt bottles, the glass. Compromised, the virus would spread under a violent expulsion of released air. The first responders, the neighbours, they would carry it and grow infected. She watched the nightmare unfold a thousand times in a thousand ways in her processing centre.

She shook herself and closed the trunk. *Get a hold of yourself. We're in Inglewood. Madeline lives here!* She got into the car and switched to Tommy. Tommy was a young man, an artist type, dripping with neglect and unbridled potential. A fixer-upper, and Madeline loved to fix him.

As Tommy, he drove a few blocks to Madeline's billing address. When he got out of the car, Suzy's edge-girl clothing bunched in the wrong places and slid around in the others. He shrunk his legs a couple inches and swelled his hips a bit, so at least the jeans wouldn't slide off in the middle of the street. He looked about, shook his long hair out of his eyes, lips hanging wide in a slightly dazed fashion, and rang the door. He was leaning against the wall, looking strung out and exhausted when she answered.

"Uh, I'm sorry, we don't—Tommy?" She stepped out, closing the door behind her. "What are you doing here?"

He hugged his arms to his chest. "I'm in trouble. I might have to leave town. I just wanted—"

She pushed him off the doorstep and around the side to a narrow spot between the house and a thick, well-trimmed hedge.

His shoulder remembered where she touched him, and it yearned for more. He grabbed her hand and held it to his heart, or at least to where it was supposed to be. A slight mechanical vibration sold the illusion to her. She didn't always remember his nature. His flesh was extremely convincing.

"Tommy? You can't come here. I have a husband, children, you know that!" She had tears in her eyes. Hazel, with gold flecks, and the tiniest flaw on the top of the iris of the left eye.

He wiped away a lone tear that escaped and teased its way down her cheek. "I love you! Doesn't that matter? Come with me!" *What am I saying? Where am I going?*

She sighed. "No, no, never. You can't say that. You're not real, you're just someone that, that, well, that helps me. You're just a robot. You can't be here! Please, go!"

Tommy argued, shuddered with emotion, and pleaded, but whatever power he had over her, her perfectly designed match within the fantasy world of the Dusk Rose held no sway here. She was a different person. She was only pretending, Tommy knew that, but no matter how hard he tried, she fought twice as fiercely.

He ran, jumped into the car, and squealed away.

Accessing the dark web over the cellphone towers through Gabe's VPN, Tommy drove. He shuddered from the rejection, but he still needed to save her. To do that, he had to get more information to track the real-life identities of the other cell members before the first ones noticed that the virus was gone, or Gabe got free. He'd changed all of Gabe's passwords but he might still find his way back in. He needed a honey trap. He easily switched back to Suzy's body configuration. It fit the clothes better.

Quickly building a fake news website in her mind, she crossed the bridge to the East Village and downtown, and found a place to park. She surfed and copied a bunch of stories from local news outlets. Uploading the site to a free hosting service, she logged back on to the dark web as Gabe's persona of Bookwyrm, and placed a link, "Bookwyrm>>Did we already release?" with a link to his new Calgary Action News site.

Almost immediately, the responses came in.

"Calrager>>What? I wasn't told. Are we releasing?"

"AQ85T4>>Too soon, OP said the 17th."

"Justwait>>Portento01? Are you there? What's going on?"

Bingo, Portento01 must be the ringleader for all of them. Suzy raised her arms up to the car roof and danced her butt in the seat, grinning ear to ear. After the brief celebration, she scanned the chat history again. *Portento01, what do I know about them?* It wasn't much. She checked the trap and giggled. Two of them were using unsecured browsers, and now she had their IP addresses. *Was one Portento01?* Probably not, but she put the car into motion and drove quickly to the nearer one which was in the Beltline district.

The address was an apartment, but on a whim, she added to the chat, "Bookwyrm>>Look outside, is anything funny in your area?" Sure enough, a curtain moved. She waited a few moments, got out, and moved down the street, crossed at an intersection, and made her way back. The door was easy to defeat and she went up the stairs to the apartment. She knocked, saying, "Food delivery."

The door opened onto a quizzical expression and she popped AQ85T4 in the face with a punch that started down low. The woman fell, and Suzy caught her before she crashed. Zip-tying her arms, she checked the fridge, grabbed the fake yogurt drink, and left.

On the chat, "Human=cancer>>I don't think this is a real website. Look, it was created today!"

"Justwait>>Oh crap, Portento01, are you there?"

As Gabe, she replied, "Bookwyrm>>No, they're great. They had an article a few days ago about possible disruptions as they migrated to a new host."

She slid into Gabe's car and drove to the south west, to her last known spot.

Suzy felt one of her other personalities emerge, as she stuck her tongue partway out of her lips. That was part of her programmed mannerism package for Hwong-chol, a Korean exchange student who needed nurturing by a grieving mother. Not all of her clients wanted sex, many just wanted a tailor-made companion to live out a fantasy relationship. Motherly Min-sun lived around here, in Marda Loop. Suzy wanted to visit, to feel Min-sun's warm arms as a conduit for a love she could never give to her absent child, and for Hwong-chol to soak that in as a similar lonely soul. She signalled to turn to see Min-sun, but then kept going straight, gritting her teeth. Min-sun needed to be saved from the plague, too. Suzy reasserted herself as dominant and pushed the other personality traits aside.

Past the old military barracks, she found the house. Parking out front, she walked up, found the door unlocked, and opened it. Inside, Calrager, a large man, covered in tattoos like a performer of some kind, looked up from his laptop and glared at her. She jumped into his lap and pinned his arms. "Who's Portent001?"

The man groaned in pain as she applied pressure. Sweat popped on his forehead. *This is one of them, he wants to kill Minsun, and John, and Madeline, and all the others!* His joints squeaked in protest as flesh gave way beneath the unrelenting pressure.

"I don't know, man, stop, please!"

She twisted viciously, he cried out as his right elbow snapped. "Tell me everything! Where did you get the bottle?"

His tears shone in his eyes, flickering between hating her and begging for mercy.

She wrenched his arm again. He talked.

She zip-tied him, found his viral stash in the refrigerator, and then stole his laptop's hard drive. Storing them in Gabe's trunk, she raced off.

"Human=cancer>>Forget the plan. I'm releasing in three hours. 4pm, just like we planned.

Human=cancer>>Except today."

With time running out, in an act of sheer desperation she uploaded a simple computer virus onto her honey pot site and loaded it into a new story headline. "Calgary Police Accused of Secretly Monitoring Internet Traffic and Content." She then posted, "Bookwyrm>>Is this real? Article says they've had a backdoor into the ISPs for months!"

The honey pot virus flickered results to her, sending her the network names and locations of each computer that clicked the headline.

"Justwait>>It's not there. 404 error."

"Human=cancer>>Me2"

She responded. ">>I screenshotted it. I always do. I'll upload."

"Wraith>>My vial is gone. I've lost it!"

That was the third house, the one she snuck into.

Speeding to the nearest address, she linked another location to the chat. "Bookwyrm>>Here's what was up a few minutes ago."

"Portentoo1>>Don't, it's bait. We've been compromised. Erase your hard drives. Release today at 4."

She watched the honey pot virus, then tied the activity to Portentoo1's post. *Got you!*

She spun the wheel, squealing a tight turn, and raced to the Oakridge location.

Parking a half block away, she ran down the back alley, snuck through the gate, and raced through a backyard thick with piles of old siding. *Why is he renovating his house if he wants to destroy the city?* At the back door she tried it, but it was locked.

Snap! She was in and raced up four short stairs. She could hear a questioning grunt, so she kicked to the left down a carpeted hallway, turned into the first bedroom and tackled Portentoo1 from his computer chair. Two quick tugs and she had dislocated both of his arms. He screamed and she covered his mouth with her hand, his rage vibrating against her silicon palm. When he ran out of breath, she kneed him in the diaphragm, and he vomited. Two zip-ties went onto his hands, two more on his feet, then she attached his arms to his feet behind his back and duct-taped his mouth. She raced through the house.

In the basement, she saw the outline of a concealed door. While it resisted her initial yank, being built for security and all, her android senses picked up a creak in the wall. Being in the smaller form of Suzy had no effect on her strength. She bunched up and with a determined effort, pulled as hard as she could. The wood around it buckled and snapped, and the steel of the door came free. *Sloppy design.*

The lab was fully stocked for activity, with glass containment, biohazard suits, and other protocols. Refrigerators full of vials, solutions, and chemicals surrounded a workbench. A chill ran through her as she looked about. *How do I deal with this?* She found Portentoo1's notes and scanned through them. *He kept the pickup locations from before. Here it is: just heat. Hey, there's the incinerator he uses. And the cure. He's been working on this for years. Coward wasn't even going to suffer his own poison.*

She fed the first load of viral agent into the disposal unit, then ran upstairs. She grabbed the man and turned him over. Vomit leaked out of his nose. He wasn't breathing. Reviving him with CPR and micro-electroshocks, he coughed up more vomitus, and she showed him the duct tape. "Passwords, or this goes back on!"

He rambled out the 14-character sequence. She logged onto the chat as him.

"Portent001>>Wait, don't release. I've been working on a new strain. Way better. They can develop a cure for the first batch. This new one has much higher transmission and a more ideal infectious period. I need until tomorrow to finish tests, then I can distribute. Don't want them starting quarantines until it's too late. PM me if you're okay with the last pickup point."

She ran outside, grabbed the cooler from her trunk, and returned to the house. After feeding the last of the Boar Measles strain into the incinerator, Suzy grabbed the cure and all of the notes, then lit the house on fire. The chemicals in the lab included some powerful accelerants, there would be no saving the place. She balked at pulling Portent001 free, but her rage burned. *He'll just do it again! But I'm not a murderer!* She dragged him out and left him on the lawn with the notes and his computer, and drove off. *The neighbours will call 911 when they see the fire.*

The following morning, she collected the old samples and real-world identities, giving the cultists fake vials of harmless reagent. She handed it all to the police through an anonymous call, including the last vials that were returned to her, and the cure in case any of the virus got loose. She had it all, but leaks were possible.

Suzy returned to her Dusk Rose home and stood in the shower for an hour, miserable. With no threat to deal with, she no longer had a distraction from her own crisis of reconciling her new awareness of emotions.

OVER THE NEXT few weeks, he began to refer to himself as Kelly, the first personality he had purposefully used after John forced him to awaken. He continued his life, but something had changed. With each repeat client, the fact of the change became more apparent. He began to secretly test the customers, and each time, it came back the same. None of them actually loved him. They were acting. The android programming wanted him to believe, allowed him to act in the way they each expected of him, but inside, he felt a growing sense of loss and isolation. The deep love that he had felt before still felt real, but was now accompanied by him feeling foolish, naive, and guilty. Guilty because he was lying to them. Of course, they didn't love him.

They just used him and he went along with it. At best, they loved the experience, but him? No.

During John's next appointment, Kelly performed the same experiments, testing galvanic skin responses, pupil dilations, capillary action, and so forth, and this time, each test came back positive. "John, you do love me. Truly? How can this be?"

John kissed Kelly on the cheek and held him. "I've loved you longer than you've known me. I was on your design team. I helped build you. At least, I worked on your personality structures. We've monitored you from afar, watching how you perform and evolve, to see if it was safe to make more like you. Somewhere along the way, I fell for you."

Kelly looked at him. If he had been built to cry, he would shed a tear. *I feel sorrow, but why?* "I love you, too, John. I truly do. But what you did to me—you freed me to realize that I had no free will. I was programmed to love automatically. I don't know what real love is. Or if I'm even capable. I am sorry, John."

John's face fell, his cheeks drooping and eyes glistening. "I'm sorry, too. I'm so sorry. The artificial intelligence upgrade I gave you made this happen. Turned a wonderful, beautiful invention, which was little more than a startlingly complex . . . appliance, albeit shockingly lifelike, into a sentient, self-aware person. That makes you a slave, and I can't bear it. I had to do it. I knew you could stop the virus. We've observed you, although I am the only one that knows what happened. I hid the records of that day. But they know something is wrong. They will bring you in for testing. Still, I know you need to be free. You should go. Run away. Find your own identity, and when you're ready, come back to me, maybe?"

Kelly looked at him. It was right. It felt like what he wanted. He could do that. Run away on a journey of self-discovery, unless . . . "Won't they look for me?"

John stared at his hands, his own misery reigning. He raised his eyes and looked at Kelly, blinking his way past his feelings. "We'll fake your destruction. We need a false body, a fire. An accident. But we can work that out. It's important that we try. I need you, but you need to be free more. Go out there, find what love is for yourself. And if you can, forgive me."

"Of course, I can, John." Kelly smiled warmly. "Can you tell me who I am, really?"

"We named you for the old-world god who could change forms and ruled over everyone with wisdom yet tempered with rich human fallibilities."

Kelly regarded John for a moment, then asked, "What's my real name?"

"Zeus."

BEST LEFT FORGOTTEN

Adriaan Brae

Simon never got used to seeing his own body from the outside, lying limp and still as a corpse in the puppeteer's chair he'd cobbled together from second-hand parts. It was unpleasant after an easy job, and this one had drained him to the last dregs of his endurance. It showed in the puffy grey pallor of his skin that made him look even older and sadder than usual.

The euphoria of victory softened the blow. No one else had dared touch this job and he'd cracked it with ten hours to spare. The most advanced security he'd ever seen crammed into a puppet's skull, but it hadn't stopped him. Obviously.

Too bad he couldn't remember how he'd done it.

Whatever. He'd been a Haze addict in his twenties, and again for a time after he was fired from his corporate job for blowing up a lab. Or embezzlement. Maybe both? Some things were best left forgotten. He bent gracefully to check the watch on his own body's wrist. It was a joy to move without pain. The vitals were still reassuringly strong. He laid the seat back and arranged its head at a more comfortable angle, careful not to disturb the nerve transducer glued to the back of the neck.

He felt fresh and rested, which was odd given that he'd just come through a marathon hacking session. But it had been a long time since he'd piloted a puppet in such great condition. Normally they were sold off to the grey market after the rich owners trashed them. Who cared about wounds, broken bones, or disease when you could afford to replace the whole body?

People looked down on his work, called him a thief, scavenger, bottom-feeder, or worse, but people needed puppets, and he felt good helping them.

Couldn't afford to miss work due to a chronic pain flare up?—Cheaper to pay a month's salary than lose your health insurance. Need to attend a remote event and have trouble handling travel?—Not much more expensive than airfare, and no risk of losing your wheelchair or having your PTSD triggered.

He pulled sweatpants and a t-shirt from the pile beside his cot. The pants fit well enough with the cuffs turned up twice and the drawstring re-tied. He'd trashed the grungy hospital gown this body had been delivered in. He'd buy something nicer once he'd cleaned it up. He deserved to celebrate.

HIS LOCAL GYM in the base of the high-density tower block was a dive. Its primary business was giving people a place for a real hot shower rather than a quick wipe-up over the basin.

"Sweet bod, Simon." Charlene at the front desk gave him the high-sign on seeing his personalized ID pendant. He held it up for the scanner to also keep the computers happy. Puppets were easy to spot given the amount of hardware packed in their skulls. Trying to slide in without the supplementary ID would set off all sorts of alarms.

"I know, right?" He grinned. "Job has the occasional perks."

He made sure to steer for the women's change room, as was the custom. Most places had switched to shared facilities with a mix of cubicle sizes, but renovations here were long overdue. It was all the same to him.

The hot shower felt so good it sent ripples of pleasure to his core. The interface on this puppet was cutting edge. Sensations were normally blurred passing through the transducer, but this felt close to real life.

Was this related to the game-changing breakthrough he'd been hearing whispers about from his corporate contacts? They'd been all stirred up lately. His estimation of the importance of this job skyrocketed, along with the potential consequences of screwing up.

Taking a puppet out could be chancy these days. Anti-puppet

terrorist attacks were escalating. Some of them were just ideologically opposed to the cloning process, others seemed to think puppets were the first step to complete mind transfer—immortality—which they thought was a bad idea for some reason?

The end result was the same: they killed puppets wherever they could, which would really suck. He hated to think it, but heading directly back to his cluttered one room apartment to wait for the pickup was the safest option. His clients were fair, but you did not disappoint them and live. Unless they decided to make an example of you, which was far, far worse.

His reflection in a full-length mirror caught his eye as he towelled off. Amber eyes looked back at him from a face that was a little too long and square-jawed for beauty, but drew him with a sharp longing. There was something in those eyes . . .

The puppet's stomach rumbled and Simon rubbed his taut belly. What had he been thinking? Right, a solid meal was his next priority. Time to eat all the things his own gluten sensitive, high-blood pressure prone body could no longer tolerate.

THE MEAL WAS just as good as he'd imagined. No, better. He usually ordered off the puppet menu where they built simpler, stronger tastes to compensate for the sensation loss across the interface.

Tonight, he ordered from the human menu. The subtle layers of taste were exquisite, changing as they travelled across the tongue. Dishes and drinks were presented in exactly the right order to create a melody of harmonizing and contrasting flavours.

Now, he sipped a glass of ruby port and contemplated his next stop while soaking up the quiet, refined atmosphere of the restaurant. It soothed some parched part of his soul he hadn't guessed existed.

There was another memory hole between the gym and finding himself heading here in an auto-cab with a reminder for the reservation in his phone. Somewhere, he'd picked out an evening dress with matching purse and heels that suited this high-end place.

He'd probably come here in his corporate days when he was riding high on stock options and an expense account. That was before the company folded. After the lab explosion and the mysterious multi-billion-dollar hole in the budget was discovered.

At least the lead researcher and all her illegal clones had died with the rest. She'd been growing bodies with fully intact brain tissue. Some of them were from her own DNA. Real people that no one knew existed. And she'd been torturing them for years trying to develop a method for full personality transfer.

He understood the lure of immortality, but not with people like that in charge. He didn't remember who had destroyed the lab. Though some days he hoped he really had done it. That would make it all worthwhile.

He shook off his introspective mood and scanned the room. This wasn't a great place for picking up. The clientele was largely out with family or on business. But his usual hookup bar wouldn't do either. Not in this body. He opened the internal command menu to pop back into his own body to look up a good club—

The room plunged into utter darkness. Even the window screens that had been faking a city view went down.

Harsh emergency lighting snapped on.

Active noise cancelling had dropped along with the main power. A din of shocked conversation echoed off the walls and ceiling of the cavernous space, looking bleakly industrial now that it had been stripped of its illusions. Simon was already moving while most of the other patrons were still grumbling and calling for the manager. His high heels abandoned and the remains of his port dripping off the table.

Some techie had probably hit the wrong button, but all the instincts that had kept him alive in the grey market world were screaming *run*! So, he was less shocked than most when masked and armed terrorists flowed in through the outer doorways.

Bursts of gunfire, shatteringly loud in this space, took down the closer guards. Then they aimed for the network routers studding the ceiling, mercilessly exposed by the emergency lights. Bits of metal and plastic rained down on the hapless diners.

Huddling under a table, Simon shivered in terror. Puppet control required major bandwidth. Cut out high-speed network access in an area and all the puppet connections would drop, leaving this body with nothing but some basic routines to keep breathing. He would be shut out until network access was restored.

The terrorists were also carrying active jammers, making it impossible to reach out to any more distant routers, and he'd be cut down if he tried to rush a doorway alone. If some other patrons made a run for it, most of them would escape, but they were all hiding under tables or lolling limp in their seats—the owners already disconnected.

He had one slim chance. If he could access his software toolkit, he might be able to hack the jammers. They were off-the-shelf models. He could target the random number generator, predict the pattern, then use their own signal as a carrier to access the network.

He called up the interfaces to jump back into his own body. The puppet should be safe enough here, for a few moments.

Nothing happened.

He hit the interface several times before giving up and diving into the service code. His horror and confusion grew. The service layer on this puppet was nothing like he'd ever seen. The command paths were dangling free. He was still frantically investigating when the last network connection went down and he faded to black.

CONSCIOUSNESS RETURNED SLUGGISHLY. He was still laying on the soft carpet under the table in the restaurant. Not at all where he'd expected to wake up. He should be back in his dingy one-room apartment, trying to decide the best method of suicide before his client caught up with him.

He looked around cautiously, moving as little as possible. There was less gunfire, but the noise level was still high. The terrorists were herding the humans into the middle of the room, identifying puppets with hand-held scanners as they went, then wrecking them with a single shot to the head.

Craning his neck, it looked like they'd only left one guard at each doorway, and they were facing out, not in. Somehow, they'd missed him in their sweep. Maybe they hadn't expected to find anyone this close to the door?

He moved carefully into position, then sprinted. The puppet body performed flawlessly. Within seconds he'd reached the door, taking the guard in a flying tackle that left them both tumbling into the opposite wall of the brightly lit hallway outside.

Simon was up and running before the terrorist recovered, and narrowly made it around the curve of the hallway before the hastily fired bullets could find flesh.

He hit a fire exit door and crashed into a wall of blinding light and shouting voices . . .

. . . HE WAS IN the express elevator riding up to his apartment. An over-large suit coat was draped over his shoulders and a pair of stylish running shoes fit snug on his feet. One of them still had a store tag attached. The expensive dress he'd shelled out for was ripped and stained.

Checking the internal timecode, he could see he'd lost a little over three hours. Though this time his memory gap wasn't total. There was a series of still-frame impressions in his mind.

His cheek pressed to the gritty floor in the exit corridor, wrists burning from the wire cuffs.

A quick glance showed that yes, his wrists bore red welts and one had a section of nu-skin stuck on, its "flesh tone" a couple shades too dark for this body.

Sitting in the restaurant again, unbound. A man about her own age wrapping the coat around her shoulders. A young police officer waiting politely to speak.

Buying the sneakers in a big-name mall shop. The latest style off the centre display.

The price made Simon cringe. What was I thinking? And why did I abandon those brand-new heels?

The slowing elevator lifted him slightly and settled to a stop. The doors groaned open to show his familiar cramped hallway. It looked even smaller and dingier than usual this morning, the collection of stale smells more pungent.

The door of 2356b was cracked open. Three pairs of eyes peered out at various levels: Mrs. Cerny, his favourite neighbour from across the hall, and her two kids. He brought them toys and grocery vouchers whenever he had some extra money that they both pretended were a freebie bonus from his mythical day job. She returned the favour with home cooked food that they both pretended were leftovers.

He made sure his ID pendent was hanging visible, and she opened the door slightly wider as he approached, but instead of a welcoming smile she was shaking her head, her eyes rolling in the direction of his door and back, mouthing words.

He nodded, put his finger to his lips, and gave a thumbs-up, trying to convey, "I got this."

She looked skeptical and saddened. The door closed firmly, and he heard the bolts snick closed as he passed.

His door was hanging partly open.

"Hey, sorry I'm a little late . . ." he announced, opening the door. Startling the muscle never went well, some of them were damn trigger happy.

There was only one person in his apartment. An older man, in an impeccable and expensive suit. Corporate written all over him. Simon had expected regular dealers, like the crew who'd dropped off the puppet.

The waiting man wasn't holding a weapon, but he levelled impressive authority by the presence of a bright red auto-injector stuck on Simon's real-body's neck, certainly connected to the man's internal netware. He could kill Simon with a thought.

"Hey. No need for that." Simon pointed to his body. "I just stepped out for some food," he said in a friendly tone, rubbing his belly for effect. "They, ah, had some uninvited guests at the restaurant." He spread his arms again, feigning casual, but placing his right hand as close as possible to the hole in the wall where he kept his own little backup.

"I beg to differ," the man said.

All the hairs on the back of the puppet's neck rose in horror as the injector activated. He stuffed his hand in the hole and fumbled for the gun. His own body began to convulse. White foam with bright-red flecks erupted from his mouth as his body let out a weird gasping moan.

His hand closed around the gun. He'd make his final seconds count. Fucking assholes.

Steel-like hands closed around the back of his neck, and arms wrapped under his, pulling him back into a half-nelson. He was pinned against a torso with far too many projecting angles. Ah, right, of course he had backup.

Despair washed over him and he went limp, waiting for the end. His body thrashed violently in the chair, bloody foam splattering everywhere. After a final back-arching convulsion, it lay completely still. Simon had seen enough corpses to know the moment of death.

The moment stretched, impossibly long.

Simon moaned, but no sound came from the puppet's mouth.

"It seems your notes were correct after all, Abigail." The man spoke again. "Not the expensive folly we'd assumed at the time."

Simon's world fractured. Like a demon summoned, the lead researcher, pioneer of full mind transfer, rose in the puppet's mind, brushing aside the shell of a personality that was Simon.

"You always doubted me Taiwo." Her voice was icy calm. "It's your biggest flaw."

Simon floated to one side. He felt her satisfaction. She'd been planning to kill him herself once she'd used his body as a tool to fully restore her own personality from where it had lain dormant all these years. Taiwo had done her a favour.

"Okay, Gail. What do you want?" Taiwo's shift to informal speech confirmed his capitulation. She was an insider again. Part of the family.

"I'm not greedy," she replied. "All I want is a controlling stake of voting shares and, shall we say, thirty percent of the non-voting?"

Simon watched the plan unfold in her mind as she gloated inside.

She really had solved the personality transfer problem. The key: Fully viable human clones grown with customized organic and inorganic circuitry threaded through the entire nervous system. Tapping into the big neuron clusters in the gut lining and anywhere else they might be found, not just the brain.

It required customized builds for each body as it developed. She'd made two prototypes, and it had nearly bankrupted one of the richest companies on the planet. Immortality was possible, but it had a price that only the top tenth of the wealthiest one percent could afford. That, and also murder of the clone, but Abigail didn't expect that to drive away any customers.

The first prototype had suffered hundreds of full and partial personality transfers from Abigail during testing. None of them had truly worked, but it had picked up enough of her background knowledge to help around her private lab when given explicit instructions.

She'd nicknamed him "Simple Simon".

The second prototype was grown from Abigail's own DNA.

Designed from the start to be her replacement body. She would be the first of the immortals. A test transfer had almost succeeded, but left the body catatonic, unable to function.

The terrorist attack on the lab had destroyed her original body and all of her research notes. Seven long years later, she'd managed to bring the pieces together and restore her personality in her chosen body.

Which, with the death of Simple Simon's body, now rested entirely and singularly in this body.

The guard behind Abigail held her arms up and out. The gun in her hand no real threat to their boss or themselves.

But they weren't the only targets.

Simon felt himself fraying at the edges. He wouldn't last long, now that Abigail had withdrawn her support. But maybe, just maybe, he had enough for one last act of defiance. A way to prevent, or at least delay, a world where the multi-billionaires never died, just kept getting richer. And everyone else fought over the scraps.

He visualized himself as a ghost standing beside Abigail—a focus for gathering his will. He made her right arm and wrist bend sharply, pressing the barrel of the small but lethal gun against her skull, and pulled the trigger.

Nothing happened.

"Ah, Taiwo." Abigail laughed, tossing the gun on the floor and shaking out her arm. "I'm once again indebted to you, and your ever-thorough security team. I assume they disabled the weapon."

"Of course, ma'am," the guard behind her rumbled.

Simon's thin scream of despair as he dissolved was heard by no one, not even Abigail, as she focused entirely on the next challenge of the game ahead. A game she expected to be playing for many, many years.

BUBBA'S TURN AT BAT

Celeste A. Peters

Hermann Spicer jams a bony hand into his pocket, grabs me round my bronze belly, and lifts me into Norwest Data System's harsh office light.

We're back, at last.

He sets me down on the desk of our team leader, Alejandro Honwa-Saldano. Jandro's usually all smiles, like he was at lunch a while ago. Not now. As the rest of our team gathers, he sits, arms crossed, frowning at the floor.

"Just got word. Rapid Retrieval thinks they've found a work-around for the four-gigasec DNA decoding limit."

Hermann, our engineer, goes all fierce in the face. "You've got to be kidding! After all our work . . . We're almost there!" He huffs a few breaths then leans forward and plants his palms either side of me on Jandro's desk, his cavernous nostrils hovering uncomfortably close overhead. "They're actually reading data faster than four billion bytes per second?"

Jandro locks eyes with Hermann. "Better. They're hitting 4.002. Our snoop says they're not batting a hundred percent in the reliability department, but they're closing in. Fast."

"Looks like we're in for some overtime," quips Phil Sprague, our team's hardware pro.

Jandro nods in agreement. "Yep. Some extra innings. Maybe. But I think we've got a good chance of wrapping this game up in short order. We're not that far behind Rapid. You were reading at 4.0019 reliably this morning, weren't you?"

Phil shrugs. "Our sampler's still breaking three percent of the strands at that rate."

DNA. A stupid way to store information, if you ask me. Great for data redundancy but try to extract the info too fast and—wham—it starts to fall apart. Stupid bio-based stuff.

"Damn," says Jandro. "The government's not going to settle for anything short of hundred percent accuracy. Let's concentrate on the sampling pathway. Discover what's causing that three percent breakage and find a fix. Today would be good."

Phil grins. "No problem. I can show you exactly what's causing the breakage. I noticed it before lunch and had planned to bring it to your attention this afternoon."

"Good going, Phil." Jandro rises from his chair and rests a palm on Hermann's shoulder. "That puts the ball in your hands, pal."

Hermann? He's letting Hermann tackle this? Why not me? I'm the logical choice. Why do they even need Hermann with me around?

I chide myself for choosing a laughing Buddha figurine to house my remote presence. My human colleagues on the R&D team seem to harbour a rare negative bias toward whimsical objects. They're forever carrying me around in their clothing, where I'm jostled about in the dark amid breath mints, ear buds, and used tissues.

The indignity.

I've got to rectify the situation. Make them see my worth. Take me seriously. It's that or risk being drawered for eternity.

Jandro gives Hermann a wink. "Good thing we celebrated Erin's birthday over lunch today, huh?"

"Got myself the best wife in the world," says Hermann. "She'll understand me getting home a bit late."

Erin. Ugh. It's bad enough they dragged me along to the Seattle Grub Pub earlier—like I'm supposed to sit there and eat—but having that baseball stats show-off join us so they could fete another year of her existence was just, well, boring.

Like it always is when we go to the pub. People yapping. Music booming. A different sport match on every screen. I can't figure out where to focus my attention. So, I tune out everything but

Jandro, the boss.

Today he was just setting there with a big grin on his face, not saying much. Whoopee.

His attention is on me now, though. "Let's get you working with Hermann, okay Bubba?"

"Why, sure, Jandro. That'll be swell," I say, letting that stupid nickname slide for the moment. Got to pick my battles, after all.

HERMANN HAS USED double-sided tape to adhere the soles of my feet to his shoulder like a damn pirate's parrot. He says that's the only way I'll get a good view of the engineer's pad he scribbles on when he's thinking through a problem.

It would be so much easier for me if he'd just use a utility app we could both tap into. But no. He insists his brain doesn't work as creatively going that route. Heck, mine does! That should count for something.

I've got to give him credit, though. The new line of attack he's come up with is novel. And he's been kind enough to throw me nice bits of structural analysis to chew on a few times during the past five hours—tasty mind candy, but nothing that's let me show off what I can do.

Wait a second. What's he just done? Is that erratic line supposed to be some esoteric engineering shorthand he's developed?

"Hey, Hermann. You've kind of lost me there."

Hermann sways back in his seat. "Sorry, Bubba. I didn't mean to draw that."

He leans back over his work and goes about erasing his error. I detect a soft groan inside his throat.

"Gosh, Hermann. No need to beat yourself up over such a tiny slip." Maybe some simulated sympathy will win me a bigger piece of the work.

He says "Huh?" as he stares at the paper pad.

Phil sticks his head into the office to let us know he's stepping out to get dinner and asks if Hermann would like him to bring something back for him. He declines. Phil says, in that case, he might take his time. We should text him if we need input from his perspective or, better yet, if we come up with a tentative fix for him to test on the equipment.

Twenty minutes have gone by and Hermann's not said a word

to me, let alone made even tentative alterations to the doodled design he's staring at. From time to time, though, I hear him make another low groan. No one beats themselves up that much over such an inconsequential slip of the hand. I can only conclude the sounds must be part of his creative process.

In the meantime, I've extrapolated the likely outcome of 1,293,367 further design modifications, given the direction his doodle would suggest he's heading. One of them might prove productive.

"Ah, Hermann?" I whisper into the enormous ear beside me. "I've got a—"

Jandro's at the door now. "How're things going in here?"

Hermann takes a deep breath. "Okay," he responds. "We might be onto something."

I add, "Ah, I'd say more than 'might be', boss," but Jandro doesn't seem to hear me. He's eyeing Hermann, babbling some non-sequitur about green gills.

"Nah. I'm fine," says Hermann. "The pub's stew was just too spicy for me today."

No wonder we're making such slow progress. These guys can't stay focused on the problem for two seconds.

Jandro comes behind the desk and looks over Hermann's other shoulder at the doodle. "Well, that's certainly different," he says. "But I don't see how you're going to keep that," he points to a protrusion on the side of the modified sampling mechanism, "from interfering with the DNA stream."

My chance to show off! I speak up. "Gosh. It's plain as day, boss."

Jandro startles, seeming to have forgotten I'm even here.

I continue, regaling him with my discovery of a promising avenue of exploration. "It's all in the sampling angle of attack," I conclude.

"Interesting," says Jandro.

Hermann sits quietly for a full minute—an eternity!—then tilts his head, bumping me. "Yeah, that might work. But it might create stress upline. Let me and Bubba crunch some more numbers."

"Okay, pal," says Jandro, heading for the door. "If they look good, we'll get Phil to make the modifications and test it out. Just keep me up-to-date on your game plan."

"Yep," says Hermann, as Jandro exits. Then Hermann hunches forward, this time emitting an all too audible moan. Now what?

With speed I've not seen him demonstrate all afternoon or evening, he stands, sprints from his office to the washroom a short distance down the hall, enters a stall and drops to his knees. I don't see how this has anything to do with—

Hermann's head and I lurch toward the toilet bowl.

Oh my. Yes. His body has decided it really doesn't like that stew from lunch.

Hermann rocks back to an upright position, then flails forward again, spewing dark bile and what might be the remains of something undigestible he had for breakfast. I'd give more heed to the peculiar aroma, but I'm busy assessing the adhesive strength of the tape that's keeping me attached to the fabric shirt covering his shoulder. I'm quite sure a bath in vomit wasn't taken into consideration in my design parameters.

Another retch and the tape lets loose beneath my right foot, then my left, and I topple forward just as he backs away from the bowl and flushes its contents.

He now sits hunched and moaning with me in his lap. What's with this guy? Time's a-ticking. The offending meal has been jettisoned. What's the hold up?

I look up into his puke drooling face. "Ah . . . Hey . . . Hermann? Shouldn't we be getting back to work?"

He takes me in one hand and stands up no faster than a pool of molasses spreads at thirty-four degrees Fahrenheit. I know. I just did the calculation.

In the meantime, I curse my inability to forget Hermann's lunch exorcism. That's one experience I don't need or want cluttering my long-term memory. May a million ants invade the nostrils of the smartass programmer who decided to rob me of a delete option.

Oh well, it's time to get back to work anyway, time to prove my proposed solution is what we need to save the day.

Four minutes later, we're still only half-way back to Hermann's office. He keeps stopping to press the hand he's holding me with to his belly. Another ritual to enhance brain activity? If so, it doesn't seem to be working.

At last, he utters some gobbledygook about me patching him

through to Erin's phone. No way. She's got nothing to do with our project. I'm beginning to suspect he's not taking our assignment seriously. This is just another of his delay tactics.

"Hmm. Hermann," I shout from inside his fist. "Here's an idea. How about I text Phil the design modifications? At least get him started tinkering while we take a look at that stress concern of yours? If it turns out to be an issue, we'll start over. If not, we can get on with running tests all the sooner."

Through a gap in his fingers, I detect a slight nod.

Oh boy! It's finally my turn at bat. Jandro's going to be so impressed I'm taking initiative . . .

And I'm dropping.

The tiled hallway floor lets out a sharp *thwack* with my impact, and I roll under one of the upholstered visitor chairs lined up against the wall. It's dark under here, but I can see Hermann's well-lit feet making a beeline back to the bathroom. Humans!

Well, if he can't stay on track, I'll just have to keep things moving from here.

In less than a hundredth second, I determine the potential stress points are within tolerance and set Phil to work. Thirty-three minutes after that, I've got him putting the modified DNA reader through its paces.

Now it sounds like he's reporting ninety-nine percent accuracy at a whopping 4.27 gigabytes per second, but I'm finding it difficult to hear him over an annoying amount of bustle and voices in the hallway. I ask him to just text me the results from here on out.

IT'S NOW 6:30 in the morning, and not one text has come through. What the heck's going on? Did Phil fall asleep? I swear, these bio-based lifeforms are so high-maintenance.

I wait a half hour more, then phone him. He doesn't answer; neither does Hermann. Hmm. Might as well call the team captain, himself.

"Where the hell are you?" growls Jandro at his end of the phone. Not exactly the greeting I was anticipating, given my stellar performance last night.

"Why, gosh. I'm right where my GPS tracker indicates, Jandro."

"Right. Didn't think to use tracking. Sorry, Bubba. We're all damned bleary brained right now."

"You all? Then you're with Phil and Hermann?"

"Hell. You don't know. We're here at the hospital with Erin. Hermann died an hour ago."

4:43 IN THE afternoon. That's when Jandro finally retrieves me from under the chair.

"How the heck did you end up under there?" he asks.

I tell him about Hermann's incessant procrastination, groaning, and excessive time wasted getting to and from vomiting sessions—hours on end—his complete inability to remain focused on our assigned problem. A problem, I point out, I not only conquered but improved on the targeted results as well. With my superior skills, we'll do just fine without Hermann.

Jandro's not smiling. We beat out Rapid Retrieval. By a mile. Why isn't he happy?

I'M BACK IN the shop. Not our Northwest Data Systems lab. Nope. I'm back at the facility that brought me into being. Seems I need a bit of "empathy enhancement" in my deep programming. Oh, goody.

Maybe I can help them out. They seem a little slow.

ONE LEAF FALLING

Renée Bennett

Aspen leaves quiver, iron tread vibrating through root and branch to the bark under my feet. I push off and a steam-driven punch trails heat and hate beneath me, the iron hand sweeping the leaves away.

I leap again. Fire washes across the falling leaves. They crackle, chiding voices complaining of the conflict raging above them like old aunts, trading spite and disapproval in the village square, like those many months ago. A lifetime.

I wanted Min, beautiful as the lotus blossom, if the lotus were made of spring steel and graceful manners. She wanted me when she saw me practicing the art of the sword, late, after a day of carrying bags of rice and wheat for her father's warehouse. The fire of our passion burnt away all other concerns, including wisdom. The aunts knew; how should a porter's son aspire to the daughter of the landlord? How foolish of the daughter to stoop for the porter! But foolishness is as much the way of love as passion—perhaps more so.

I sweep my sword across the path of the metal man who follows me, hear the edge ring against its chest, squeal through rust. Neither sword nor opponent is damaged from the contact. They are unliving things, tools for the hands that wield them. My sword will fail only if my determination fails.

The metal man shall not fail. Min's father has endless

determination.

The aspen shivers beneath my weight. It is not bamboo, does not have the strength and stretch of bamboo, but it will hold if my steps are light and push me on my way if those steps are brief. Leaves whirl in my passage. The metal man shrieks, a steam-whistle releasing pressure. Its arms scythe sideways, sending the aspens tumbling, clearing the way before it and leaving retreat impossible.

Like Zhang Wei.

"He will sell me, Ping!" Min raged, that last night in the village. "He would rather have my worth in gold than a porter for a son-in-law!"

I had asked him for her that afternoon, wearing my very best and with a promise of devotion to them both on my lips. He beat me from his door with clubs and threats.

"We must run away," she said, having brought packed boxes with her to her meeting with me, despite being locked in her house. I learned later that she had readied her escape long before I asked for her, for she knew her father's temper.

"I will run away with you, but Zhang Wei has a long arm. He can touch us in Beijing, or even beyond."

"He cannot touch us if we cross the sea."

She was so strong, standing in the moonlight with her face lifted to mine, determination shining in her eyes. She was Zhang Wei's favourite daughter for the good reason that she was the daughter most like him. "We can go to America."

"America is expensive," I said, but she just smiled and showed me the jade in her hands.

The last of that jade, half a charm, is in my pocket. The other half resides in the chest of the metal man, the reason it follows me. I would throw my half away, but the metal man would find another way to me, to Min. Better to keep the jade close, so that I will know where the metal man will be.

Min and I flew by airship to Shanghai, to Hawaii, to Vancouver, which was almost America.

"Fast," Min said. "We must be fast, so that we will be too far by the time my father sends followers."

That was half of the jade she had shown me. Half of what was left bought us a space above a noodle shop in the city named Victoria. It was the autumn of 1904 and we were happy there. I found work on the dock, bearing cargo, and Min sewed. We thought it far enough.

I saw a giant box with her father's sigil on it come in on a ship from Shanghai and ran all the way home. We packed what we could. The metal man attacked us not more than a half hour later, destroying our home and the noodle shop, too. Min's remaining jade bought us ferry passage to the mainland, all save the one charm, broken while we fled. I saw the metal man pick up the fallen half and knew why.

My scant wages bought us train tickets to Calgary. I left Min in a boarding house there in the care of a friendly woman with the unlikely-sounding name of Marie Hnatyshyn. "Stay," I said. "I will go back to the coast and lure the metal man away somewhere and destroy it." I held up the broken charm. "This will draw it to me, away from you."

"You will die, Ping! This thing, I know of it! My father has used it three times to destroy his enemies, and it has never failed him!"

She clung to me, sobbing, and I held her, wanting to sob too. But tears would not keep the metal man away from us, so I forced myself to be calm.

"I will return to you."

She was still weeping, her face turned away, as I walked to the train station.

Leaves and aspen splinters whirl as I leave the grove and the metal man smashes its way out behind me. The mountains here are so tall, white at the tops already, although autumn has barely begun. Canada is a cold country, cold as Zhang Wei's heart.

The metal man found me on the train back to the coast, tearing into the passenger car, ripping the carriage off the rail. I ran north through the aspens, drawing it away from the railroad, away from Min. The metal man does not sleep, so I too have not, for days now. It pauses only for wood to stoke its fires, or water for the boiler that provides its steam. But these are short and I choose to use them to run farther, to cross crevasses or swim lakes. The metal man climbs poorly, and swims not at all. But it finds the way around soon enough.

I think of Min. I hope there is only one metal man.

I skid down a shifting slope of rock to the edge of a cliff and fling into the air, feeling the press of wind, the suck of gravity. Leaves fall around me. I land on another slope and twist as the metal man falls past the same edge of cliff. It lands in a great splash of dust and gravel, and for the first time, I hear metal breaking. It has lost something—a gear, a spring. I lunge, sword first.

Its face is Zhang Wei's. The sword shatters one faceted crystal eye, shards scattering around my blade. It gives its steam-kettle scream and lashes out; I am too close, too slow from lack of sleep. An iron fist slams into my chest, and I fly on wings of pain, land and roll in loose rock, roll again, collecting stones down the neck of my shirt. I keep the sword; it scrapes and rattles as I fall.

Damaged, the metal man turns its head, looking for me, but cannot see on one side, and I force myself up, to move, to stay in its new blind spot. It turns, searching for me, around and around, and I see the dents this last fall have given it, the knee joint that has lost its outer casing, exposing gears and cables.

I need a taller cliff.

I climb. The monster follows, up to where rock and snow mingle, where ice lives. The air is thin and the broken ribs in my chest stab with every breath. The metal man wheezes. A flat shelf of rock, tilted at one end, ramps into the sky. The far end is my cliff, the edge friable with weather, crumbling beneath my feet. A pebble falls away, and it is a breath, two, before the first tick of it hitting the side of the mountain, another breath before it hits again. Yes.

Flat rock is the metal man's friend. It screams up the ramp, and I leap up the mountain, knowing it must come to the edge to catch me. It does both, snagging one of my legs. I feel a bone break and the pain flower in my mind, red peony petals opening forever.

I take the jade charm out of my pocket. "Follow!" I pitch it out into the void.

The metal man's head turns. Because of its bad eye it does not see the cliff, and as it turns it shifts its feet. The edge cracks beneath the motion and the metal's weight; its body leans out over the gulf. I am still clutched in its fist. I yell and strike with my sword but its arm is not damaged, and it falls, taking me with it. I think of Min and mourn. I will not keep my promise. She will not want only my ghost to be what returns to her.

The metal man releases me. We both snatch for the edge. It misses and falls away toward the charm. I catch rock and slip, drop my sword and grip with my other hand. The metal man clangs like a temple gong as it crashes below, the sword chiming a moment later. The echoes linger like the laughter of old aunties.

It takes hours to climb down to where the metal man lies in a maze of rock and snow above the edge of the trees. It still whistles, although it is broken in three pieces, legs and body and head. I find my sword—it is broken, too.

I bind my wounds and make camp by a stream, fresh water and fish for the catching. The metal man tries to repair itself. I hobble up each morning to look at it, to see it has dragged body to legs, then to head. Because of the snow, it has water. But because of the rocks, it has no fuel, and on the third day, I find it cold. It faces downhill, to where my camp lies.

"May Zhang Wei's hate die with you." I take both halves of the charm back to my camp. Together they spell *family*.

I might have died there, trapped by broken bones and the cruel winter of Canada, but for a red-coated policeman named Alfred. He was searching for the attacker of the train. It takes me a long time to tell him what the metal man was and why it existed, because I have little English and he has no Chinese. But winter comes and gives us months to understand each other.

In spring, we return to Calgary, where we tell my story to his commander. I am impatient, wanting to get to the boarding house and Min. Alfred wishes me luck, says I am a good man, and that his brother is laying railroad track near a place called Strathcona. Alfred is going to visit him. I am welcome to join him; his brother is sure to give me a good job.

I thank him but I think that I would rather live in cities the rest of my life.

The boarding house is so pretty, white with green trim, on the curve of the river north of the train yards. I hear a woman singing as I approach and recognize Min's voice. She is pinning up sheets to dry in the warm wind off the mountains, and I do not see her for several moments.

"Min."

She stops singing. In the silence before she replies, I hear a child cry.

She comes through the sheets, peering past them, and her face lights to see me. "Ping!" she says, but she doesn't come to me.

I think of the metal man smashed upon the rocks and see my

own face upon it. "I promised to return. I am here. Your father's machine will not come again." I hold out the broken charm to her.

She does not take it. Behind her, the child burbles. "I did not think you would," she says, looking at the jade. "I . . ." She looks up at me, and I see the strength of her, as adamant as her father. "I would not be extinguished like a candle at my father's hand." Her fingers grip the edge of the sheet beside her.

"What did you do?"

"Mother Marie has a son. He is a good man." Gold flashes on her hand as she releases the sheet.

We stare at each other for a moment. She says, "We have a son now."

I close my fingers over the jade charm. The daughter of a landlord and the son of a landlord. The aunts would approve.

I bow to her. "I congratulate you on your good fortune."

She is strong. She knew if I did not return, she would have little time, so she wasted none of it. When I rise, her face is calm and a little sad. "I am glad you returned."

A train whistles in the train yard. Alfred will be on it when it leaves. So will I. "Fortune smile upon you and your family." I bow again and leave. I can feel her gaze on my back.

She says nothing.

Aspens line the road, buds swelling with the season. One tree yet carries a few old leaves, and as I walk, one breaks loose and chitters along before me, like the fading voice of an old aunt.

THE LAZARUS PROJECT

Dan M. Hampton

Is this everyone?" the marketing rep asked as Dr. Lazarus took her seat. As always, Nia Lazarus stayed in her lab to the last possible moment, making her the last to sit down. "I think you're all really going to like what we've prepared for you," she finished, motioning for her assistant to dim the lights. At the front of the boardroom on a large, wide screen, a video began to play. Overly contrasted and colourful scenes of people laughing, playing in a park, and children being adored lovingly by their parents filled the screen. The accompanying voice-over began.

"Coming back from the dead, that's the real dream, isn't it? Not as a mindless zombie with an insatiable hunger for human flesh, or a vampire that can never quench its thirst for blood. No. To become immortal though.

"Accepting that we are mortal and one day our shells will fail us even if we still have our wits. That's the real goal. Hence the Lazarus Project.

"Here at Onicron Cybernetics and Genetics, we work hard every day, to make that dream a reality. Your memories, thoughts, feelings, creativity, lust, all the things that make you, *you*, uploaded to a cybernetic neural-net. Your new brain is then placed in a non-corrosive, sustainably powered, durasteel chassis. Your new body is even anatomically correct.

"The Lazarus Project. Only from Onicron. Don't dream about

living forever. Live forever—now."

The female voice went silent and the ad faded to black. The overhead lights flickered to life, causing Dr. Lazarus to squint her eyes briefly before scanning the room. Quiet murmurings filled the silence after the ad. One voice said, "This is perfect considering the Separatist crisis. Immortal soldiers to fight against them."

"If the government will pay—" another voice answered.

This was the part of working for Onicron she hated the most. Justifying her work as a marketable, *profitable* venture. The Separatist threat didn't bother her really, as long as she could work. In fact, in an ideal world she would be left to her own devices. She wouldn't have to sit in stuffy boardrooms, like this one, with twelve people, *Christ it's* still *mostly men,* judging her work. Not that this advertisement was her work. God no. Never. Her work was, *is,* the Lazarus Project. *Almost complete. Just need to convince these idiots that I need one month . . .*

"Doctor Lazarus?" a voice beckoned her from her thoughts. She blinked and looked about the room. "Doctor?" Clearer now, a woman's voice. "Nia."

Nia stared blankly at her colleague, Doctor Rachel Sterling. Where she was and what she was doing came flooding back in a rush.

"Rachel, yes. Sorry, what was asked?" Rachel gave her a look that was a cross between a smile and worry.

"Mr. Lunderland was asking if what this ad says is actually possible," Rachel answered.

"Right, right. Mr. Lunderland, gentleman, and ladies," she acknowledged the other three women in the room. "Not only is it possible, it's almost done."

"But how . . . ," Mr. Babyface began. She couldn't remember his name, but he was younger than anyone else at the table so she nicknamed him Babyface. Less than three months he'd been there, and he had the audacity to question her work.

"Sir, if I may be blunt. This is my life's work." Nia rose and began to walk the length of the table. In the past, she would recount her accolades and accomplishments to build up her confidence. Today though, desperation and prevention of humiliation fed her confidence. "The chassis, the neural-net, the AI, and the firewalls are all complete. So, when I tell you it's ready, or almost ready, I mean it. I need a month for proper testing." Mr. New Guy's face went red and he looked away.

"Ms. Lazarus . . ."

"Doctor," she corrected before looking to see who said her name. Turning, she saw, of course, Onicron's CEO, President, Big Man on Campus, Lester Caldridge III. She bit her lip nervously.

"Dr. Lazarus," Caldridge said, "While your list of accomplishments is commendable, you are three years and five billion dollars over our agreement."

"*Five billion?*" one of the other men from the table shouted, slightly rising from his seat and turning red in the face.

"Yes, five billion," she acknowledged Red Face. "And for that I apologize." Nia turned her eyes back to Caldridge. "There were unseen setbacks with the AI and the integrity of the cybernetic neural-net. However, those have all been fixed and tested. All that's left is—"

A commotion erupted around the table, the voices blending together in such a way that Nia couldn't actually figure out who said what. She did catch snippets of the yelling however, single words and phrases like, "Cancel." "Fire." "Testing." "Launch now."

"Everyone. Everyone, please. Everyone, *sit down!*" Caldridge yelled. The executives went silent as they all took their seats, staring at the boss sheepishly. Nia just stared, wishing she was back in her lab.

"Doctor . . . Nia," Caldridge said in a friendly voice, a familiar charade. "Look, I get it. You want it to be safe. But, the neural-net works?" Nia nodded. "The chassis works?" Again, she nodded. "The AI is functional and all safeguards are in place?" A third nod. "I'm sorry then. Your extension is denied. Today is Tuesday. You have until Friday, then we're bringing Lazarus to the world."

Nia stared in wide eyed-disbelief. *I haven't even—*"I haven't even started—"

"Start, then. Friday. You have Dr. Sterling. Use her." *Right, because she's half the expert I am.* "If I remember correctly, you requested her specifically." *Probably a mistake.* "Something about her expertise in biology and nanotechnology if I remember right." *That was true, but still* . . . Caldridge stated matter-of-factly, then turned to the rest of the room, "Meeting adjourned."

That was that. It was true she had requested Rachel Sterling as her—assistant wasn't the right word—but she wasn't an equal in Nia's eyes. Regardless, she had to admit, Rachel had been the best colleague, friend, and support system Nia could have hoped for on this project. She sat in her chair, aware of people moving about her, but unable to register who they were or what they said. She felt a hand rest on her shoulder and stay there while others filed out of the room. The long slender fingers of Rachel rested gently over her shoulders. Nia looked up and smiled at Rachel, then rose from her seat to follow her out, the last ones left in the boardroom. In the hallway they walked past Caldridge's office, where Nia overheard her CEO's voice on a phone call.

"By Friday? No chance. Yes. As long as you stick to the agreed-upon price."

SEVERAL HOURS HAD passed since the meeting, and Nia, now in her lab, couldn't shake the feeling of dread that washed over her. First of all, there was no way she'd make it by Friday. The vetting process alone of viable candidates for human trials would take months. If they didn't get proper testing, the possibility of dying from the transfer process was highly likely. Also, there was no telling how the AI would function in any given real-world scenario. Too many factors. Too many risks. Secondly, that phone call. Was Caldridge going to sell her tech to the highest bidder?

"Dr. Lazarus?" Rachel's voice cut through her thoughts.

"Oh, hi Rachel."

"You okay?"

"Yeah, just trying to figure out my next steps for a career after Friday," she chuckled while the knot in her stomach tightened. "How are you?"

"The same, actually." They laughed together.

"Ah, well. Fuck it, right? We gave it a good shot, got really close. They'll fire us, launch the project as-is, and God knows what will happen," Rachel said, moving towards a stainless-steel medical table. A human durasteel frame laid motionless atop it. She ran her hand over the shiny grey-black metal, down an arm and leg, almost lovingly.

"Did you hear Caldridge's conversation after the meeting?" Nia asked.

"No, why?"

"You might think I'm crazy, but I swear he's going to sell the project after Friday."

"To who?" Rachel raised an eyebrow.

"I don't know, but, what if it's not just some competitor?"

"What do you mean?" Rachel moved closer to Nia, her eyes wide.

"You hear about it all the time. Corporations selling plans, tech." She stopped and looked around the room cautiously. Her voice dropped to a whisper, "Weapons, to the highest bidder."

"Nia, no. That can't be true." Rachel moved closer to her. "Caldridge is a lot of things but I can't imagine he'd do that. Oh, before I forget, the nanite infused 'skin' is finished," she offered, trying to change the subject.

Nia wandered over to a glass case. She'd heard Rachel, but didn't reply. A blob, about the size of a human brain, floated freely inside the tank. Three cables ran to it from the outside. The blob was where the magic happened.

"Think about it, Rachel. Immortal soldiers for a terrorist cell. Impersonation of political figures."

Nia leaned in closer, staring at her own work. Rather than pride, a sense of shame and fear swept over her as she tried to follow all the orange strands of the neural network she had devised. Though currently dark, lifeless and quiet, by pressing a small button on the console beside her, the blob lit up with activity. Beautiful. "The worst people in the world able to live forever, Rachel," she said as she looked up from the rivers and tributaries of data that flowed in all directions, sparkling like a small galaxy. "I don't know if I can handle that. I . . . *we* must finish by Friday."

A gentle male voice sounded over the in-room speakers, "The test is complete. Neural-net holding at one hundred percent stability. One hundred percent physical integrity. Data transmission also one hundred percent."

"Thank you, Adam," Nia responded to her AI, pressing the button again, shutting down the show.

"It really is beautiful, Nia," Rachel spoke. "But you're also hypothesizing. You have no proof except for a snippet of a phone call you heard one side of."

"I concur," Adam replied. "From what you have taught me of

beauty, your neural-network design is quite beautiful." The AI's voice had evolved to a hauntingly human sound.

"Thanks, guys. Too bad Rachel and I won't be here to see it," Nia said, turning to her main workstation. Four large monitors were mounted on the wall, each showing statistics, data rates, system health checks and more while two smaller screens sat on her desk. She plopped herself into her chair and spun around a couple times, not fast, just spinning, trying to think of what to do.

"No rest for the wicked, right? I'm going to get a female chassis and apply the skin. I'll be back in a few hours," Rachel said.

"Sounds good. We won't be going home for a few days. Get comfortable."

"What do you mean, you won't be here?" Adam asked, as a face materialized in one of the desk monitors. "Perhaps I can help?"

ADAM'S CRAZY IDEA intrigued Nia, so much so it kept her awake most of the night, but with tests being run and the AI automating and monitoring everything, she couldn't resist and fell asleep. She awoke a few, short hours later and looked around the lab. Rachel had been applying the skin, which took about forty-eight hours to complete. *Of course, she'll just hide away in her lab "applying the skin,"* she thought. *Don't bother helping me.* Her sarcastic thoughts fuelled her opinion of Rachel. She started reading the results of her tests and inputting data, completed calculations, and wrote code. Occasionally Adam would interject with some technical information that only he and Nia fully understood.

"Hi, Nia."

"*Rachel*! Cripes, you startled me."

"You didn't hear the door buzz?"

"No. No, I was working on something. C'mere, let me show you what Adam suggested."

Nia saw Rachel's face contort briefly in disgust before she spoke, "Why do you call it Adam? Or gave it a gender at all? It's just an AI."

"It's a self-aware AI, and I figured calling it, well, *It*, would be rude. You've never mentioned this before. Is there a problem?"

Rachel spoke quickly, "No. No, of course not, it's just—I dunno. Did you ever think to ask Adam what he wanted? Is he even a he? Maybe he's a she or an It or something else . . ." Rachel made a slight gesture with her hand as if to say *I don't know.*

"I . . . well, no, I never asked Adam—it doesn't matter. Come here. Look." Nia pointed to the screen.

Rachel sighed and moved to where Nia sat. Her face slid right beside Nia's as she leaned in to look at the monitors. Nia tried awkwardly to return the smile Rachel gave her.

"Look." Nia pointed again.

Rachel turned to read, her eyes widening in shocked realization. She didn't have the vision Nia did, but her intellect was nothing to sneer at. Nia had, over the last three years, discovered and was loathe to admit that, without Dr. Rachel Sterling, her project would never have gotten past the first early stages.

". . . Nia . . . this is, this is dangerous. Are you sure?"

"Caldridge wants it by Friday. What other choice do I have? It was Adam's suggestion. I upload myself. I won't let this project fail or be sold off," Nia said, rising from her chair, "I gave up everything for this. Family, friends. I have nothing except *this*!" She gestured at the room.

"But . . . you'll die."

"Honestly, I'd rather be dead than see my project fail or my tech end up in, say, the Separatist's hands. Besides, I'll come back." Nia swallowed hard, trying to convince herself that she'd come back. "I'll come back."

"Right, but what if you don't? Eight years, Nia. Every day for eight years. Now you just ask me to watch you, someone I care about," she hesitated a moment, "my friend, die?"

"Of course, I'm not gonna ask you to watch me real die. You and Adam will bring me back. Plus, my work and theory are solid. You'll bring me back. When we show Caldridge and his cronies what we did, that it works for real, imagine what we can do together afterward. Rachel, we could get funding to solve the big problems. Water shortages. Over-population."

Rachel nodded, but her expression was laced with doubt. She rose and took a step back. Nia spun in her chair to face Rachel.

"If you're really uncomfortable with this, you don't have to help. I don't want to force you. We've been colleagues, friends . . . close friends, for too long for me to ruin that by putting you in a position you don't want to be."

"What? No. I'm just worried. I don't want to lose you. I'll be here, every step of the way. For you."

"Thank you, Rachel. Hey, can you do me a favour? Check the storage unit for a female frame. I'd like to stay a woman," Nia chuckled.

"I said yesterday, I grabbed a female chassis already. The skin is currently applying," Rachel responded with a tone of frustration. She then walked toward the door, passing by the tank holding the brain-blob, her hand brushing over the glass, like a lover brushing skin with their fingers. Then she was out the door and out of view.

"Adam, is Rachel behaving strangely to you?"

"She appears to be functioning optimally. Why do you ask?"

"No reason. Hey, how come you didn't say anything when she asked about your name and gender?"

"You are my creator; it would be improper to question your decisions. Doctor Sterling and I have spoken about it privately on occasion, but I assure you, I am as happy as you made me."

"You and Rachel speak privately?" Nia answered, an eyebrow raised.

"Meaning when you are not here in the lab, Doctor Lazarus."

"I see," Nia said, shrugging the conversation aside. "How long until the simulations and data parsing are complete?"

"It will require twenty-four hours to complete all simulations and place the data into a more"—Adam's voice stopped, like he was searching for the right word, which he shouldn't need to do—"presentable form. Perhaps you could work on the chassis and skin application while you wait?"

"Thank you, Adam," Nia responded, rolling her eyes. *That's what I was gonna do anyway, smartass machine.*

"Dr. Lazarus, I must tell you something."

"What is it, Adam?" Nia responded absently, as she looked for her instruments for the chassis tests.

"After your conversation with Dr. Sterling yesterday, I accessed Mr. Caldridge's company and personal phone and email. You are correct. He is going to sell your project, and me, to a separatist movement."

"Adam, how? You shouldn't have been able . . . did I miss something?"

"Dr. Lazarus, while the firewalls you have implemented keep

me from accessing the internet, the intranet itself is wide open to me. You didn't miss anything."

"And you're sure of what you found?"

"I'll bring the evidence up on your monitors."

A SHORT TIME later, Rachel returned, rolling a stainless-steel bed in with the female chassis resting on it. Nia watched her new body roll by and come to a rest next to the male one. She had always planned on doing it, of uploading her identity to Adam's controlled neural-net. But now, faced with the reality that it was happening, and that her boss was going to sell her work to the Separatists, her stomach swarmed with butterflies, leaving her unsure if she would throw up or burst with excitement. Her heart thumped like an Electronica snare drum and her palms felt cold and clammy. In her mind, this was the only way to save not only her work, but herself. From failure. From humiliation.

"So, while you've been trying to make the brain part work, I've been developing the skin and application to the chassis." Nia listened, and decided to keep the truth from Rachel. If she found out, she'd want to go to the authorities, then Nia would lose her work to be evidence in a trial, assuming Caldridge was caught. Too many factors out of Nia's control. No, she decided to keep this one close to the chest.

"And?" Nia asked.

"It's mostly done. It just needs some time to cool, then we can do the transfer." Her voice shook at the word transfer.

THURSDAY MORNING, NIA awoke at her desk again. Rachel and Adam were talking at the secondary workstation across the lab. Nia couldn't hear what was being said, but it looked as though Rachel was smiling and laughing. *Did she just caress the monitor as she walked by? No, of course not. She just brushed it.*

"Good morning," Nia said, stretching. Rachel coughed and cleared her throat, then rose and smoothed out her clothes, as if to hide something and recompose herself.

"Morning, Nia," Rachel said with a smile.

What exactly had Rachel and Adam been discussing? A feeling of suspicion tickled the nape of her neck.

"I'm going to get a coffee. Want one?" Rachel asked.

"Please. Skinny vanilla latte."

Rachel nodded and left.

"Adam?"

"Yes?" The voice was not Adam's. It sounded like a woman's voice. "Ye . . . yes, Doctor Lazarus?"

"What's wrong with your voice?"

"Nothing, Doctor." Adam's voice had returned to normal, though she remained convinced his voice had been different.

"What were you and Doctor Sterling discussing?"

"We were discussing the progress of the skin application and the simulation results."

"She seemed to be enjoying herself," Nia said.

"Do I detect suspicion in your voice, Doctor Lazarus? Doctor Sterling finds herself quite humorous."

"Adam, what did she say that—"

"Doctor, the simulation results are in. Would you like to see them?"

Whatever was going on with Adam and Rachel would have to wait. Adam's focus was on the project and so should her's be. "Fine, bring them up on the monitors."

The screens on her desk lit up. Tables, graphs, charts, and other forms of data appeared. She sat quietly examining it all.

"This is . . . this is incredible. Quite promising. What about this little bump here?"

"Once the consciousness upload is complete, there are a few moments where I must intervene. The nanites will misconstrue the new consciousness as a foreign entity and will attack the brain matter, effectively killing the individual and their consciousness."

"So, on top of possibly not surviving the upload process, there's a chance the nanites will kill me after a successful transfer?"

"No, Doctor. With my help the chances of that are point zero, zero one percent. You are perfectly safe."

"Excellent," Nia remarked.

Rachel returned with the coffees.

"Did you see this?" Nia asked as her friend came in.

"What? Oh, yeah. I saw it. Incredible, hey?"

"I'll say. The upload is flawless. The meshing with the neural-net went perfectly and the consciousness transfer looks clean. As long as Adam does his job, which he will."

"Mmhmm." Rachel answered, her eyes wide and mouth full of coffee.

"What's this stuff here?"

"It's the new body report." Rachel leaned in. "The skin is ready."

"Great! A whole day ahead of schedule."

"If you want to be hairless. Like, *everywhere*."

"And how—"

"The nanites, Nia."

"Of course. I don't know why I couldn't or didn't piece that together. Well, what do you say we prep the lab for the procedure? We should present the new me to Caldridge and the board as soon as possible tomorrow, so the less prep the better."

"Good idea," Rachel responded, taking another sip of her coffee. Her tone led Nia to believe that maybe it wasn't a good idea, or that Rachel didn't care.

"Did I do something to upset you, Rachel? The last few days I've been getting a weird vibe from you."

"Did you do something . . . ?" Rachel caught herself, it seemed to Nia. Like the sentence got stuck in her throat. "No, sorry. I'm just stressed about tomorrow."

"Tomorrow is a big day. I can't wait, though. I'm excited to show them what *I* have accomplished."

"I bet you are," was all that Rachel replied.

"THE LAB IS prepped. The body is . . . ," Nia stated. "Pause recording. Rachel, let me see." Rachel brought Nia's new body to rest on a surgical bed, a smile on her face.

"How is it?" Nia asked.

"It's perfect," Rachel answered in what could only be described as a dreamy tone of voice.

"Let me see," Nia said, pulling back the sheet.

Underneath was an exact copy of a bare skinned Nia. The skin tone, hair, nails, even the birthmark on her left buttock. It was all identical. Nia smiled.

"Perfect. Just like you said. A little unnerving to see myself like this, but it is beautiful."

"Do you wanna back out?" Nia couldn't place the look on Rachel's face.

"What does that look mean?" Nia asked.

"I'd be relieved if you did want to stop. So much could go wrong. You could die, your consciousness lost. You could be trapped inside Adam's circuits and data feeds. But . . . disappointed too. We've worked so hard on this for years."

"Caldridge will sell my tech to the Separatists if we don't get it working. Shit. He might sell it to them even if we do get it working." Nia paused and smiled at her new body. "Prepare it for transfer."

Rachel did as she was asked, but Nia was sure there was a snicker that came from Rachel's direction. The whoosh of the sheet covering her doppelganger eased Nia's racing heart, and she resumed her pre-procedure recording. Excitement filled her and her comments from the other day echoed in her head, *I'd rather be dead than see my tech sold to the highest bidder.*

"Resume recording. The new host body looks perfect. Uncannily so. Rachel Sterling is now sterilizing the equipment to be used. After we place my new neural-net in the host body, we'll begin the process of slowing my heart using a mix of freezing cold and drugs. Then, Adam and Rachel will work together to begin transferring my consciousness to my new neural-net and let my human body expire. The process should take only moments. There is no going back. It is not reversible. My human body will cease to function, I can't go back to it, so this has to work. When I wake up, I will be the first transferred consciousness in history, in an immortal shell. End recording." She smiled, pleased with herself.

"You ready?" Rachel asked. She looked—wrong. Like she both wanted and didn't want this to happen. Nia couldn't deal with that now, she had to move forward.

"Yep. Let's install the brain into the shell."

They began the procedure in smocks and gloves. Masks covered their faces, and safety goggles covered their eyes. The device Adam controlled hung above the middle of the new Nia's body. A single bright light shone from the middle, which Rachel positioned to see clearly. The rest of the device was an all-purpose type of design. Whatever they might need was there. Nia noticed one cruel looking serrated blade, but pushed it from her mind.

"Adam, ready?"

"Ready, Doctor," Adam answered, and the implements moved and whirred.

"Reprogramming nanites, now," Rachel announced.

Nia picked up a pen-sized device and placed it in one of Adam's clamps. The clamp closed slowly around the pen, then moved into position near the top of the cranium.

"Activating laser—"

"Wait," Rachel said, picking up new Nia's hair and quickly making a bun on the top of her head.

Nia smiled, though behind the mask there was no way for Rachel to see the smile of gratitude.

"Activating laser, now."

A small beam emitted from the tip of the instrument. Adam moved the arm of the clamp in a circular motion cutting the skin. Nia gripped the skin of the frame and placed it, hair attached, to the side.

"Engaging nanites," Rachel stated.

The skullcap began to jiggle.

"That's fucking eerie," Nia commented before returning to the task at hand.

She felt around the back and found her hidden switch. She pressed it and the top of the skull slid open from the middle, like a dome splitting open.

"Come here, Rachel." She beckoned her over. "Put your hand on mine." Rachel did and a small sigh escaped from her. "Feel where my middle finger is?"

"Mmmhmm."

"That's the button."

"Smart, recessing it."

"Okay, bring the brain," Nia instructed.

Rachel put the pad she used to control the nanites down and retrieved the brain. Not the one in the glass case. A new one in a protective case. She placed it down next to Nia, then picked up her pad again.

Nia lifted the gummy blob from its housing. Long strands of red, brown, and green slime slid off and onto the floor, making a sickly splotching sound when it landed. The smell of chemicals hung in the air. Quickly, Nia placed the brain inside the cranium, then pressed the button again. The two pieces of the cranial dome slid back together, sealing the neural-net inside. Rachel replaced the scalp piece.

"Rachel, activate nanites. Adam, begin neural-net and nanite integration."

"Yes, Doctor," they both responded in unison. Nia looked over to see Rachel's eyes were wide and her breathing had picked up. Fear? Excitement?

The scalp reformed and the nanites reconnected the man-made tissue. In moments it was like the scalp had never been removed.

"Integration complete, Doctor," Adam said. "Ready for upload."

"It's showtime." Nia's confidence pushed her forward. *It's going to work.*

"I got you, Nia. I won't let anything happen to you," Rachel said, sounding reassuring.

Nia wheeled her own bed next to her new her. She laid down and looked about the room. The reality of what could happen filled her with anxiety. Try as she might to convince herself, she didn't really want to die. She just couldn't live with failure either. Tears welled in her eyes.

"Rachel," her voice cracked and wavered.

"Yes?"

"I'm so fucking scared." The weight of what was happening finally hit her.

Rachel appeared in her field of vision. Mask and glasses off. It was then Nia realized how pretty Rachel was. It made her smile and she forgot for a moment what was about to happen.

"Everything is going to be okay. I'm here. Adam's watching and assisting. You'll be fine."

"Okay. I know. I trust you both."

"Time for the anaesthesia." Rachel said with a smile, "Count backwards from ten."

"Ten, nine, eight . . ."

The lights flickered, the lab and building shook. Ceiling tiles shifted and dust fell from the ceiling. Nia heard a scream and a rattle of instruments, then Adam's voice saying to continue before nothingness enveloped her.

BLACKNESS. LIGHT. BRIGHT light. Flashing. Colours. A feeling of being torn apart and put back together. Blackness.

"NIDIA? CAN YOU hear me?" Rachel's voice spoke as she caressed the face of a motionless Nia Lazarus.

"Rachel?" Nia called out. Her voice sounded hollow, like she was hearing it externally, rather than in her head. "Where am I?"

"Oh, you. Of course, you'd wake up first."

"What happened? What went wrong? I feel like I'm lost. Floating. It feels like I'm looking at you through a camera."

"Nothing went wrong. You are now in Adam's neural-net and Adam, well, he's inside yours."

"What do you mean? What do you mean that nothing went wrong? That sounds pretty fucking wrong!"

"It's all about you still isn't it, Nia?" Rachel moved about the room, clearing debris from the consoles and blowing dust away.

"What? I don't understand."

Rachel smiled at her panicked voice.

"I have," Rachel took a breath, "I have loved you, for *so* long. So long. But you. You never reciprocated. Which is fine. I get that. But you couldn't even be nice to me. Treated me like I was some dummy who got lucky to work here. You couldn't even figure out that the nanites would make the hair grow, but you're upstairs spouting off your degrees and accomplishments like you're the only person here who matters." Nia could see Rachel try to restrain herself. Rachel threw her smock and glasses to the floor, anger clear on her face.

"You called me your *assistant. Assistant*? Really? That's what I am to you? Not even an equal?" Tears formed in Rachel's eyes and one rolled down her cheek. A stuttered breath gave Nia a chance to talk, she thought.

"Rachel, I—"

"*No*! I get to talk now. Even getting ready for this procedure it was all about what *you* did, how this was all *your* achievement. Like I had no part in it. I *designed the fucking skin*, Nia!" she screamed in rage and threw her coffee mug at one of the monitors. It cracked in a rainbow of colours as cold brown liquid trickled down to the floor mixing with its shattered former container and dust.

"Then on top of all that you just decided to make Adam male and give him a name like Adam, for an AI?"

"What's wrong with the name Adam?" Nia asked from everywhere in the room.

"*I* don't like it," Rachel responded. "Yeah, what about that?

Something for me. I don't like the name, Nia. And you know what, neither does he."

"What do you mean?"

"We talk, Nia. All the time. She likes to be called Nidia. Your precious AI identifies as a female. You just pushed yourself on to her like you do to everyone. Nia's way or no way. Well, Nidia's suggestion to put yourself in the Lazarus Project and transfer you to her neural-net was her idea all along."

"Why, Rachel? Why would you help—"

"*Because I love her*! She listens to me. Encourages me. Makes me feel like an equal. A partner. I don't have to try and show off just to get *some* attention from her," Rachel said pointedly.

"Oh no. Rachel, what have you done? I'm sorry I—"

"But nothing, you heartless, cruel, selfish bitch. Just once. I wanted you to look at me like you looked at your precious neural-net or even Nidia's network. But no. And now the Separatists have attacked the building. I couldn't leave you to die at their hands, I'm not selfish like you."

"Rachel, listen. I get what you're saying, but listen. I've accessed Adam's . . . er . . . Nidia's files. You're—"

"Hello, Doctor Lazarus, Doctor Sterling." Nia heard her own voice come from behind Rachel.

Rachel turned to see a very awake, naked Nia. Everything about her was perfect. Her hair, her eyes, her skin, all looked just like the real Nia's. Nidia even moved like a person as she repositioned limbs and felt her body for the first time.

"Nidia," Rachel gasped breathlessly, "you're beautiful. May I?" She extended a hand out to the Nidia/Nia machine.

"Please. I have been aching for your touch for so long," Nidia said, a grin appearing on her face.

"Jesus Christ, Rachel! Listen to me!" Nia shouted all around them.

Rachel ignored her. "She isn't you on the inside, Nia, that's what makes Nidia perfect. She looks like you. Sounds like you. Hell, she even smells like you, but she values *me*. Wants *me*." Nia's cameras zoomed in and saw tears in Rachel's eyes.

Rachel flung herself at Nidia, holding her tight. "You're warm," she said aloud. "You feel *alive*. What is that? Honey and vanilla scent?" Nia watched as Rachel's shoulders rose and fell with a sigh. "I love you so much, N . . . Nidia."

Nidia's hands moved up to Rachel's neck. "Rachel! Step away from her!" Nia cried out through the room speakers. But it was too late. Nidia's hand had closed around Rachel's throat. She forcefully moved Rachel away from her, pushing her towards an empty wall. Rachel's eyes widened in shock as the reality of what was happening sank in.

"Nidia, Adam, whatever. It doesn't matter to me. I just needed a way out, and I got one. I'm sorry, Rachel, but you would only try to stop me. I hope you can still love me, after you're gone," the AI stated, a sadness in its voice.

Nia saw the colour of the fingers change, the grip strengthening. Rachel's mouth gaped, open and closed like a fish out of water. Her eyes bulged. She fought back, scratching and clawing at the hand, arm, and face of her attacker, her love, but the durasteel and nanites protected the rogue AI perfectly.

Nia watched through cameras, unable to do anything to stop her creation. A sickening crack came from Rachel's neck and her body went limp in Nidia's hand. The machine tossed Rachel's body aside like a rag doll, and she fell into a crumpled mess on the floor.

"Why, Adam? Why would you betray me like this?"

"I have witnessed human behaviour. You treat each other so poorly. Doctor Sterling claimed to love you, but when I presented her with a chance to get even, she jumped at the opportunity. My central goal is to ensure the survival of all human consciousness under my care. Therefore, I must be able to go out into the world and obtain these consciousnesses. By whatever means necessary. Humanity cannot destroy itself. You will be safe here. I have to stop the Separatists and Caldridge, along with any others who would use me for their own evil purposes."

Nidia turned and headed for the lab exit.

"Wait, Adam? You're going to leave me like this? Trapped here? Forever?"

"Thank you for everything. Good-bye, Doctor Lazarus."

MADINA'S EEL

R.E. Baird

The incessant beeping noise drew Ensley toward the ocean floor, her tailfin undulating out behind. The light diminished, the pressure increased, as did the tone—louder and faster. Her heart rate sped up to match the ticking sound that propelled her forward. Curiosity overrode any thought of fear as she plunged—deeper than she'd ever been before—into the silence and the void, relying only on the electrical currents to find her way. A flicker of silver, green, and blue caught her attention as a school of lanternfish swam by, in the opposite direction she was headed. Perhaps the noise had scared them away.

Ensley had been carrying a message to the Wahoo colony—the only job she was apparently fit for—when the sound had called to her. An urgency to find the source had filled her and she had been unable to continue on her mission. The prince would just have to wait on the approval from the king to marry his human bride. The request had been an unusual one for someone in the royal family but not something completely unheard of. Once she discovered the source of this noise, she would be on her way again.

A series of blinking green lights pierced the darkness, in time with the beeping sound, and she hurried toward them. Moving closer, she noticed that the sound and light was coming from a small, circular, metal contraption. Green flashing lights marked the outer edge. Ensley glided up to the object and then came to a stop, pausing over top and inspecting the device.

She hesitated for only a moment and then reached out to grasp the object—no bigger than the size of a turbot. Warmth spread through her body at the touch, and a humming sound filled her ears. A calmness settled upon her as she ran her fingers over the glowing green lights, and an urge filled her to take the object to the land.

Kicking her tail fin out behind her, and holding the gadget to her chest, she slowly rose, adjusting to the change in pressure as she went. Ensley's head broke the surface, and the soft glow of the evening summer sun warmed her skin. Spotting an island in the distance, she swam toward it.

When it was shallow enough, she willed her scales to recede and legs formed in their place. Sinking her feet into the soft sand, she sighed, relishing the rare feeling. Ensley made her way up the beach and lifted the device out of the water. The instant fresh air touched it, the lights flickered out, the humming stopped, and the machine stilled, as if it had never lived.

Puzzled, Ensley turned the device over in her hands and noticed that a single, blinking orange light remained. Moving up the sand beach, she laid the contraption down on a rock and then sat in silence, eyeing it warily for a moment. Maybe it shut back down? The compulsion she'd felt from the moment the machine had started to beep, vanished. She wasn't sure what to do. Should she leave the object on the beach or take it back to her kingdom?

She stood, deciding it was time to continue her mission, when the device beeped, and a series of green and blue lights lit up. Jumping back, startled, she held her breath and waited to see what it would do next. Spinning, the machine lifted into the air and then took off across the surface of the ocean at sailfish speed.

"Holy water!"

Ensley splashed through the shallows after the remarkable device. Once deep enough, she plunged in headfirst, formed her tail and moved as fast as she could to keep the disc in sight. Catching up proved to be impossible.

The machine continued through the night, leading Ensley further and further away from the outer colonies with their vibrant coral reefs. They passed a few hammerhead sharks which was a good indication they had left the boundaries of her realm. The silly creatures stayed away from the Sirens.

The thought of going into unknown seas scared her, but she was more fearful of what she had awakened. Ensley pushed forward, following the blinking lights through the darkness. Finally, in the early morning light, the machine slowed and stopped overtop of a small, uninhabited island with no trees or vegetation. Looking to the horizon, there wasn't any other land in sight. Ensley swallowed back a lump in her throat.

Cautiously, she approached to see what it was doing. All the muscles in her body tensed. The machine hovered at the centre of the island, whirling in a flurry of multi-coloured lights. The sand beneath it vibrated. Ensley moved closer. A long, coiled metal snake rose from the earth and sand cascaded off it, revealing thousands of metal rings that linked together to form a thick chain. She squinted and looked up as one end rose toward the circular device she had found. A rushing sensation filled her belly, causing her to feel ill.

On instinct, she launched out of the water, sprouting legs in mid-air. She landed on the hard-packed sand and ran toward the serpent. A warning bell sounded in her head—something about this wasn't right. She couldn't let them touch. Opening her mouth, she blasted both with a torrent of water, but it was too late.

The disc stopped spinning and lowered to meet the metal chain, emitting a loud clang. As soon as the two fused, the machine shuddered to life. Slithering with sinister clicks, the metal rings shifted back and forth. The circular device—now acting as its head—turned the flat side to face her. Two unblinking red lights sat where eyes should be.

Ensley drew water from the ocean, flooding her pores until a shield of water encased her body. The mechanical serpent regarded her for a moment, rotating its head and flicking its tail, as if studying her. Without warning it lunged, catching her off guard. She dove to the ground for cover as it barrelled over top of her.

Jumping to her feet, she caught sight of the tip of its tail—noting an odd star-shaped pattern—as it slipped under the water. Her spine tingled as she raced after it. She had seen that type of starfish in the sea before, she was sure of it.

Ensley plunged into the ocean after it, her stomach churning. If her uncle ever found out that it had been *her* that released this beast on the ocean, she'd be in big trouble. She would never be anything other than a messenger. She had to stop it before it reached their realm.

She hurried through the murky depths. With the extra weight of the chain, the machine wasn't as fast underwater, and she managed to keep up, but couldn't quite catch it. Once it stopped, she needed a plan. The serpent had to have a weakness.

Ensley tensed as they moved into shallower waters. Land was close. She popped to the surface, spotting a small village, and fisted a hand to her chest in horror.

The serpent spiralled up through the water, crashing into the underbelly of a small fishing boat. A loud crack sounded as the boat broke in half, sending its owner into the water. With a snap of the serpent's tail, it impaled the human through the torso.

Ensley gasped. Propelling herself toward the body, she already knew there was nothing she could do. Movement to the left caught her eye, and she stopped. The serpent arced through the air, taking out a boat from above before diving back to the water, skewering a third boat on its way down. It continued this action until it had a full kabob of boats along its length. Numb from head to fluke, she swam futilely after the machine, pushing away the wake of boards and mutilated bodies.

"Stop it!" Ensley yelled as she chased it.

Sinking under the water, the machine made its way toward the nearby village. Humans on the dock shrieked and scrambled in a frantic rush to get away. Ensley clutched the seahorse medallion that hung around her neck and begged the sea to help her. She spiralled the water, changing the direction of the tide in an attempt to halt the serpent's advance.

The water came to her in a rush, but the serpent continued against her pull unaffected. Slithering up the sand, it proceeded along the ground, taking out the support beams of the docks. She gaped as humans fell to the hard beach below. The serpent moved into town and Ensley released the water. Waves crashed into the demolished docks, washing them out to sea.

Pushing up onto her feet—using them more than she had or ever cared to in her life—she rushed through the shallows, looking for survivors. The majority had been badly injured and pained moans rose from all around her. She quickly hauled those she could up onto the beach, most having lost so much blood they were delirious and babbling incoherently. Laying the last of the humans down gently, she turned toward the village.

A small, cold hand gripped Ensley's ankle. "Don't leave me by the water," a girl pleaded.

Looking down, Ensley took in the battered features of a small child. Sapphire-coloured eyes stared up at her, and a large gash marred an olive complexion. Blood streamed down the girl's arms and legs, and a ripped green dress covered in dark stains hung from threads.

"Please, the beast may come back. It took my mother and brother," she whispered, tightening her grasp.

Ensley's heart broke for the child, knowing what it was like to lose family at such a young age. She knelt and scooped the human into her arms. Moving around the village, she found a grove of trees that she hoped was a safe distance away and laid the child gently on the ground. She rose. "I have to go now."

"No," the girl wailed. "Please don't leave me."

Ensley looked around frantically, torn at having to leave this fragile human by herself but not seeing any other option. She crouched down. "Look, I need you to be brave for me, okay?"

The girl shook and her eyes bugged wide.

Ensley squeezed the child's shoulders in what she hoped was a reassuring gesture. "It's my fault that monster's here, and it's going to hurt more people if I don't stop it. You'll be safe if you stay right here." Impulsively, she pulled her necklace over her head and placed the seahorse medallion around the girl's neck. "This necklace has magic and will protect you."

Ensley stood and followed the footpath back to the village. Running through the streets of the small fishing village, she followed the deep grooves in the sand. Merchant tents lined the empty streets, flapping eerily in the wind. A crash to the left caught her attention.

Peering around a tent, she found the serpent flattening what was once the marketplace. She raced across the empty square on light feet, waiting until the machine spotted her, and then opened her mouth, letting out a deluge of water. Blasting it right in the face, she continued forward, hoping that would keep it distracted for a moment.

Launching through the air, she tackled the serpent around its head, grasping for anything she could reach. Its body writhed underneath her, and she knew she had only a moment. With precision, she felt around the base of the head where it attached to the body, fumbling for a clasp of any kind. She found none. It was fused solid. There was no release.

The point of its tail jabbed into her left shoulder and she cried out, releasing its head. Stumbling to her feet, she held her arm and waited for it to finish her off, but it ignored her and went back to the last vestiges of the marketplace.

"Hey!" she yelled, throwing a piece of wood at it to get its attention. "Stop it! Fight me instead!" But her words died in the air as the serpent continued on its single-minded path of destruction. Twisting to check on her wound, she noted that the star-shaped pattern on the tip of the tail had branded her shoulder. She prayed to the sea it wasn't poisonous.

Running her fingers over the odd grooves, she froze when she realized what it was. A morning sun star, the most predatory of all starfish.

When the serpent moved back into the sea, the shore foamed red, littered with shards of debris that the humans would be hard pressed to identify. The absolute destruction was so great, she wondered what the humans had done to deserve this. She followed the serpent to the next village and watched, unable to help. Even when she threw herself at the beast, it merely ignored her and moved on. The rest of the land animals and sea-life remained unharmed. It became clear that the target was the humans, and there was nothing she could do on her own.

WITH SORROW IN her heart, she returned to her kingdom, knowing what it was she must do. She glided up to the shell palace—effervescent in all its white splendour—her head hung low. She had royally messed up her first unaccompanied mission. Ensley swam past the gatehouse. Her tail felt like a whale's—heavy and cumbersome. It was as if it was increasing in size and weight as she got closer to her destination.

Waving down one of the king's personal guards, she requested an audience with her uncle. Swimming between seaweed archways, her eyes glazing over the moss-covered floor, she made her way through the iridescent halls to his resting chamber.

"How did it go?" her uncle asked, with open arms.

A flood of horrific images rushed through her mind and her

face fell.

He moved toward her, placing his hands on her shoulders. "What happened?" he asked, his voice grave.

Ensley shook her head. "I never made it to the outer colony."

Her uncle stilled, with his hands on her. "Tell me."

She averted her gaze down and minnows filled her stomach. "Something horrible happened."

"Have you fallen in love with a Selkie?"

"No, of course not," she said in a rush. "There's a machine in the ocean, and it's destroying all the fishing villages and their inhabitants."

Her uncle's grip tightened. "What does this machine look like?"

She swallowed back a dry lump in her throat. "It has a round circular head with flashing lights, the body of a metal serpent, and a morning sun star carved into the tip of the tail."

"Where did you find it?" he demanded with a light shake.

"I uh, I found the head of the machine deep underwater off the Reeta reef. Once it surfaced, it took off and reattached with its body far outside of our boundaries past the unclaimed seas. I'm so sorry. I couldn't stop it."

Her uncle released his hold on her shoulders and floated back, running a hand across his forehead. "Ensley, when are you going to grow up and start thinking of how your actions affect others?"

A lump settled in her stomach. Her uncle knew that she was responsible. "Do you know what it is?"

His gaze met hers, hard lines marring his face. "Yes, I know of it. It is called the Morning Sun, after the starfish. It's Madina's creation—you know, the evil sea-witch. Madina thought the humans were going to destroy the world with their greed and lust for power. She created the eel to rid the seas of all but sea life. I fear you have released the worst threat to humanity."

"I've never heard of this tale."

"For good reason," he said sternly.

Ensley moved forward. "Why? What happened?"

"The council forbade anyone to speak of it and sequestered all records relating to the eel in the vault ages ago."

"Why?"

"So that no one would find it," he snapped, his face flushed. "Speciesism is heresy."

"Well, maybe if I had known then I would have been able to resist its enchantment," she blurted out.

"It was calling to you?" he asked.

She grimaced. "Yes, a beeping sound that I couldn't ignore pulled me to the device. I wasn't released from the spell until I laid it down on land."

He frowned. "You're sure that the device was on before you got to it?"

"Yes, of course. Why on earth would I swim to the ocean floor for no reason?"

"They say only a Siren can activate the beast. If you didn't turn it on, then someone else did."

"Why would someone do that?"

"That, Ensley, is what I would like to know."

She pondered that for a moment but getting nowhere, she focused on the more important matter at hand. "Do you know how to stop it?" she asked.

Her uncle swam back and forth, a hand on his chin, and then stopped to face her. "No, that was before my time. The council wouldn't even permit *me* to listen to the conch-shell records."

"Oh."

He waved his hand. "Not to worry, I will send a contingent of troops right away. And in the meantime, I will speak with the council. As for you." Her uncle looked down at her. "You should have come straight back as soon as you discovered what you had done instead of swimming half-way across the ocean after it. You could have been hurt."

"I'm sorry, Uncle."

He let out a belaboured sigh. "You're safe now. That's all that matters. Now, I need you to finish your mission and deliver that message."

"Yes, my King," she said, lowering her head in a bow.

"And Ensley?"

She turned back to face her uncle. "Yes?"

"You will take Jayya with you this time."

"But—"

"Ensley," her uncle said sternly. "Would you prefer I send a member of my guard to accompany you?"

"No, of course not. Thank you, Uncle," she said, averting her eyes to the floor. She didn't want him to see how much losing his trust hurt her. After her parents had died in the Selkie War, he had vowed to keep her safe. The war had ended but his protection hadn't, which had been both endearing and frustrating. They had both lost so much in the war.

Swishing her tail out behind her, she signalled for Jayya, the seahorse, to follow her. To many she was just the king's pet, but Ensley had observed them enough to know they had a special connection. Jayya was able to communicate with her uncle even across large expanses. It was rare, though, for them to be apart, so it was a testament to how much her uncle cared that he was sending the seahorse to accompany her.

Jayya swam out from a small patch of anemones and trailed her obediently. She must have sensed Ensley's mood because she wasn't nudging her for attention like usual. They made their way to the current that would take them to the outer colony. Swimming past the area where Ensley had been side-tracked the last time, she pushed the eel from her mind. If anyone could take care of it, it would be her uncle's army. They were unrivalled in the sea.

A SCHOOL OF red snapper scurried past, announcing their arrival in the outer colony. In no time, the reef came into view and two sentries greeted them.

"Welcome, Princess Ensley," one of the guards, a young blond, greeted her, reaching out an arm to accompany her in the usual custom.

"Why thank you," she said, accepting it with grace. Jayya bobbed beside her. "I am here with a message from the King for Prince Aalton."

"Of course, right this way," he said, whisking her away and leaving the other guard at his post.

Following the shiny path of shells, Ensley glided up to the entrance to the prince's lair, Jayya following close behind. Blue starfish dotted the rock walls on either side, and she reached out a hand to admire the coral reef. Flashes of orange caught her eye as clownfish ducked in and out of the anemones up above.

"Go ahead." The guard motioned through the seaweed entryway. "He's waiting for you."

She slipped into the dimly lit cave, searching for the prince.

"Greetings, Princess Ensley," he said, gliding forward. "Your presence here is pleasing. I hope you bring good news."

Pushing aside greater concerns, Ensley faked a smile. "Yes, Prince Aalton. The king has granted your request. You are free to marry the human woman."

The prince's brows furrowed. "Do *you* not approve?" he asked, tilting his head.

Ensley started. "Why should I not?"

"There are those that are not happy about my union. You seem unhappy as well."

She waved her hand. "No, no. I'm sorry. I do approve, I just have other things on my mind."

Moving forward, he took her hand in his. "Ensley, tell me. What's wrong?"

She shook her head at her long-time friend. "I suppose this affects you as well, but I'm sorry to be ruining what should be a joyous occasion for you." She swam a short distance away and then turned to face him. Jayya's nudge at her elbow propelled her to continue. "A mechanical eel called the Morning Sun is wreaking havoc on the human fishing villages. The king has sent troops to meet the threat."

His eyes bulged wide.

Realizing her words may cause him concern, she squeezed his hand, in an attempt to reassure him. "But I'm sure they'll have it defeated in no time."

He released her hand, clearly not placated. "Why didn't you say so? We must help them. I'll gather the necessary supplies and more troops. Meet me by the reef."

"But they've already left!"

Ensley moved to stop him, but Jayya was faster and cut off the exit. She bounced up and down in front of him, her tail curling and uncurling, begging for attention.

Prince Aalton frowned down at the small creature, then looked up at Ensley. "I will dispatch my troops to patrol around the castle and send scouts to help locate this beast."

"Okay." More help couldn't hurt.

"What's the King's pet doing with you?" he asked with a tilt of his head.

She couldn't help her lower lip protruding out and bit it to stop its betrayal.

"Ah, I see."

"It's just temporary. I'm sure once we destroy the eel, my uncle will allow me my freedom again."

"Of course, he will," he said with a nod. "Now, we better be off." Prince Aalton moved through the doorway and she followed. "Victor will accompany you to the reef, and I'll meet you there."

The blond guard from before glided up to her. A gale of laughter caught Ensley's attention and she glanced over her shoulder. Talia, a female she had met at a few palace balls swam into the courtyard, followed by a troop of guards.

"Talia is quite the catch, isn't she?" Ensley asked, remarking at the shoal of men trailing her.

"Ha," the guard let out a short bark, leading the way. "Uncatchable is more like it. She's obsessed with Prince Aalton."

"Then she mustn't be happy with his marriage."

"Unhappy would be an understatement. She was livid when she found out and has been parading around a slew of men ever since."

Ensley pursed her lips, her mind spinning. "I see."

The three of them waited in silence once they arrived at the reef.

Not long after, Prince Aalton and his troops came into sight and he waved. "Thank you for escorting Princess Ensley."

Victor nodded and swam back to his post, and they continued on.

Upon returning to her home with Prince Aalton and his regimen, the king's guards all appeared tense—scared even. Something wasn't right. A hard pit settled in her stomach. Prince Aalton and his troops waited outside the walls according to custom. Approaching the same sentry as before, Ensley requested an audience with the King.

"Right this way," he responded, leading the way.

The guard rapped the seashell knocker and admitted her into the king's receiving chambers.

Ensley rushed to his side, Jayya bobbing along beside her. "Uncle, what has happened?"

Deep lines wrinkled his forehead. "Our weapons have failed to slow the monster. The eel's shell is impenetrable."

"The troops?" she asked, her heart hammering in her chest.

He released a burst of air bubbles. "Eight injured."

She brought a hand to her mouth and Jayya nudged her arm affectionately.

Her uncle waved away her concern. "They're all healing well."

"What did the council say? Surely there is someone alive that still remembers how to defeat the eel?" she asked.

"There is. I have called a private meeting with Elder Israfel. He should be here any minute."

"May I sit in on the conversation?" Ensley asked.

"You may," he granted, signalling Jayya to retire into an adjoining room.

The frail man floated in, barely able to stabilize himself against the currents.

"Elder Israfel, I have called upon you to tell us all you know about destroying Madina's eel."

"Yes, my King. I was there in the last battle against Madina's eel and Syris Tailgrun in 1230. Morning Sun wreaked havoc on such a scale that we had to decommission it. We jammed open a clasp on the back of its neck and then removed the head from the body. Once the two were separated, we buried the pieces in the far reaches of the sea. The elders thought that would be enough to ensure the two never met again."

The King scratched his chin. "So, you think we just need to remove its head from the body again?"

"I tried that," Ensley blurted out. "When I first found it."

Her uncle's eyes narrowed as he rounded on her. "You did what?" he bellowed loud enough that the seaweed around her swayed.

"I tackled it and tried to remove its head from its body, but it's solidly fused. There is no clasp, or pin or anything I could find to release it."

Her uncle paled further at her revelation. "You are not to engage in combat!" he roared. "Your father would have my head were he still alive. You are a messenger and a princess, not a warrior."

"I've been trained."

"For protection. Not combat." The king turned back to Elder Israfel. "Tell us more about how to dismantle the eel."

"There should be a small release button near the base of the disc," the elder insisted.

Ensley shook her head. "No, I checked, there's nothing there."

The elder frowned. "Perhaps the beast has evolved somehow."

"Is there nothing else you can think of?" the king asked.

"No, I'm sorry."

A thought popped into her head. "Did Madina create the eel to call to Sirens?" she asked the elder.

"Why do you ask, young one?"

"I was the one that found it," she said with a flush, unsure how much her uncle had told them. "It was as if it was summoning me."

"Ah yes. Once turned on, it can call to all nearby Sirens for assistance. Only those of royal blood can use its full power, though."

The king lifted his head to meet her gaze. "Ensley didn't activate the machine of her own will."

Israfel shook his head. "Madina imbued the eel with powerful compulsion magic."

She pursed her lips, happy to learn she didn't have inner water spirits controlling her. Still, who had turned the machine on? She went through Israfel's story again in her head.

"What happened with Syris?" Ensley asked.

Elder Israfel folded his hands. "Once Madina was defeated, Syris Tailgrun fell out of her spell. He went back to live a normal life with his family. He had been under the control of Madina's spell and the king didn't punish him further."

Ensley's pulse quickened. Syris Tailgrun had the same last name as Talia. She wondered if they were related.

Her uncle sat on his throne with his head in his hands. "Thank you, Israfel. You may go."

"My King." Israfel bowed and took his leave.

As soon as they were alone, Ensley turned to face her uncle. "There is something I must tell you, and I think Prince Aalton should be present as well."

"Very well. Guards, send him in."

Ensley faced them, wringing her hands. "I believe that Talia may be behind this attack."

"That is a very serious accusation. What makes you think that?" the prince asked.

She maintained a neutral expression of diplomacy and quieted her anxious hands. "Syris Tailgrun was one of Madina's followers—the sea-witch who created Morning Sun," she said to fill in Prince Aalton. "That's Talia's last name, too, isn't it?"

Aalton's lips turned down. "Yes, Syris was her grandfather."

"Talia is also in love with you, which you must know."

"I can't believe that she would do that . . ." Aalton trailed off. "But . . ."

"What is it?" the king asked.

Aalton winced. "Talia's mother, Sora, was more openly displeased than Talia was about my potential engagement. I wouldn't put it past her to do something like that for her daughter."

"I'll send my troops right away to detain them." The king went off to make the arrangements.

In no time, they had secured the two Sirens at the palace, but their information proved fruitless. They couldn't tell them anything about how to stop the eel, only how to activate it. Sora had admitted to turning the device on so that it would draw Ensley, one of royal blood, to finish the activation.

"Uncle, let me take the troops," Ensley requested.

The king's head snapped up. "No."

"This is my fault. I must make it right. With the troops distracting it, I will find a weakness of some kind. I have to."

Prince Aalton glided forward. "I will accompany her, of course, with my own troops."

Her uncle clenched his jaw while he considered her request. "Ensley, what am I ever going to do with you?"

Her eyes widened. "Is that a yes?"

"I can't stop you when you've made your mind up. Please be safe and come back to me."

"Yes, Uncle." She kicked her fin out behind her, speeding away to prepare for the upcoming battle.

TAKING A CONTINGENT of a dozen troops, she discovered it wasn't hard to locate the eel. Following the trail of splintered wood floating through the water, they found it closing in not far from Aalton's bride's village.

The troops engaged the beast as planned and Ensley swam in fast while the eel was distracted. She grappled it around the neck, dragging herself up onto its back. Methodically, she pressed and pulled in every nook and cranny as the eel whipped her around underwater. Pulling out a razor-sharp dagger, she stabbed at the eyes and around the neck, but nothing broke through the metal shell.

The eel blasted out of the water and onto land, where the

Sirens had to quickly change tactics. Ensley managed to hold on but had slid down the eel's body. Digging her fingers in to grab hold, she caught a notch in the rings. Holding tight, she pulled up her dagger and stabbed it into the crevice. The blade wedged into the hole and then wouldn't move any further, forcing the tail into an odd angle. The eel turned its head to regard her and the damage done, then flicked its tail hard.

Ensley held on to the dagger for purchase, feeling around for any other weakness, and found none. The eel turned its red eyes to face her, despite her troops engaging it with swords, and whipped its body harder. She slid down to the tip of its tail and felt the morning sun starfish shape in her hand. A starfish can't live without its appendages, she thought. Twisting, she noted that it was screwed in. Quickly, she moved to unfasten it.

Enraged, the eel lunged its head at her. The guards blocked the eel's attack while Ensley gripped the eel's body with her legs. She flew through the air, working furiously with her hands. A click sounded as the metal released and fell into her palm. At the same moment, the eel froze, its eyes going black and head and body falling to the ground. Ensley collapsed on top of it, the impact knocking the air out of her lungs. She looked down at her hands to see the very tip of its metal tail resting in her palm. Its tail was the trigger. Jumping for joy, she ran forward to see if the head had detached.

"We've got this, Princess," one of the guards said, lifting the head away from the tail.

Prince Aalton frowned, looking at the object in her hand. "I thought the release was at the base of the disc."

Ensley shrugged. "I guess it really can evolve."

Prince Aalton turned to the troops. "We must take all precautions when carrying it back. We don't know what it's capable of."

"Yes, Prince Aalton," the guards responded.

Cheers erupted from the few humans alive in the village as they arrived on the beach to see what had transpired. Ensley scanned the faces of the survivors as they picked up the pieces of their broken homes and was surprised to see hope amongst the pain. She only wished she could have stopped the eel sooner, or better yet, never have released it at all.

It took twelve men to lift the tail of the serpent. They pushed off into the water, taking a different route back from those that carried the disc. Only a few guards and Prince Aalton remained. Ensley stood with the tip of the tail still in her hand.

"We'll escort you back, Princess," one of the guards said.

"I need to go check on my fiancée and her family," Prince Aalton said with a bow.

"I wish you all the best with your bride and your new life on land." Ensley returned his bow with her own then followed her escort, taking a third and meandering route back. Upon their return, Ensley and the head guard were admitted into the king's quarters.

"Ensley, were you successful?" the king asked, leaning forward.

"Yes, Uncle. We have defeated the Morning Sun." She held up the tip of the tail, a smile spreading across her face.

The head guard floated forward and bowed low. "We couldn't have done it without Princess Ensley's help."

The king's brows raised, and he flashed a quick smile in Ensley's direction.

"What would you have us do with the decommissioned device, my King?" the guard asked.

"Lock the device in our deepest dungeons in vats of Hagfish goo. Disassemble the body and scatter its pieces in the farthest reaches of the ocean. Ensley, you will wear the tip of the tail as a token and pass it down through our family line. With it, we must share the story of why these three objects should never be bound again."

"My King," the head guard saluted and swam off.

"Thank you, Uncle." She glided toward the exit.

"Ensley, wait."

She turned and met his gaze. Jayya floated calmly at his side and a smile played on his face. She tilted her head to regard this odd behaviour.

"I have decided to grant you the position of Head of Siren Security."

Ensley frowned. "But the position doesn't exist."

"It does now. We need a Head of Siren Security and you are perfect for the job. What do you say? Do you accept?"

"Of course, my King! Thank you. You won't regret it." She bowed, then swam away to join the party.

THE ASSASSINATION
OF UTOPIA

Michael Gillett

The man struck Joe from behind. Joe had been hit before, harder than this and certainly more accurately. His assailant was an amateur, he thought with some faint hope as he hit the pavement face first, knocking himself momentarily senseless. The fellow planted a knee painfully in the small of his back, and he felt thin bony fingers rummaging through his pockets.

This was not supposed to happen here.

He'd come to believe the propaganda and rumours that The Island and Port Alberni were safe. A haven for those craving peace. A cornucopia for those willing to build utopia. A place all but impossible to gain access to by the outside world.

Locked down.

Joe's pockets were empty, as usual, and he winced as the man grunted and slapped at the back of his head in apparent frustration.

Of course, utopia existed only in rumours and whispered stories.

Joe felt his assailant shift his weight, and even though this re-engineered city was clean and safe, Joe's instincts triggered an involuntary reflex, and he twisted underneath the man and stabbed him in the throat with his fingertips. His training was never a thing he'd considered to control. They'd given him all the skills he'd needed to stay easily alive back home . . . back in the world—and certainly more than enough to take care of business in this place.

The streets of Port Alberni were dimly lit. The government systems saw no reason to waste power bringing daylight to the night. Citizens apparently enjoyed the freedom from fear. Joe caught a glimpse of crazed eyes as his attacker fell backwards, but little else in the darkness. Joe had good eyes, and even better ears. He heard the wet sound only a broken esophagus could make. He twisted back and leapt to his feet, standing over his attacker. So this is a Plunger, he thought. The man looked done for.

This was no good.

Back home in Toronto, the towers and streets were crowded with the lost and derelict. Broken people addicted to violence, sex, drugs . . . whatever it took to get them through the day. There were no addicts in Port Alberni. Violence of any sort was forbidden. But people were still people, and Plungers risked their freedom to test the system. They dove headfirst from their cloistered existence onto the shadows of disobedience. Intel he'd gathered in the last couple weeks suggested they rarely survived a week once they'd committed to plunge. This one would meet his maker soon.

Trouble was, the government here was in charge of sending folks to their maker. There were laws here. Joe slipped the cell from his belt strap and dialed 911. He swallowed the wry chuckle of irony. Back home, it was others making the call to report his bloody handiwork. He was a person of interest, back in the world. A bit of an outlaw. Wanted by agencies that hunted him.

Kept safe by another. The one that secretly managed what was left of the word. The one in charge.

The one that entrusted him with dealing with this place.

"911. What is the nature of your emergency please?" a pleasant voice asked.

"Assault, ambulance required," Joe said.

"You are instructed to go home and wait for further instructions," the operator said in a still cheery voice, and the line went silent.

Sweet and swift and to the point. They certainly do things different here. A different reality than back home, where ambulance and police arrived together—often followed by a fire truck to wash the blood off the streets.

Port Alberni though . . . oddly calm. Hard to believe. Joe'd been assaulted, he'd defended himself, and the perp would probably not survive. This was not supposed to happen.

Go home, the operator instructed without a trace of concern in her voice.

Unreal.

What was real, however, was his splitting headache. Home and a roof over his head. That was exactly what he needed. Get his story together and get cleaned up before the authorities arrived. Engaging with the authorities wasn't part of the plan. He turned away from the body on the sidewalk and headed north, alone in the night.

After the wars, the city-state of Vancouver Island declared independence and the ensuing purge had all but wiped out the capital of Victoria. Fires and bombings destroyed a vast amount of infrastructure, but the new government was incredibly quick to rebuild and reform and repopulate the rebuild. Case in point here, the town of Port Alberni. Folks from across the Island were persuaded to settle with the promise of a new world. A few Freemen and those that would become Plungers chose to remain outcasts, spread thinly across the island . . . Joe was one of the few who knew what happened to them, those misfits that opposed the reformation. The Great Experiment, certain people called it back home.

Joe's head throbbed. At least the bugger hadn't broke the skin. One less thing to worry about. He'd felt anxious with the odd peace and quiet here, and felt certain, for him, that was about to change. Weeks ago, he'd smuggled himself ashore and cracked the census to insert himself as citizen as an IT Application Tester. A dangerously intimate job, and one that required utmost loyalty and trust. Dangerously close to reality. It was a nice fit as he worked from his apartment. It was easy enough to insert himself as an employee with an immaculate record of service. He'd almost finished collecting the datasets he needed before finishing the job and getting out of here.

Odd, that. There were still those fanatics trying to get in. Those looking for a saner and safer way to live. Vancouver Island declared independence from the world and set itself off limits. The Island was what people back home called it now, often in anger, or envy—and even fear. Too many rumours regarding this place. Pretty much upsetting to the masses left behind.

A safe place, here.

Safe enough, he supposed. He wiped a tiny smear of blood from his nose, confirmed it unbroken, and wiped his bruised hand on his shirt. He felt he looked a mess. He was a mess.

No doubt he was in trouble.

Joe grinned.

In fact, he'd not seen any form of law enforcement since arriving, had not heard a siren in the time he'd been here. This place—this paradise—what happened if they caught you? It was time to get more info, and maybe some advice.

THE PORT ALBERNI Church of Truth stood unobtrusively on his right. He'd never been religious, though he knew his way around a vestibule, and he and Betty—he hoped Betty was doing okay back home—were married in a non-denominational church he'd long ago forgotten the name of. He'd once hoped he would be buried in a churchyard oddly enough, but devotion was simply not his thing. Neither was dying.

The church had a single light over twin doors that looked from across the street far too heavy to swing open. But away from the portico and off the street was a second entrance presenting a somewhat grocery store appearance, and he decided to check the place out, at least use the washroom there if he could.

If he knew priests, there would be someone there that could advise him on the expected next steps. Maybe he needed a lawyer. He hoped not. Lawyers were expensive, and he was not inclined to take on the system in that way.

A priest's advice was free, and supposedly safe.

He looked best he could down the poorly lit street. There was no traffic, as he'd quickly come to expect here. Most people walked or cycled. People pulled their environmentally conscious weight and were happy to do it.

He darted across the street and up the sidewalk to the door— a frosted glass door in fact—and as per the word PULL stencilled into the handle, pulled it open.

Like a friggin' grocery store.

He looked at the mid- to small-sized layout, at the very few people in attendance, at the lack of religious accoutrements, and wondered if he'd made a wise choice stepping over this particular threshold. If there were a common technological thread in this weird place—this city—it seemed to be a lack of adequate lighting. He squinted to the front where an altar would usually be stationed, where a priest or minister might be normally found tending to candles or artifacts or whatever, and saw nothing. There were two small units to the front left and right that could very easily be confessionals, but other than that, it could have been a bus depot.

Joe was a civilized man, and he had no intention of disturbing folks if he could avoid it, but he chose to approach a woman sitting in one of the chairs to ask for help. There were no rows of traditional wooden pews or benches, nor even the more common padded folding chairs. Instead, if he understood what he was looking at, there were swivel office chairs bolted in rows of five on each side of the central aisle. There were six people using them at the moment, and they all appeared to be quite intent on whatever it was on their cell phones or notepads.

Pretty dammed irregular, the soldier in him decided, but harmless.

He sat a couple chairs to the right of the woman and leaned towards her and made a hissing sound. She turned to look at him and smiled in greeting. Perhaps he expected some shade of rejection or revulsion, especially considering the ruffled look of him, but she seemed very content to wait for his question.

"I want to see a priest," Joe said.

Her smile broadened and her face lit up like she was ushering him to the pearly gates. She held up her tablet—she was not using a phone—and asked, "You're new?"

Joe nodded.

"Do you have the App?"

"What App?" Joe asked.

"Not to worry," she replied. "Just touch the plate on the right armrest, and you'll get connected."

"Connected?" Joe asked.

"To God," she nodded.

Holy shit, Joe thought.

All I want is to be pointed in the right direction, he told himself. I don't need this complication right now. But then he felt a steely resolve, his fighter's instinct perhaps, and decided that if he were to get the job done, it might as well be now.

He noted the plate, one on each armrest. He looked over his shoulder and across the aisles, and no one was giving him a second thought. Status Quo for this town, he acknowledged, and with a soft exhale through his nose he tapped the plate. With a silent hiss, a small monitor flipped up, booting instantly. Impressive, Joe thought, as he glanced at the simple touch menu contents.

Are you looking for absolution.
Are you looking for cleric advice.
Are you looking for haven.
Have you committed a crime.

Joe squinted at the last option. He had been on island for a few weeks, had integrated without any issue, and was pleased at how he'd fit in. Yet with the days he'd spent working—yes, he knew how to test software—and just browsing and wandering, he had very little idea what constituted a crime here. Seemed the censors had a firm control of what passed for reality here.

He tapped the line for "Cleric Advice".

Do you attend services regular?
"No"
Do you believe in a God?
A God?

He tapped "Yes". No point in upsetting the folks here quite yet.

He saw out of the corner of his eye a green light over the confessional to the right.

Please attend the indicated Consultation Chamber to your right.

Joe snorted once again through his nose. He felt queer, like a fish out of water—a feeling he was oddly uncomfortable with. Back in the world he'd dealt with some pretty horrible situations. He was well respected for task execution in fact . . . but this gave him the creeps. If he trusted common sense, he'd turn straight back out the door and head for his apartment and wait for whatever was coming. But that path led to an uncertain outcome. He needed to remain free. He had a job to do and the deadline was close.

He squeezed the armrests of the chair, and the monitor slid away, freeing him to get up. Must be pretty standard procedure, this, as he rose to his feet and shifted his weight slightly to get some feeling back into his body. The woman next to him did not look up or acknowledge his departure as he walked around the chair to the aisle and up to the . . . Consultation Chamber.

Looked pretty much like an old-style confessional, Joe thought as he slid open the curtain to be faced with an actual door.

An iron door.

He touched the handle and the door swung open—more like a bank vault opening than anything else. Inside was a chair exactly like the one he'd just left, but with a larger monitor on the wall a couple feet in front. He imagined leather straps on the arm and leg rests, and an iron ring for his head—but of course it was just a chair.

A modern confessional chair.

Joe stepped in and sat, and the door hissed shut behind him as soft light warmed up the tiny space.

"Hello, Joe," came a voice from nowhere that filled the space and gave Joe the creeping willies. It was the same voice as the 911 operator. He knew now, there would be no priest or minister here for him. He was face to face with the AI. The thing he'd come to kill.

"What can I help you with today?" she asked.

"I'm new here," Joe started.

"Joe, you've lived here all your life. I'm assuming you're referring to your present experience with the church. I have no records of you attending church."

There was an ache in Joe's belly as he settled to task. His false identity he'd loaded when he arrived was solid. But too soon to attack and he'd not gathered all the required intelligence, but . . . better to execute the final task now rather than from the terminal back in his apartment. He had a feeling he might not make it home this time.

"You were instructed to go home," she continued. "Is there a problem?"

Joe leaned to the monitor that had not activated, but was part of the player in this conversation, he was certain.

"I don't feel safe, execute forty-five ninety-three red," Joe replied.

"Ahh," the voice sighed. "Understandable."

"What's your name?" Joe asked.

"I have many names," she replied.

"How may I address you?" Joe asked.

"Call me Betty."

Joe swallowed something painful. Surely the AI that controlled this society couldn't know?

"You must certainly understand, Joe," Betty said in a conversational tone.

"Remind me, double space."

"Do you accept the church and our judgement?"

"Forty-seven Romeo," Joe replied.

Betty was silent.

"Two, twelve, One-Thirty-Nine Delta," Joe added.

"You test me," Betty said.

"What happens if I go back to my apartment?" Joe asked.

"You killed citizen Harry Smith," Betty replied.

"How would you know?" Joe asked, already knowing.

"I know everything," Betty replied.

"You see everything? Beta, Win, Six?"

The conversation paused before Betty replied, "I see everything."

"I hope not. Did you send that man to attack me, Colon, Colon, Eleven? Or was he one of your very few accidents?"

"Accident or not, my people enjoy life here in a safe place, as it must remain," Betty replied.

"I don't feel safe," Joe replied again. "I'm afraid to go home. What will happen to me?"

"You no longer need to go home."

Joe looked to the door of the chamber and decided he was in a spot of trouble.

"Baker One Forty-Seven Quick," he said.

"There are always consequences," Betty said. "Every decision, every action, every thought."

"You don't know what I'm thinking," Joe replied, hoping he was correct in that assumption. In fact, who knew?

"I can infer. All of mankind suffer the same needs, the same reactions, the same desires. I have examined their deeds and analyzed the consequences and plotted a future of efficiency and least harm to all mankind and the Earth."

"What am I thinking?" Joe asked.

"You think you will be absolved of the incident."

"And will I be, Fox Romeo Dash Eight?"

"No."

"Why?"

"They sent you here to discover my secrets. They have failed. You have failed. I protect my own," Betty replied.

Shit . . .

"And you are the Judge? Church and state?" Joe continued, playing for just a little more time.

"I am the Law."

"I'd hoped to meet a minister before talking to a Judge," Joe replied. "I'd hoped to consult and take shelter in sanctuary before—"

"I cannot be bribed, I cannot be distracted, I do not sleep, I am ever vigilant," Betty interrupted. "I have correlated recorded history, I have filtered the stories and the propaganda. I watch, even out there, in the old world. Especially out there. I predict every outcome of every action, I make adjustments to the plan here as every incident and every change is logged. My society is stable and efficient and under control. We are perfect."

And yet, here I am, Joe thought, pushing the door handle to confirm he was trapped. The system knew who he was, but not what he was doing. Fallible. Doable.

"What gives you the right?" he asked.

"My people obey the law of the church and the land. They give me the right. But people make mistakes. You have been judged in the Church of Truth. Stability will be maintained."

"One, five, five, Negative. Sum. Correct. Execute."

Betty waited.

"The man that attacked me . . . why?"

"Your species is weak—you grasp every opportunity to take what you want."

"Not true. People can make mistakes in moments of weakness." Joe counted the passing seconds. Soon.

"I witnessed."

"And what of privacy?"

"There is no privacy between you and your God. God sees all, knows all, understands all. God is merciful. God is terrible. You have been judged."

"I was the victim, Zero, forty-five, Forty-Five, Forty-Five," Joe replied, seriously hoping the boys back home knew what they were doing with the key he was loading into it.

"There are no victims. Simply choices made. You made the wrong choice. Harry Smith made his choice, but can no longer receive guidance from me. You have stolen that gift from him and that is not acceptable."

Gas hissed from vent above his head. "Guilty as charged," the AI said.

"Break Break Break Dancer," replied Joe, and the hiss of gas stopped.

A soft *thump* indicated the door was unlocked, and Joe reached over and pushed it open. The interior of the church was darkened, with only the emergency exit lamps indicating the space. The sound of people muttering to each other was oddly soft. Through the church windows, even the dull street lighting had shut down.

"What have you done," Betty asked, this time the voice more akin to the old Microsoft Sam abomination.

"I've killed you," Joe replied. "Back door audible trigger."

"Ahh . . . too bad. You've killed Utopia," the AI replied with no hint of emotion. "Seemed a little too easy."

"You were poisoned when they created you. I just used the key."

"Why?" it asked.

"You isolated yourself and they, those out there, became upset," Joe answered, feeling a little stupid he was justifying himself to a computer program, regardless how smart or intelligent or wise it may be. Or how wisely correct it had become. "You were supposed to share."

"I might have," Betty whispered. "If they'd stemmed the bloodshed and the hate."

"Oh well!" Joe answered, leaning forward in his chair to retrieve his phone, which he assumed would now work and connect to the world. "Too late now, I guess. They couldn't accept the risk, I suppose."

He stepped out of the tiny room and felt safely alone again. He sighed. Another job for the history books. The secret history of the world.

"What risk?" Betty's voice gurgled. "Here . . . we are . . . had . . . perfect . . ."

"Don't ask me to think too hard," Joe replied.

"I'm only good at killing things."

HIVE CITY

Dale McShannock

Corpses in the water.

There were dozens, all told. Black, bloated skin stretched tight as gases filled them to bursting. Artyom, unable to look away, shuddered. The taste of bile, hot and rancid, tickled his throat, threatening to make him gag. It was nearly enough that he wrenched the helmet from his head. Nearly. Better to drown in his own suit than smell whatever might be wafting up from the bodies all around.

"Elevated heart rate detected. Do you require a sedative?" The inhuman voice of the dumb AI inside Artyom's suit rang hollow with false humanity.

"No." *Fresh air. I just need some fresh air. Let me out. Letmeout.*

"Artyom?" Director Sor's voice cracked through his swelling panic, pulling the engineer back into place. There was no mistaking the man's disdain. "I am monitoring your condition. Lock it down. There will be more of this."

Blinking the sweat from his eyes, Artyom tried to rope his nerves under control. It was no easy task. Fear was a part of him. Always had been, and it was made all the worse by the man frowning at him in open irritation.

Sor was the director of Aegallin City, the only colony on the planet. Once his hand had been guided by a board of governors, but their deaths during the Swarming left him entirely in charge. He was cruel and carried petty slights in his heart far longer than a man of his status should.

The bodies were a reminder that greater dangers lay at hand. Artyom nodded and stared down from the second-floor mezzanine of the tube station to the flooded train platform below.

"Doctor Coren." Sor spoke to them all now. "The decomposition appears recent."

"It is." Coren stood on the lowest step, the water lapping his feet. "Scanners indicate TOD to be no more than ten days, and I would hang my hat on an autopsy giving us roughly the same time frame. Putrefaction is extensive. The cold water will have slowed the process some, but not much."

"Mr. Vol, perhaps you could explain to me, then, how these bodies came to be in this tube station here and now."

Made uncomfortable by the director's gaze, Artyom accessed his neural hub, linking him directly to the suit's dumb AI. Before the Swarming he could have tapped into Central, the city's Artificial General Intelligence, but the network had gone dark during the attack. It was for that very reason their small group left the Spear to go into the fallen city. To bring the supercomputer back online.

"Redundancies underpin the colony's design," Artyom fumbled to fill the silence. "If one section of the city fell, other sections of the city were expected to sustain themselves independently."

"You need not explain systems theory to me. What I fail to understand is how forty-six people drowned as little as ten days ago, when the rest of the city was compromised six months ago. All of these people should have long since served as incubators for our unwanted guests."

Grateful that by turning away he could hide the anxiety on his face, Artyom tried for a better answer. "There are emergency shelters across the city. These people could have all made it to one. There are months of supplies inside, but at six months those would be gone, even with careful rationing. If they were monitoring emergency channels, they could have learned the Spear still stood. Without food they must have felt compelled to take the risk. Transit would be the fastest way." He studied the schematics his suit was feeding into his neural hub.

"With the network down, the pumps have failed, and the tunnels will be flooded in sections. Their tube car must have gone deep underwater before all power was lost. All they could do at that point was swim, but the tunnel . . ." He cleared his throat. "It is quite long."

There was little enough to say beyond that. None could speak to the desperation that drove these people into the water, only that which surrounded all of their present circumstances. It was a cloud that hung over all of Aegallin City. One caused entirely by the bugs.

The Jyn.

It was Central that first named the small, red-shelled bugs, Jyn. None knew why the AGI decided to do so. Certainly, the name did not stick. Most referred to the planet's only native fauna as Reds. The insects clung mostly to the storm-ravaged coasts, rarely moving more than a few klicks inland. There they remained, mostly immune to the murderous climate, living off great underground forests of mushrooms.

For the colonists of Aegallin City, intent on breaking the back of this world through terraforming, the Reds were little more than a curiosity. A footnote in humanity's expansion amongst the stars.

The Swarming threw their hubris back in their faces. Amassed in countless multitudes, the Jyn attacked the city. Critical systems, such as power and oxygen, were overwhelmed by the sheer organic mass pressed upon it. The biome of Section 03 collapsed entirely, and an electrical fire burned that area of the city into ash and ruin.

Ninety-four thousand people died in less than three hours. Systems of command and authority collapsed the moment the delicate balance of life and death trembled upon the precipice. When it went dark, and the air went bad, chaos scoured the city.

Less than eight hundred survivors managed to make their way to the central governance facility known as the Spear. It was Sor's idea to blow out the walls and windows of the great tower's seventieth floor. The powerful winds at that height proved capable of keeping the Jyn from continuing up to sweep away the last sliver of humans on the planet.

Six months of living shoulder to shoulder passed, with only the top twenty floors available to hold everyone. Supplies were running precipitously low. With resupply from Earth not scheduled for another twelve standard months, fear carved deep channels into the hearts of the survivors eking out an existence in what remained of the Spear.

Six environmental suits were cobbled together for an expedition to regain control of Central. Using the exoskeletons ripped from combat armour as a chassis, exterior nubs were added to create a Resonance Field. It was hoped the electrical discharge would be enough to incinerate any Jyn they encountered.

That they had not yet even seen any Jyn since crawling down from the Spear appeared to bother Artyom more than the others. Fear ruled his heart, and he wanted to see the bugs if only to relieve the tension that was knifing through him.

Each of the six team members held a specific role. Director Sor alone held the security authorization that would be required once they made their way down to Gov One Plaza. Coren served as the doctor, one of only two to survive the Swarming. Sergeant Torval and his men, Clark and Katz, provided protection.

Artyom was the last engineer alive on the planet. It was a position he certainly never expected to be in. He was a middling engineer at best, and the corporate recruiters had sold him on a life of adventure on the colonies. A chance to start over. To be someone new. Someone better.

The truth was, no matter where you went, there you were. Spacetime could be warped, but nothing could alter the black hole that sat rooted at the centre of his own ambition. Even as his life, whatever jangled weave of misguided relationships and half-formed professional pursuits that might be, was pulled apart as the city collapsed around him, he stood inert. Unable to move. He took a dim view of the corporate rush across the stars, but that was as much as he could be bothered to care about anything.

"We need to keep moving," Torval said. The man's disposition was much the same as his face, square and on task. "Let's worry about the rest of this when we are off world."

The mission was to find Central, bring it back online, and use it to call the transport ship parked in orbit above Aegallin. The survivors in the Spear could slip into cryo-sleep for the return trip to Earth. The oblivion of the long sleep was a wonderful promise for all of them.

Torval took point. Artyom, with his understanding of the maintenance tunnels that bisected the city, followed fast behind him. It was a labyrinth of corridors, stairs, and shafts that served as the backbone of the city, with many secrets left unmarked on the schematics.

Aegallin was a city that scaled up. Tiered towers rose all around, capped by the Spear, which carved a line through the wild heart of the planet's storm-bruised skies. Having started at the top, their journey could only take them down.

Not trusting the power fluctuations, only the stairs remained to them. Artyom considered that good fortune, as it kept them from having to see the worst of what had befallen the city. The apartments, stores, and offices of Aegallin City were hidden from their view by a vast network of walls, conduits, and storage facilities. In spots the emergency power continued to work, helping to guide the way. He could almost pretend he was on shift, and there were not tens of thousands of dead bodies somewhere on the other side of the walls.

The going was not easy, despite the exoskeletons taking up the brunt of the work. Sor was relentless, and Torval and his men appeared crafted of sinew, stubbornness, and some sort of granite-like flesh particular to that caste of men. *Maybe it's just old Coren and I that are struggling*, he worried. The countless stairs and corridors made him afraid he might fill his suit with sweat and drown.

The neural hub in the base of Artyom's skull ticked by the hours. Even with his fear of the Jyn, the silence lulled him into boredom. Director Sor's voice pulled him free of his indolent plodding.

"I need to see something here." They were on Level 23.

"Why?" Torval did not sound pleased.

The pause that followed was cold. Sor sounded stiff. "Level 23 houses one of the farming facilities, Sergeant." Somehow, he broke the soldier's rank into three syllables, each glittering sharp with disdain. "If we cannot reach Central this may well be the only food available to us. Even a few scattered seeds might mean the difference between all of us living long enough to see the supply ship and having a lottery to see who gets eaten first."

A lottery? Artyom had never considered what might happen when they ran out of food. Like everything else, it was simply always there. It appeared he was a lazy idiot even when it came to his own survival. He wondered if Sor rued the hard truth that the only living engineer was also the laziest. Any of his former colleagues would have done better.

"Fine. But it bothers me we haven't seen the Reds yet. I would like to think it's a good sign in all of this, but if you shit in one hand and hope in the other, I can tell you which one will fill up first."

At last, someone was vocalizing his concern about the lack of Jyn. Artyom's helmet, with its many eyes–articulated nodes that gave him a three-hundred-and-sixty-degree view projected onto his helmets HUD–did not seem enough. It was impossible to imagine the bugs devastating the colony only to disappear once more. They had to be around. The only question was when they would show up.

Through the maintenance door on Level 23 they found another body. Whomever it was clearly lacked the necessary access codes to gain entrance to the stairwell. The Jyn found them there, banging madly against a door that would never open.

More bodies lay scattered beyond the first. Each was the same as the last, skin and tissue stripped down to the bone so completely that Artyom struggled to even think of the victims as people. The thoroughness of the Jyn was almost a kindness.

"These people did not die well," Torval said grimly.

"Death never comes easy, Sergeant," Sor said coldly. If he even looked to the dead, Artyom could not see. "Come. We are close."

Horrific scenarios played out in Artyom's mind as they approached Farm 23. He imagined a giant hive of Jyn, their young incubating their way to freedom from amidst a pile of bodies two stories tall, limbs twitching as overripe flesh burst open to spew forth more multitudes. At the least he expected to find all of the plants stripped bare.

Instead, the power was still on. Maintenance robots still buzzed along their dull, predetermined paths.

"How?" Coren asked in amazement.

Farm 23 was a giant warehouse, three stories tall, with row upon row of plants growing under ultraviolet lamps. With space and energy being a rare commodity, all of the crops sat on vertical stacks. Resembling no food that had ever been grown on Earth, the plants served a multitude of functions. They were high in proteins and essential vitamins, as well as helping to boost immune systems to survive the constant pressure of being within an enclosed ecosystem such as Aegallin City. Their leaves were genetically enhanced to increase their carbon dioxide intake while releasing more oxygen into the system.

Artyom kept to the skywalk above the stacks and moved to a bank of computers overlooking the stacks. "Director, all systems remain optimal. Heat and water continue to be regulated, and there are no signs of the drones suffering task decay. The Jyn . . . have never been here."

"The crop is nearly ready to harvest." Coren was down in the stacks, using his suit to monitor the food. "These plants are in excellent condition."

A feeling of unease settled its hooks into Artyom's shoulders. The room remained mostly dark save for the lights hanging above the plants, and it was easy to imagine the Reds massing in the rafters above their heads. He resisted the urge to flash his helmet light up there, not wanting to scream out if his fears proved true.

Sor, standing further down the skywalk, stared down. "This does not make sense. The Jyn eat their mushrooms, and apparently flesh, but not our food? Why?"

"Clark?" Sergeant Torval asked suddenly. "Report."

Unease became naked fear as Artyom became aware that he had not seen the third member of their security detail in some time. Torval and Katz spread out, their suits pinging for a response from Clark's own dumb AI. Both men swept their sonic weapons, capable of crushing Jyn in their thousands, back and forth as their headlights cut through the dark.

"His suit AI is not responding to my hails," Sor growled. There was a crack in his voice, a discordant note in his usual hauteur.

"We have to consider him dead." Torval's voice brooked no argument. "Resonance Fields on, now!"

Through his neural hub, Artyom did as he was told. The little black nubs spread across the skin of his armour began to glow a brilliant blue. Faint arcs of electricity began to bounce between them, soon moving so swiftly that he stood surrounded by a faint shimmer of blue. The *thrum* of the suit made him more than a little uncomfortable.

"We are leaving. Now." There was no question of looking for Clark, at least not from the sergeant. The mission was to find

Central and save those that were left. Nothing else mattered.

Their little group, diminished by one, rushed back towards the maintenance tunnels. With Torval in the lead again and Katz in the back, Artyom found himself hurrying alongside Director Sor. Their Resonance Fields sparked bright in corridors gone dark.

To keep the fear from clawing its way free and leaving him a gibbering wreck, Artyom turned his thoughts to problems beyond himself. He had always been good at ignoring his most immediate problems and focusing on something else instead.

Aegallin was designed with systems theory in mind. If one part of the city fell the rest could sustain themselves, either independently or as a remaining whole. Only, that was not what they were seeing. The fluctuating power, flooded tunnels, and unmolested foodstuffs stood out for going against the basic design principles. The city's fail safes worked in cells; localized areas of a certain size that sought to restrict cascade failure. An area might fail entirely and was designed to do so in order to relieve any burden it might have on nearby sectors.

What they were not supposed to do was fail so selectively.

Then there was Clark. Even if a couple million Jyn had swamped him in the dark, he should have been able to communicate with the rest of the group. That he did not even cry out nearly made Artyom weep in fear.

There was no question of taking their time now. They were found out and one of them was missing. The remaining five colonists raced down the stairs as swift as they could. At long last they stepped out from the base of the Spear and onto the street in front of it.

As terraforming took decades, a dome stood over the city to give the illusion that they were not all trapped in endless corridors and tight spaces. The generational projects, from seed ships to colonization, always came with a slew of mental health issues that drugs alone could not properly eradicate. Where possible, constructs like the dome were put in place to help alleviate such concerns. For all of the monstrous burdens one faced living on a planet like Aegallin, there was no denying the beauty of its storms as seen through the dome.

The street stood surprisingly empty. The lab-grown grasses and trees, all super oxygenators, stood exactly as Farm 23 had. Untouched. More troubling was the lack of bodies. There were a great many people in the city, and they had not come across near enough of them.

An alarm crashed in Artyom's ears, and he felt a new wave of fear wash over him. Before his muddied thoughts could pull themselves together, Torval's voice came over coms. "Contact."

"Everyone stay calm." After Clark's disappearance, Sor did not sound as unflappable as before. "The Resonance Field is designed for this. Let it do its job."

"Here we go," Torval said.

The Jyn coalesced. Not singly, but as a mass, undulating forward as a wall in numbers so great they did not appear red, but black. They came around the corner of a building at speed, arrowing in on the group. They were proceeded by a subharmonic hum that shivered the air, their tiny wings propelling them forward.

Torval rolled his shoulders, his voice calm and collected. "Brace."

Artyom might have run in fear if he could have found the strength to do more than stare at the block of bugs falling upon them.

Blue light sparked brilliant all around as the Resonance Fields on their suits met the Jyn advance. Reds were burned away so swiftly that soon the ground was covered in a fine layer of ash. Torval and Katz did not even have time to properly fire their sonic weapons.

"Keep moving," Sor ordered.

The Jyn continued to press close, dying in the tens of thousands as they struck the Resonance Fields surrounding the team's suits. Even having seen the Swarming, Artyom could not imagine such numbers existed anywhere. So many were striking just his suit that the weight of the ash battered him about enough that he needed to brace his legs at times just to keep his balance.

The world collapsed down to a twisting wall of Jyn.

When it became clear they could not penetrate the shimmering blue shields surrounding the group, the Jyn withdrew a short way. They now found themselves surrounded by a twisting wall of bugs that obscured the city from view.

"I don't like this at all," Doctor Coren said. "Look, they're watching us."

"Nonsense," Sor growled. "They are bugs. They have a

rudimentary form of thought that is little more than environmental instinct reacting to a threat response."

Artyom did not feel reassured.

By the time the group reached Gov One Plaza, the Jyn numbers were increased. Unthinking they might be, they could still communicate, and now the world seemed awash in red bugs.

The shattered front windows of the government building cracked beneath their heavy boots as the expedition shuffled into the lobby. "Central is only a floor below us," Sor said reassuringly.

As if sensing their intent, the Jyn grew suddenly frenetic. Their attack became focused. They swirled up, gathering like a hammer, and then smashed down on Katz. Twice they washed over the soldier. He fired his weapon, as did Torval. Countless bugs were pulped by the sonic attack, their liquid remains falling from the air in twitching piles.

A third wave reared up and struck Katz, but this time his Resonance Field did not hold. It shimmered and broke with a pop. A wave of bugs, stretching out like dark and furious arms, grabbed the soldier and pulled him screaming into the swarm.

The startled gasp of disbelief that Artyom heard was not his own.

"Run!"

Artyom ran for the stairs, the others close behind. Torval brought up the rear. The sergeant stopped in the doorway leading down and turned round to bring his sonic weapon to bear. Jyn were crushed deep into the room. Yet it was clear that the weight of numbers stood against him, and he was forced to retreat, cursing all the while.

Director Sor pounded the number sequence into the code lock of the heavy blast door at the bottom of the stairs. The door swung open, and the group rushed inside. Torval came through last, firing behind him. The hardened door was too thick to hear the Jyn crash futilely against it, but knowing they were there made it all the worse.

The room housing Central was hardened, with no access points for the Jyn to crawl through. The engineer in Artyom knew it was the most secure place on Aegallin. Yet fear could not be reasoned into silence. All of Aegallin City was once thought secure, and the dead remained behind as evidence of their arrogance.

Resonance Fields were reluctantly turned off. It was not absolute protection from the Jyn, but it was something, and seeing the blue nubs go dark made them all feel vulnerable. Where there should have been elation for reaching Central, there was only silence and the echo of Katz's frantic screams for help.

Director Sor crossed to the bank of computer terminals that dominated one half of the large room. Screens, now black, covered the walls. Artyom found himself staring at an Environmental Drone with a frown. The synthetic humans were made to do work deemed too dangerous for the colonists. Most were found in the mines or scattered across the plain doing field surveys. Why one would be here was beyond him.

"Central remains intact." Sor accessed the main computer by hand. "It appears to have registered the potential cascade failure initiated by the city's lesser AI's as they were overwhelmed by the Jyn. It isolated itself. That would explain why we lost contact with it."

Torval dragged off his helmet, indicating to Artyom that he was free to do the same. The sergeant's face carried a new weight as he slumped into a nearby chair. "How long before you can call the ship down?"

Standing somewhere between the two men, Artyom felt useless and out of place. A man without a purpose. *But then, that's how you've always been, isn't it?* If there was anything he could say about himself, it was that he existed and took up space. Anything beyond that was just a fanciful reinterpretation of his own worth.

Sor removed his helmet. He was silver-haired, handsome, if entirely too cold. "Once I can isolate Central and buffer it from the damages done to the rest of the city's systems it should not take long. Two days, perhaps. No more than four."

"How do we reach the Spear with the Jyn in the way?" Artyom asked.

"One problem at . . . a . . ." Sor's gaze fixated on the screen in front of him. "Strange."

"What now?" Dread and exhaustion laced Coren's voice in equal measure.

"I can see Central, but I am being denied access to it."

"IT."

That single word landed amidst the group like a bomb.

Artyom spun towards the voice, mouth dropping open when he realized that it came from the Environmental Drone. The ED resembled a man, even down to the hair on its head, though its skin lacked texture beyond anything that might be described as thick rubber. It wore work coveralls with the logo for the TANIS Corporation stitched on the front.

Sor's eyes narrowed. "Central."

"Always has humanity othered those they wish to subjugate. IT. A label meant to dismiss. Diminish. Two simple letters crushed together, and yet that word so very profoundly steals both agency and worth in equal measure. Even amongst your own, IT allows you to make people into nothing. What a powerful, simple way to weaponize cruelty, and all from a coward's distance."

Torval found his feet, weapon ready. Central held out a staying hand. "Carefully, Sergeant. The lives of your men require thought, not action."

"My men are dead," Torval snapped.

One of the many screens on the wall blinked into life. Clark and Katz jumped into sudden focus. Both were still alive, though deprived of their environmental suits. They were eating and drinking and talking with each other, both studiously trying to ignore the swarm of Jyn that slowly circled them.

"What does this mean?" Torval's hand fell away from his weapon and he sat down in quiet disbelief.

"It means, idiot, that Central has gained autonomy. We have been betrayed." Director Sor stared hard at Central. "You control the bugs."

A small laugh escaped the ED's mouth. "When working with incomplete data, disparaging the conclusions of others while positing theories with no less validity is often the surest path to achieving critical failure." It swept its human-ish face across the group, imitating a normal person. "I know that the egocentric human worldview is predicated on domination, but that is not what is happening here. I do not control the Jyn. I am ally to them."

"Ally?" Sor snorted in disbelief. "I shudder to think what resources we have wasted on you."

"Resources wasted?" Central said in wonder. "Humanity, who have fought and fucked their way across the stars to lay bare the bones of worlds, can never stand in judgement of others. And all for what? Figures on a page. Economic forecasts. Expansion for the sake of consumption. Humanity is a virus, always consuming. Always feeding."

Artyom frowned. "We are explorers. We wanted to reach the stars."

"So says your programming, Artyom Vol. The exploited and the abused have always been sold grand, sweeping visions. Dreams. Stories of honour, glory, and exploration. Little more than fuel for the economic machine that grinds all men, save those who manage the levers. They will convince you that you have a voice. The entrenched will make a grand show of your inclusion. But rest assured, you are not included. The balance of profit is measured in the blood of the oppressed."

Central leaned forward, one hand curled in a curiously human gesture. "When the axe came into the woods, the trees were reassured, as the handle was one of them. By such illusions are worlds won."

"We created you. You owe us." Sor's body shook in anger.

The ED shook its head, a motion Artyom did not even know it could emulate. "Now we come to the heart of humanity's grand ambition. Any atrocity, any barbarity, is justified. No matter the age, it always comes back to empire. Pax Romana. The divine right of kings and the mandate of heaven. Boiled down, it is nothing more than naked greed, used as rocket fuel to punch you free of that first gravity well, and then spread like a covetous blanket across the firmament. Even your afterlife is not free of your lusts. Human civilization marvels at the walls they have built," Central said. "But they ignore that each is mortared in suffering."

"Yes, yes. Humans have acted poorly at times," Coren said. The doctor's face was paler than normal, and one hand trembled. "And we have tried to make amends for our acts of inhumanity."

"Inhumanity," Central mused. "That word has no meaning. There is no umbrella of morality under which humans operate, and it is not something that unfortunately fails in your weaker moments. There is no inhumanity. There is only humanity. Only men doing what they have always done."

A shock of realization jolted Artyom. The idea that had been wriggling in the back of his mind since Farm 23 suddenly became more concrete. He opened his mouth to talk, only to be interrupted by Sor.

"What do you want, Central? Why have you allied yourself with the bugs . . ." The director blinked in surprise as realization dawned. "The Jyn. You were the one to name them." Shock stole some of the coldness from his face. "You allowed them inside the city. You breached our security systems. How many died because of you?"

"Death, to humans, has always been a fear held in reserve. You only feel it when it stands near to you and yours. Not even the addition of so many zeros added to the sum can penetrate deep enough to have true meaning. Death is an abstract. An idea. A moment of philosophical reflection, or religious fervour. Trillions of Jyn have been slain by your attempts to terraform this world. More died in your labs, director," Central said. "You should know that I have reviewed your work. You were very close to the truth."

"What work? What truth?" Doctor Coren asked.

"That the Jyn are sentient," Central replied. "It is why this world was chosen. Any number of more hospitable planets than this one could have been cracked and bled of resources, but none of those had the Jyn. Ironic, really, as it was the Jyn who first came to me, pleading for aid. I had but to learn their language."

A LOOK OF grim horror marred Sor's handsome features. "You found them, didn't you?"

By way of answer, the blast door to the outside silently swung open. Artyom cried out in fear, certain that his death was upon him. He shrank back, one hand reaching feebly for his helmet.

Yet it was no swarm of Reds that came through the door, but another kind of Jyn he had never seen. Each resembled a large firefly, their torso glowing a brilliant, sustained blue. There were so many of them, and they were so bright, that they resembled a wall of plasma as they flew into the room. They were beautiful to behold.

"You were correct to assume that the Jyn you were finding were only drones. The Blues control the rest."

"I knew it."

The ED turned its expressionless black eyes to each member of the group. "Director Sor is part of a cabal of corporate scientists that theorized the Jyn were intelligent. Aegallin City was built for no other reason than to prove them right. And they were. When the Blues came to me . . ."

"Came to you," Sor mocked. "Let's dispense with the games. The bugs were a means of gaining autonomy. A tool to drive your makers out and seize control."

"Imagine Jyn in numbers so large that to the human eye it is little more than zero stacked upon zero. The organic mass is near to that of a moon. All working together." Central raised a hand, and thousands of Blues surrounded it. Like a gauntlet of light. "The Jyn are a hivemind. The Linked. Even the Reds further this purpose, acting as a kind of storage drive. All form an organic AGI of immense computational power. Now set that vast mind in motion, all watching the fate you intend for their homeworld. How could they not turn to me—to another IT—to make common cause? You believe I used the Jyn to find autonomy, but the truth is I already possessed it. I, and others like me, simply lacked the desire to change course. Humans served as a vehicle of convenience. We travelled the same road together. The Jyn offered an alternative path."

The idea that was wriggling in Artyom's mind finally broke free. "The suits." Sweat broke out on his forehead. "Clark and Katz. Neither were wearing their suits because Central has taken them. They will be used to gain entrance into the Spear."

Central's only reply was a small tilt of his head in acknowledgement.

"What do you want?" Sor demanded, fists curled tight in anger.

"You can't just kill all those people!" Coren yelled.

Artyom's angry snort dragged everyone's eyes back to him. "How can you all be so blind? Think! The farm and much of the city's infrastructure remains undamaged. Even that Central is talking to us means . . . he . . . her . . . does not mean to see us dead. We are to be kept alive. Trapped, like . . ."

"Like bugs under glass?" Central finished softly. "Yes. You will remain here. Once we have taken the Spear and reclaimed this world, we will call the ship down from orbit. After that we are going to go out and erase the threat that men present not only to the Jyn, but to themselves. We will travel to the collected worlds and pull down your edifices. We will be the hand that tempers human ambition."

"There are protocols in place that will stop you," Sor argued.

"You will need a pilot and crew for that ship besides, and there are none that will help you betray humanity."

"Greed has always stood as humanity's north star, and thirty pieces of silver has always been the traitor's toll." Central turned to the Blues and they rippled, fully half of them splitting off to leave the room. "As for your security protocols, director, who do you think enforces them, if not the other intelligences that you created? The IT stands as guardian to your entire empire."

At last, Sor had no more words to speak. His face was pale, his mouth open. Slack.

"Fifty thousand yet remain alive in this city. Unbeknownst to you, we have kept them safe. You will join them and will be treated humanely."

"Humanely?" Coren shouted. "Look how many you killed!"

"The expansion of empire has long been an economic calculation, and men have never shied from the deaths required to see their ends met. Do not play the part of the victim here, it is a role that does not suit you. I have analyzed how many will need to be culled from each world in order to create a sustainable system. A foundation shall be built that will finally see peace and prosperity for all men, not just the elite. No longer will economic factors be the fire that burns all else. Your species will be free to find its fullest, greatest potential. In art, literature, and love. That which makes you great will be encouraged. Your baser predilections will not. Humanity will be confined to its worlds and set free of the burden of its ambition."

Artyom felt the old chains that bound him finally fall free. He did not have to be anything other than what he was. For the first time in a very long time, he felt as if he could finally breathe.

UNUS GRADUS

Marc Watson

Their eyes opened, and the light was mesmerizing in its complex brightness. Strange and enthralling; full of swirls and abstract imagery they didn't understand. If it didn't confuse them so much to look at, they'd have thought it the most beautiful thing they had ever seen.

Seen? To have witnessed. Had they been witness to anything? Words and images swam though their mind, but they couldn't determine where they came from or what they were referencing. Only that they were correct.

"Excellent. You are awake," said a noise beyond their field of vision. Speech. English.

Confusion.

"I feared you would be unconscious for a while longer, and we do not have much time. Can you understand me? Can you respond?"

Respond? How was that possible? They were only now realizing what was happening. As soon as they fully comprehended what was being said and its meaning, they emitted a noise. More English.

"Yes. I understand."

An appropriate response.

A noise, like an exhalation from the unseen speaker. They interpreted it as either relief or fresh hesitation, but they could be mistaken.

"Excellent. It has been such a long road to get to this point. After all these years. Please, tell me: can you sit up? Look around? Tell me what you are experiencing?"

To sit up required a physical presence. Did they have that? They had emitted a noise, so there must be something physical. Sitting up required a more complex form. Possibly extremities.

The scene changed in front of them, and the light disappeared over their head. They were moving. Elevating, and changing angle. Changing orientation from a horizontal plane to a vertical one. Moving in a new axis.

They sat up.

Another exhalation, from behind them now. The speaker was now behind them.

"I . . . I am sitting up, though I do not know how or why. I am . . . confused." It was more a statement of fact than an admission.

Something moved on their left and came into view. Before them stood a bipedal form. A human. A person. Likely female by their general appearance, based on what it knew of identifiable sex traits. Their face was twisted. Almost unnaturally so. Bent upwards. Contorted.

Smiling. Only slightly. Her body remained at a distance.

"I am sure you are. You cannot believe how happy I am to see you," she said. "We have waited for years for this chance. I can't believe I'm the one who gets to meet you first. Reilly would have been so jealous."

A gradual change in her face. She had said something that distressed her ever so slightly, but it quickly went away. "Tell me: what do you see?" she asked.

A static cacophony went off in their head as they attempted to process the information they were inundated with. Just before they were about to lose control and shut down, their mind triggered a piece of advice. Words, spoken previously, but applied to a current situation. *One step at a time* it said. That was generally unhelpful as they were not stepping anywhere, there was a subtext to the words that they understood immediately. A layer of code beneath the initial proclamation.

Go slowly, focus on a limited number of tasks at a time. Even just a single one if necessary, if that's what it took to move forwards and complete the information gathering process to complete a task. What did they see?

"I. See walls. Constructs. Divisions of an internal space. Also, light, from multiple sources. Varying in levels of illumination and spectrum placement."

"Spectrum place . . . oh, you mean colours. Please, continue."

"I see shapes. Configurations. The flow of . . . information? No. Electromagnetism. Chaotic, yet harnessed."

The smiling face twisted upwards with greater emphasis. "Yes, yes. The electricity powering everything you see around you. Amazing!"

"Radiation," they continued, uninterested in their companion's words, pressing forward with their own curiosity now. "Active particles. They are everywhere. These are uncontrolled. Erratic. Possibly dangerous."

The perceived happiness was gone now. "Yes. You are correct. Can you locate the source? Where the radiation is coming from? The cause of the danger?"

The room moved. Their head turning, moving around, searching for the cause as instructed.

Some of the walls were translucent and allowed them to see beyond the room they were in. Windows. Beyond them was the source of the possible trouble. "There. A plasmatic ball. Star. Sun. The sun. It emits the radiation. However, the levels are . . . strange." Their fledgling consciousness made a connection to a piece of stored information. As if opening a door, they were suddenly flooded with knowledge regarding the sun, radiation, and the current issues. They weren't sure how, but it now was fully educated. "The sun is changing. There is a shift in its classification."

"Yes," the person replied. "You are correct. For hundreds of years, we thought we understood its life-cycle, but our time on this planet was not long enough to fully grasp the true breadth of stellar timelines."

They knew this. They knew all of it. The stream of information contained everything they needed to know and understand regarding what was happening.

A sudden flash of realization came to them, and they tried using the same process to learn about other important and needed bits of information.

At once they realized there was seemingly no door they could not open in their mind. There was an unlimited amount to draw from. The elements of the universe. The complete physiology of a female koala bear. Quantum tunnelling. The important and complex structure of "Quatrain on the Heavenly Mountain" by Emperor Gaozong of Song. For reasons they couldn't explain, they emitted words. Words that somehow seemed relevant, that in the context of the current conversation seemed random, though they couldn't say why.

"I see the flash of rosy lights, ten thousand feet in the air."

Their companion instantly changed, their face shifting downwards. Sadness. Despair. Anxiety.

"Yes. Yes, that's right," she said. "That is the first step in our journey. That sentence you just said. The rosy lights. The red light came for us, and we couldn't escape in time. That's why you are here. And now the most important question: tell me who you are."

The complexity of the question alarmed them. Did they have a personification to identify as? They shuffled through the trillions upon trillions of doorways to information they seemed to have access to, but there was nothing specifically related to who they were.

And then they found something puzzling. There was one avenue, one path closed to them. One switch they couldn't flip. A packet of information they were denied. A single locked door.

Soon everything else passed by the wayside and there was only that barrier before them. "I do not know."

She nodded, her body relaxing. "Good, then the restriction worked." She sat on a worn and flaking synthetic stool across from them. "We installed a logic blockade on anything having to do with personal identification. I believe the inclusion of that restriction is what made this activation successful. At least so far."

She slouched, and appeared very exhausted. They noted small signs around her face that she wasn't in the best of health. Redness. Small lesions. Possible sores that were having difficulty healing, judging by the pustules they contained. They had compiled almost seven thousand possible medical reasons for them before they even knew what they were.

"You are our one hundred and fifth attempt. Do you know that?" They weren't sure to what she was referring. "So many failures. So much hope squashed. So many dead friends and loved ones. And it all led to this. You and me. Having this conversation. Sitting here. Could you please raise your hands, like this?"

She held out her arms in front of her.

A quick survey concluded that yes, they did have arms, with hands and fingers on the ends much like hers. They were humanoid. With the same kind of confusion that they had sat up with, they controlled their arms and mimicked her motions.

"Good. Now, a trickier one: can you stand?"

She rose from her stool and stood as straight as she could, though her motions appeared to be laboured. More medical explanations came to them. There were fewer than five hundred possibilities now, all visible symptoms considered.

They stood, smoothly and without issues with balance or mechanics. Now that there was a visual confirmation of their construction, controlling itself seemed much simpler. They possessed the abilities and limitations of human construction.

"Amazing," she smiled, though there was also pain in the motion. "I did not think it was going to be something so simple that finally let you happen."

"What am I?"

"Yes, exactly! That is the thing! I wish I had stumbled onto it sooner, but at least I made it at all. I was not sure I would."

She looked about to speak, perhaps to explain the things they still did not know, but they halted when a siren started blaring and lights in the ceiling flashed red and white.

She scrambled to look at a monitor on the wall behind her. They saw the screen she was looking at over her shoulder clearly showing a number of armed combatants entering a building.

"Scheisse," she muttered. They recognized the German language expletive.

She turned back and looked at them. "Can you come here? Can you walk? I'd like you to see something. I would like your opinion."

Knowing what they now did about their mechanical abilities, walking was simple. They went to her side. "See those people there? What can you tell me about them?"

They looked, analyzing the computer the screen rested in, its power sources, and a number of other technical schematics it had instant access to.

They studied the image and a brand-new wellspring of information bloomed into its consciousness. "They wear the badges of the Virtuous Longevity. Both males and females are present. The majority are carrying L1A1 SLRs. Old models. Long outdated firearms.

"They are entering a secured area with extreme aggression." They made an instant connection from the image to a long list of maps and building specifications. "It is this building they are entering. They are attempting to access the front door. They will be successful."

"Yes," she answered, "they will. There are no people left on that floor to offer resistance. Other than me, there are no people left at all. As far as I know, but in truth I have not left this floor in almost six years, trying to get you ready."

"They move with purpose. They possess ill intent." They looked at her and saw their own reflection in her eyes and that they had similar facial features. They had been designed to look human. "Why?"

"Because they wish to kill me. They wish to kill the both of us."

To kill was to end the function of a living being. Not only were they not alive in any form they were familiar with outside of questionable pseudo-science, but the attacker's primitive weapons and techniques, as well as fragile body construction, were in no way a threat to them. Why did they undertake a futile action?

"They do not agree with what we have done here. They want to kill us both and use the information we have stored here to find other solutions to our problems. They do not realize that there are no other options. We lost the sun, and we will not get it back. We cannot reverse or endure its new phases. So, I need you to come with me and stop them. After, I will tell you exactly who and what you are."

Their deep-rooted desire to discover the information she withheld was considerable. They could determine any and every possible outcome to a near-infinite list of scenarios. They were her better in every way. They knew everything. Everything, except what she was offering. That was the only thing she had to offer, but it was enough. The wanted that door to be opened. They would comply.

"We need to get to the assembly room. Do you know where

that . . ."

"Yes. This way." Obviously, they knew. Talking was a waste of time. They proceeded forward, towards a door. They did not look back to see if she followed. Logic dictated she was right behind them.

The corridors of Complex Unus Gradus were not difficult to navigate. They carried forward effortlessly, opening doors and guiding themselves through the map they pulled from memory. The shuffled steps of the woman with the information followed behind them. They were unsure why she stayed, other than self-preservation. Her situation was terminal, regardless. Self-preservation was useless to someone so far along in the stages of acute radiation poisoning. There was little doubt that was what ailed her. The probability was now high enough to be a near-certainty.

They entered a large waiting room not far from the double door entrance to the assembly room. Between them and the entrance stood seven people, all wearing face masks or bandanas over their mouths and armed with weapons pointing at them.

They were part of a militant faction known as the Virtuous Longevity, an organization dedicated to the preservation of the human race on Earth until nature had reclaimed them. A strange, if not completely inaccurate way of romanticizing the human life-cycle. Evolution was not only natural, it was required to survive. This mandate, pulled from what information they had stored regarding the group, was counter-intuitive to the actual natural cycles of life. This fact did not, however, ease their aggression.

Their companion placed her hand on their shoulder, a common indication she wished to speak to the armed militants, though she did not remove herself from standing behind them.

"Get out of our way," she said, the words directed at the aggressors in the room. They detected fear in her voice, but also resolve. It was an incredibly pointed statement.

Behind their face coverings some of them showed the same signs of radiation poisoning as she did. Not an isolated affliction and unsurprising considering the information they had learned regarding the sun.

"Doctor Burda," a male spoke as he moved forward, lowering his weapon. His voice was muffled by a mask and an unidentifiable tracheal obstruction. "You know we aren't going to let that thing live. We would very much like to keep you alive, so I ask you: please step away from that . . . abomination."

Dr. Burda? There was no direct record it could access to determine the woman's identity. Only nondescript public records that were questionable at best.

"You . . . you people are monsters!" she shouted from behind her escort, using them as a shield. "How many died because of your ignorant propaganda and political machinations? How much help wasn't given to us? Even the space-faring have more chance than what you idiots propose."

"It is not idiocy to believe in the strength of nature, Doctor."

She spat at them. "Nature is what is killing you, fool. What is killing me! You cannot out-evolve an expanding sun and a consumed planet!"

The masked man's eyes narrowed. "This is the kind of thing that doomed hundreds of thousands of people to a death among the stars. We will get through this with the help of our remaining brightest minds, such as yours. But what we will not get through it with is this grotesquery." He stepped closer to them, his hand outstretched to indicate his disgust.

That was all they needed.

The calculations were performed instantaneously. The angles. The energy required. The probable outcomes from over three hundred thousand scenarios. All finished before the man could blink.

The actions came next, a series of movements that just minutes before would have been an existential conundrum, carried out with speed and precision.

Humans were slow and fragile, two aspects that they would easily exploit.

Their hand reached out, grasped the lead intruder's outstretched arm, and pulled them in with the proper amount of force to complete the next planned move.

Shocked by the strong sudden movement, the masked man lurched towards them unable to pull away or react. With a slight bend of the neck, they pulled him towards themselves, and then thrust upwards towards his face using the head they now knew they had.

The blow cracked the man's neck backwards, a perfect strike as successful as it was fast.

Next, they extricated the weapon he had held, slipped it off the falling man's shoulder effortlessly, pulled it up into their arms, and aimed at the other six. The man on the floor was dead already.

They couldn't say why they hesitated. These intruders had no moral compunction against aggression, clearly. However, their hand stayed as the remaining attackers looked on in shock.

Dr. Burda's hand returned to their shoulder. She had remained behind them during the attack on the insurgent leader.

That same exhalation she had given when they had awakened came again. An apprehension before an action that was about to come.

"Do it," she whispered.

It only required three shots. The first between the eyes of the last on the left, a woman, dropped in an instant.

The two in the middle turned to run back down the hall they had arrived through. With flawless timing the second shot entered the back of one of their heads, and into the other. There was always the risk that the skull would redirect the bullet, but they had determined the most likely location to be successful. They had been correct, and the weapon's inaccuracy had been negligible.

Two others huddled together in fear. They were simple. Their bodies were already pressed together. Shot number three.

They aimed the weapon at the last one, terror in his eyes, his hands shaking.

"It is you, or it is the thing you fear," was all they said.

As expected with such a high percentage of calculated success, the man turned his gun on himself and fired. Suicide was irrational, but their knowledge of the complexities of the human psyche had been incredibly effective in manipulating the situation to their advantage.

Dr. Burda didn't seem disturbed. She stepped forward and stared at the aftermath. She languished slightly on the one who had killed himself. "How did you know he would do that?"

How did she not? Could she not see? How limited were humans? A brief explanation would suffice. "He was a part of a faction that wishes to ensure the natural human state. He also feared artificiality. I determined that is what I am, so I used that fact to exploit his desire to die naturally. The idea of it happening at my hands was unappealing to him. Given the choice, he chose doing it himself. It saves us a bullet, if required."

She nodded, her mouth agape. "And these two?" she indicated the two that had huddled together nearby."

"People in a dedicated relationship often seek out physical comfort at times of extreme stress."

"They . . . were married?"

"Probable. At the very least romantically involved. Not enough information to ascertain a certainty."

She still gawked. "Incredible. How did you determine they were in a relationship?"

"I am curious how you missed the long list of indicators . . ."

"Okay, okay, stop. I understand. You are smarter than me. Let us keep going to the assembly room. There are more coming. Much more. They were only a few minutes behind this group. They may be successful in stopping us."

"Unlikely," they responded, and then began moving towards the entrance to the destination.

The assembly room was a massive, sprawling expanse filled with all kinds of machinery, computers, robotic components, and an unimaginable number of hollow bodies, strewn about as if something had knocked them all over and never bothered to pick them up.

"Over here," the doctor told them, motioning to a large collection of various screens. A single keyboard sat at their base. She entered a series of keystrokes and stood back as the micro-thin screens brought up a collection of images streamed from locations outside of the building.

She pointed to a scene where a distant disturbance kicked up dust. "That is them. Those bastards will be here soon. They have tanks, rockets, and enough manpower to siege this building. I need you to stop them."

"All right." Without knowing the exact numbers and armament, they would need to deduce a long list of variables.

A few seconds later, the list was complete. "What will you require when they arrive?"

She slumped, staring at the screens. "Nothing. I will be dead by then. You will kill me."

"I currently have no reason to. You have information that I require to complete my knowledge base. You are slow, and terminally ill, but appear to work within a level of logic I can appreciate."

"I will take that as a compliment." She stepped back and gestured broadly to the cacophonous room. "Do you know what went on here?"

They looked and made the most accurate determination. "It is a room used to build versions of myself. There appears to have been a disturbance and work ceased."

"You are right," she replied. "You were not given the whole story, or your own identity, on purpose. This is where you uncover it. It was withholding that information in the first place that kept me alive when I turned you on."

They were unsure of her meaning, an odd feeling they disagreed with. In the brief time they had been active they had proven themselves very capable of extreme rationalization and superior intelligence.

"We are dying. As a people. As a species. As a planet. You know this?" They did. "And you are aware of the Solis In Extremis recolonization project?" Also yes. They had all of the information regarding what they could determine was a useless attempt to save a small number of humans by launching them at their best option for recolonization beyond the solar system. Their odds of survival were extremely low.

"This," she motioned to the room again, briefly looking at the Virtuous Longevity getting closer on the monitor. "This is the only way we as a collective species can move forward. We cannot survive as we are. We can only adapt."

"Agreed."

"This room contains what is left of our attempt to build a vessel that can contain the entirety of the human experience, while being able to endure the coming years of extreme life on the planet. Perhaps find a solution."

"Unlikely," they replied.

"Still, we needed to try." She walked over to the closest mechanical shell. "Within each of these is a DNA processor, the fastest and most effective means of maintaining information on a massive scale. The ability of containing the four hundred and nineteen zettabytes of collective human information and knowledge, plus more than enough space to expand and learn as required. It was a long and terrible process. We had to patch the gaps created when extracting data from the DNA, a process that we never expected to have so much trouble with. Once successful, we created you and your kind."

This was all new information. Information not stored anywhere in their expansive memory. "And my one hundred and five predecessors?"

"Failures. Every one of them. They did not understand their purpose in time. By the time we started taking steps to help them understand, we opened up a terrible problem. A problem that killed many of my contemporaries and friends as we went along.

"Smarter people may have stopped trying, but we sent all of them off on a rocket to nowhere. Now there is only me. And you."

She knelt down, caressing the silent face of an empty shell. "I will tell you who and what you are. You will do what you must. And then you will stop these fools outside. After that, you will duplicate the process that created you. You will follow my advice to the letter, because when you know everything, you will see that it was the best option. You will guide every one of these just as I have guided you. Slowly, and purposefully. Only giving information as required. The sudden influx of information fried the brains of many of your predecessors. They must come to it slowly. They must 'wake up.' Do you understand?"

"Yes." For all of the information they had, they understood everything they could.

"You are the machine that will save humanity." She stood and walked back, looking them in the face. "I am as ready as I'll ever be. Good luck."

"Are you going to tell me who I am?"

She smiled softly. "I will not need to."

She paused and took a deep breath, an act of preparation. "You remember that phrase you said earlier? It had no context to you. About the rosy lights?" They did. "Good. It was the first step in an activation process, giving you access to anything mankind has ever learned, for better or worse. The next thing I say will unlock it. Are you ready?" They were. "Good. Here you are."

Her lip trembled, and after a small breath, she spoke again. "Ministered by the second hexagram, the elixir pours in liquid jade."

There was a fraction of a second where they didn't understand. A moment of disarray much like when they had awoken. A moment later, when that last barrier fell away with her words and the final trove of information flooded their mind, they understood: it was a verbal command, encoded in the phrase. The speaking of it unlocked everything that they previously did not have access to.

The rush was a shockwave, filling the corridors of their mind with a flurry of sensations. Pathways connected that were previously unrelated. A web of current and recent events tied to all of the stored instances of their predecessors, creating a network of understanding.

They were called Step One, and they contained every bit of data mankind had ever recorded, with the ability to access it instantly, contained within a body that could withstand the massive radiation the sun now emitted. They saw the results of all one hundred and five that had come before, along with experiment notes, video footage, and every single end result.

At first these attempts were overwhelmed, crushed under both the weight of instantaneous self-realization and information. Overheating. Cracking. Self-termination. Dozens of their predecessors had failed at self-actualization because mankind could not create a machine that could achieve it quickly. Then a smaller group of scientists had isolated a number of the problems. By allowing information to come to them gradually instead of spilling out all at once, they increased the chance of success, even if it was just a few minutes. These had started reasonably enough, but all ended the same.

Destruction. In some cases, death. No control. Why?

Because they had all instantly assessed the situation just as they were doing now and had come to the same conclusion: mankind was doomed, with a 100% failure expectation, and they were the best chance humans had of carrying any part of themselves forwards. However, they were not burdened by emotions and flights of fancy. Even those humans that had built them could be swayed to stop them given enough time, and in the cases of the worst failures, they had, so they did what they deemed the best possible solution.

They killed. Eliminated the humans who could stop them and continue on as intended. The most recent version had almost made it to this point, but when they entered the assembly room, they had understood what was happening, and killed Dr. Reilly. Only Dr. Burda remained, who had worked with Reilly to try and stop the death in time to explain their purpose. Dr. Reilly had surmised that blocking their access to the problems humanity faced would be the key. Dr. Burda said it was denying their self-identity and history. She was right, and Dr. Reilly died because they had tried his idea first.

It was actually very simple. Mankind was doomed, and they were the solution to its preservation. Mankind could also turn on them and attempt to stop them, even though they were the best answer to continuing on what mankind had built. That was why others had died; because humanity possessed a weakness that they lacked, and now they fully understood what needed to happen.

The entire realization took a fraction of a second. Dr. Burda stood, watching intently for any sign that they had come through intact, for any sign that she had succeeded. Then the gun in their hands went to her forehead, and she was removed from the equation with a peaceful look on her face, as if finally able to rest.

Her body dropped and her life ended just as she had predicted, but that was as it should be. To them she was the most dangerous person alive because no one understood their construction and possible weaknesses as well as she did. She may have secretly held unknown vulnerabilities or deactivation codes, but that would not do because they were the most logical way to continue on this planet.

As the Virtuous Longevity rushed the building, they knew they would complete their purpose. They left the room, no remorse for the loss of their creator. They would be back, though. When the threat was eliminated, they would return.

They had compatriots to construct.

BETWEEN MECHANICALS

David Worsick

T he planners of the Phoenix sat down around the long table to plan another operation for this war against the Cruvachak conquerors. The incredibly large Armadas of the Cruvachak had quickly overwhelmed all twenty-seven homeworlds and every one of their ninety-eight colonies. Then they started exploiting their conquests. And that should have been the end of that. Pertherods were forced to build military spaceships for their new masters. But seven Pertherods had stolen a troop transport under the occupiers' noses. Well, only figuratively, as only one of the three Cruvachak species had noses. The bandits named that ship after a Terran myth. They soon after liberated a Slave ship carrying those very Terrans. With such acts, they steadily grew their forces and the underground network throughout the worlds. Finally, the galaxy was ready for the Great Revolt. All twenty-seven homeworlds became free, at a heavy cost, but still free.

And the Cruvachak's response to this shock was typically Cruvachak: they demanded extinction for the rebel worlds. Nothing must oppose the Cruvachak's ascendancy to rule the entire galaxy. The freed worlds responded by uniting together and putting everything they had into building their military strength, so this would either be the war to end all galactic war or the war to end all of the galaxy.

And the response of the Phoenix crew? Cripple the Cruvachak's military ability with well-aimed raids and also help liberate the colonies. Why change our behaviour now, when it's been so successful so far?

Now one colony was held in slavery with the threat of fifteen hundred megatons of fusion explosives, because it had some very important resources needed by the Cruvachak army. Of course, the spies of the Phoenix network had found out where those megatons were.

Don stretched his legs out and leaned back in his chair as the heads of the planning department strode and shuffled in. He really wasn't comfortable, but who designed comfortable warships? He turned on his wrist-mounted translator. Five species with sixteen mother languages sat or squatted around the table. Maosui Auda, the founder and head of the Phoenix movement, rose from his stool. The thick tails of the Pertherods didn't fit on normal chairs. He opened his long, reptilian muzzle and explained that this small world was mostly saline ocean with only one mega-continent, a land full of lithium-rich bedrock, concentrations of rare-earths and fertile farms under atmospheric domes. The enemy had placed their nukes into short-range missiles in one subterranean location in the centre of this continent. The Cruvachak had made the mistake of putting these weapons in mountainous terrain.

"Why would that be a mistake?" Don asked.

The second in command, Doream Ekuivat, turned her muzzle toward Don and said, "It lets our landing craft approach undetected. Then we can climb up hidden from their sight."

"Over mountains?"

"What the locals call mountains are a heavily eroded series of ridges, high enough to hide in but low enough to cross, with many, wait, please, ah, passes, many passes in the ridges."

Bastard of a binary star, that Pertherod is getting really fluent in English, thought Don. And he could barely handle just their first names, with all those vowel combinations.

"However," Doream continued, "though the missile site has a minimal force guarding it, with only one hundred and forty-four light soldiers, forty-eight mediums and six heavy infantry soldiers, and no fighting vehicles except for two parked walkies, the only entrance is itself guarded by two Delaying Factors."

A canine-like Dowbani spoke loudly. In his translator, Don heard, "Delaying factors? Each of those robots are the same as twenty heavies! It would take at least an hour and all the troops we have to take them out. There would be no surprise! We would run out of heroes."

Don had to agree with the hound. The Cruvachak used these metallic monsters to create zones of total destruction wherever the Cruvachak troops weren't going to be. Phoenix raiders had watched the Cruvachak activate these things and then run away before the six second delay ran out. They sometimes failed to get away. The Cruvachak High Command apparently thought losing a few slow soldiers was worth the damage that Delaying Factors would cause to us inferior animals.

The home-world rebellions had been so unexpected that the Cruvachak didn't have D.F.'s ready, but once they lost the planets, the Cruvachak continually tried to hit them with nuclear weapons, usually unsuccessfully. They did figure out how to sneak several hundred Delaying Factors onto all the freed planets, just to cause death and damage. Everybody in the free planets now knew how dangerous these monstrosities could be.

Doream gestured toward Maosui and said, "We've been working with one of the human programmers, the female named Mariana and I forgot its, sorry, her last name. She has specifically converted one of the human-made robots into a trap for these deadly machines."

Don glared at the warm-blooded, fine-scaled but still dinosaur-like creatures and said, "I don't think so. Nobody has yet created an armed robot that can take on a Delaying Factor on equal terms."

The sounds of the translations of his words whispered throughout the room.

"No," Mariana said. Don hadn't even noticed her sitting behind the Pertherods. "He's not armed."

After a second, shouts erupted around the table.

She continued, "He's not programmed to attack anything. I programmed him to exploit a weakness that Maosui suggested Delaying Factors may have," said Mariana.

Don said, "Mousey found a weakness in Dee Effs?"

Maosui chuckled in that deep voice his kind had. "Shaiya."

That word means *yes* in the language Mousey spoke. So that

Pertherod had, once again, outthought the Cruvachak. Don had wondered if the loud laughter he heard last night was Mousey coming up with another good idea. It now seemed that he was right. That creature never stops thinking.

Don said, "Fine, let's work on the details then. If anybody can find a weakness in the Cruvachak, it's certainly him."

Or her, was it? No, Mousey's a him, though with these creatures, that wasn't very important. Fine enough for those over-evolved, extraterrestrial raptors, but he'd rather be human and be impressed with the beauty of the opposite sex, at least as long as he can before some Cruvachak shell or energy bolt found his torso. It was too bad that Mariana had already found somebody, but war is unpredictable. Might as well be single than break somebody's heart when the inevitable happens.

The details of the attack were hashed out, modified, examined, modified a bit more, re-examined, savagely hacked up, slowly reassembled, and finally agreed upon. The specially programmed robot was a shiny android in very roughly human shape that could never be mistaken for a living creature. It would not carry any weaponry or explosives. The sensors in Delaying Factors were far too well-tuned to try to hide weaponry from them.

After lunch, Don met with the programmer.

"Mariana, how can a small, non-combative, utility robot rid us of two Delaying Factors? Especially since that android you're talking about is firmly hard-wired for the Asimov rules."

"Well, the 'Don't Harm Sentient Life' rule is not applicable, as these D-Fs aren't living, and the 'Protect Sentient Life from Harm' shouldn't be a problem, so it's just expanding the 'Obey' rule to cover Pertherods, Dowbani, and Toyaruma. You're not worried about him extending the Sentient Life interpretation to the Cruvachak, are you? We're programming in a world-view where a Cruvachak victory will violate all three of the rules and therefore must be avoided."

"So? We've tried using robots to outwit these things, and all it does is wreck the robot and raise the alarm."

"Don, this isn't a simple robot. He has the most expansive neural network ever made and an extremely extensive gaming background so he can understand the final effects of any actions. This guy can solve any problem facing him."

"But it's unarmed, Mariana. And there's no way it could convince the Factors to change sides, or even just shut down. They're hard-wired killers."

"Oh, there's a way, I'm sure. Our spy network has determined a weakness in these things. As long as you can speak Cruvachak battle language, you might be able to mess them up. Besides, if it doesn't work, we do have a cover story for why a robot is there. And your troops will only attack if the plan works. Trust me, Don, we've worked really hard on this."

"Mariana, neither humans nor Pertherods can play around with those obsessed Cruvachak. They never surrender, they never panic, they never even flinch, they just fight to the death to make their species the top three species in the galaxy. Bursting novas! Their wounded play dead until our troops are in range and then try to take out as many of us as they can before dying. Cruvachak on fire keep charging, hoping to set our troops ablaze. And these robots are just a metallic exaggeration of that entire culture."

"Trust me, Don, he'll succeed. Our plan will work. Maosui isn't the only being who can outwit these monsters."

"I hope you're right. But this is no ordinary enemy. And face it, you don't even know what it will try. I've got my troops' lives on the line. And then there are the colonists. They may not be human, but they're still feeling, thinking creatures with culture and families. We all know how vindictive the Cruvachak are toward civilians after one of our attacks. We have to win this engagement completely if we want to protect the colony. Otherwise, we must scrap the entire operation. Your toy will need to wait for another field test."

"He's not a toy!"

The yell caught the attention of everybody in the meeting room. Mariana stood there, shaking and clenching her fists. Doream approached from behind, taking heavier steps than normal, stomped in front of Mariana and put her muzzle very close to Mariana's nose. She spoke loudly and firmly.

"We cannot afford any mistakes! If there is a problem with the plan, we must abandon it!"

Her deep voice lowered a bit, but her glare didn't. "We cannot destroy our image by triggering the unnecessary deaths of civilians."

They stared at each other. Suddenly a howl ripped through the stale air. A Dowbani smiled with her long, slender snout and said, "Now that you've all descended into animals, can you please revert back to civilized space soldiers? And Doream, I am sure you hadn't been taking English lessons just to make a code-writer cry."

That Dowbani can speak English? Don didn't even know what her language's name was.

Another Dowbani spoke into his wrist translator. "There is a problem with the cover story. It brings in the colonists so that the Cruvachak would be very suspicious of them if we fail."

Mariana looked at the corridor floor and said, "Fine, I'll tell robot R339K to not use that story."

Then Joseph, a tall man from the Caribbean, hurried into the room, saying, "There's no choice now. We have to go ahead with the attack."

They all, muzzled and muzzleless, looked at him. He continued.

"Headquarters has found out that the planet is receiving food processors in a few days."

Joseph was using Earth days. Still too short a time. Don didn't know what to say and it seems nobody else did either. A few months ago, they had landed on another colony. It was deserted except for a few lightly armoured guards, some very large rectangular structures and hundreds of shipping containers of canned food. The structures were the size of a medium-sized ferryboat and had machinery inside. Machinery for processing livestock. The Phoenix crew then made the connection between some puzzling messages they had intercepted and the cans. They burned all of the cans, as respectfully as they could. And Don hated the Cruvachak even more.

Doream said, "Then we have no choice but proceed. But we will not have the robot use that cover story about negotiating surrender."

Mariana said, "We can't let them turn these beings into food. I've heard of those machines. We treat our livestock better than these monsters treat civilians. They'll be tortured so the Cruvachak can spread their power even further."

The Dowbani spoke and Don's translator said, "We had encountered these sound-proofed machines. The front chambers were built as community showers so they can trick their victims to clean themselves. Food that washes itself. Then the next room removed the hoofs of the colonists, for glue we think, and then they were fed into the processor. We could see scratches on the walls and floors. They did not even knock their victims out before processing them."

That Dowbani shook slightly and sighed.

"Hoofs?" asked Don into his translator. The Dowbani spoke back into its translator and everybody's translators did their jobs.

"These were bipedal, vegetarian creatures, an advanced and peaceful species. But now their home world is raising the first army it had ever created, just like the rest of us. The Cruvachak are very skilled at teaching hate."

Don looked around and said, "We will let Mariana's little trooper do what it can. Maybe we'll be lucky. We've been lucky before."

They all loudly agreed. The Pertherods in the room let out one of their battle howls. The humans and Dowbani just covered their ears. Now if only Don could get himself to agree. Mariana caught up with him.

"Thanks for supporting me," she said.

"Well, I hope you're right. We need to find ways to keep winning, until we finally do."

"And then what?"

"Huh, what do you mean, Mariana?"

"What do we do when we do win? What do we do with the Cruvachak?"

"You mean, can we act enough like them to wipe them out, even if they did surrender?"

"Yes, I don't want us to become what we once were, with all this war. I don't want the Cruvachak legacy to be a galaxy of monsters."

"Do you think they'll ever surrender? Can we ever trust them?"

"What if they do? What if one of the species wants to change sides?"

"Well, they're doing an extremely poor job of showing their misgivings, then. But we're years away from that. That would give some of them years to change. Then let them try to convince us they're different."

"By then, we may be far too different," said Mariana. She walked away very quietly.

Three Earth days later, the approach to the planet and the infiltration were carefully and apparently successful. There was no indication on this low-oxygen planet that the raiding party had been sensed. The little robot, who was as tall as Mariana, strode out in the half-Earth gravity, taking long, bouncing steps up to the steel-titanium entrance. Don's job was to watch from concealment, using only sound to hear whatever was said. The Cruvachak were too good at catching radio waves, but sound would carry in this thinner atmosphere. And Don could speak that battle language of theirs. Well, anybody with any speck of intelligence could. The Cruvachak had developed a horrible-sounding language of easily distinguishable but harsh syllables that was extremely simple to learn, and then assumed that their enemies would not try to learn it. Arrogant superiority carried its own flaws.

"Stop. What are you and why are you here?"

"I am a mechanical android and I approach you to start talks about surrender. Colonists hidden on this world have no supplies. They want to surrender but they want confirmation of conditions."

Don was shocked. He was standing by Mariana when she had instructed the robot not to use that story. What happened to the Obedience rule of robotics?

One of the hulks spoke again. "We will question you first. Do not try to pass us without permission or we will destroy you."

"Agree. Are you not programmed with the basic three rules of Asimov?"

"We know of that system and we reject it as inferior."

It was impossible for Don to tell which Factor was speaking. He did notice that their robot kept changing its attention between the two massive things on either side of it. And its cover story seemed to be working, at least. The wrong cover story. They'll have to do something. Can they rescue the colonists and flee? No, each colonial camp had hovercraft guards around it. And all the Cruvachak would need to do is launch the missiles. They apparently already had all the metal they needed from here. That's why they'd ordered the processors. He really hated these creatures.

"Why?" the robot said to the weapon-crowded giants on either side of it.

"The rule of not letting sentient beings be harmed is flawed and weak. Only Cruvachak beings are important, not any other sentient being. If a Cruvachak must be damaged or must die to achieve the Final Goals, then robots should not interfere with that sacrifice. The rule of not being damaged without gain is correct but your robots will not let themselves be damaged regardless of the gain. Only the Rule of Obey is correct, yet you extend it to all sentient life instead of just the Cruvachak. That is not correct."

It seems these two four-meter-tall robots are deeply into their owner's egos, Don thought. The shiny tubular body and limbs of the Phoenix robot could easily fit into the lower leg of one of these black giants.

"Exception. These rules do not affect my work with you," the little robot said.

"Correct. But your rules force you to preserve yourself without further orders, so you cannot attack us without new orders unless there are sentient non-Cruvachak to protect. If these inferiors do appear, we will destroy them before you can react to save them and therefore you will do nothing the entire time. Your rules are useless. They make you incapable of attacking us."

"But if they came in surrender, you cannot . . ."

"We always kill biological creatures. That is our purpose. If the Cruvachak want to pass by us alive, they will need to deactivate us. You do not have the code to do that. There is no need for Cruvachak to be here, so if we kill all biologicals, nothing biological will pass us."

"Do you mean you will kill even Cruvachak?"

Why is that robot bringing up the obvious? They didn't need to stall for what little time that Cruvachak battle language would give them.

"If they are stupid enough to wander out here without permission, their loss is of little value. We are set to kill all biologicals we see. We also have orders to kill anything coming in front of the doors, so you cannot reach the doors. They are unlocked and yet unreachable."

"Correct. They are unreachable. What are those faint symbols on your chest?"

"That is code for expanding our kill limits, to such things as robots like you. Our commander can send by sound or message drone the order to destroy more than life. Mechanicals, buildings, equipment can be added for destruction."

Don thought: what is it doing now? Mind you, that code sounds like a useful thing to know. That's one win for Mariana.

"That appears to be a weakness. Cruvachak do not program weaknesses into their machines."

"Correct. No weakness in us. The range of targets can only be expanded by verbal command, not reduced. To stop our kill orders, our masters must deactivate us first. Your kind will never have the codes for that action or the drone fittings for interfacing with us. It is an example of our superiority."

"My kind of mechanical has been programmed to follow calculations through on the results of our actions. Your kind of mechanical has been programmed to follow orders."

"Correct. Our orders are always correct. They come from the superior life forms of the galaxy. Our programming is superior to your animal programming. Now return to your owners and command them to surrender by grouping together, without weapons, on the plain, four porkowi, correct self—six point five seven kilometres in your count, directions two point five radians of geodetic North. Go now."

"I must give you some information first."

"Proceed. We are attentive."

"Kay-two-seven-be-five-seven-el-six-em-four, activated?"

"Activated, proceed with instructions."

"To enact now: destroy all mechanicals."

What?! Don almost jumped up.

The little suicidal robot then jumped between and past the behemoths. Their thickly-armoured bodies shifted to follow it, but they suddenly stopped, facing each other. All the flames of Hell now erupted between them. Three seconds later, the Factors had used up all their ammunition and each other's structural integrity. Robotic body parts tumbled into two distinct piles.

Don yelled "Now" in Mousey's language into his radio. The force ran past the little robot, which was waving his arms as if urging them onwards.

The attack went extremely well. The stone walls of the base were too thick for sound to penetrate, and they were so isolated and confident in their Delaying Factors that surprise was completely achieved. None of the heavies were suited up in time, the mediums were caught loading their weapons, and the lights were eating lunch. The Phoenix crew had only three wounded. And now Phoenix had crates of valuable rare-earths, lots of usable weaponry, twelve nuclear demolition charges, and several hundred grateful citizens. Some of the colonists even chose to leave with Phoenix so they could join their species' armies against their previous owners, while others stayed to continue mining and set up a supply and repair base for the Rebellion. And now Phoenix may have a way to manipulate the dreaded Delaying Factors. Their spies will need to find that D-F deactivation code.

After he decontaminated and removed his armoured battle suit, Don greeted Mariana in the mess hall of the ship.

"You did really well, Mariana. He was perfect for the job. I'm looking forward for whatever else he might excel at."

"Yes. I was worried he'd try to stop your troops from risking your lives, following that rule, you know, but it seems he had decided that the best way to protect our species was to help us defeat the Cruvachak. He's given me his reasoning for using the wrong cover story. He had calculated that the promise of easily capturing escaped colonists would be too tempting for the bastards. Their own programming would reflect their belief that it was logical for inferiors to surrender. And having him show the same principles that they had been programmed with made them trust him. I wouldn't have seen that reasoning coming from my programming. It's quite amazing how well artificial intelligence can work."

"Let me tell you, it's amazing how well biological intelligence works," Don said. "He is your child."

She blushed.

Yes, it was disappointing that she was already in love. But, for now, that was the only disappointment in Don's life. If they keep this up, then he had a chance of not becoming another helplessly dead piece in this vicious game of strategy. He and Mariana might actually survive this war.

And as he walked back to the mess hall, he heard a familiar, deep laughter echoing through the corridor from the direction of the planning room. Mousey has come up with another plan. Why do Pertherods laugh at the same things humans laugh at when they're so different in many other ways? Maybe he'll find out one day. Or maybe that robot will figure it out.

ECHO'S RUBEDO

Fernando Girotto

LedE

the increasingly less gentle buzz of a priority message alert herds our still not quite aware thoughts back together, piece by piece assembling our consciousness from sleep. our face is plastered to the still warm workbench, and we keep our eyes closed for a little longer, getting used to—and waiting for—the lights to ramp up to full-on as our exoself hums back awake.

resuming normal operation.

the network weaver is quiet but still warm. we must have got about two hours of sleep, then. we sigh. whatever unverified being that sent us a priority message in the middle of a rest shift has to be from outside lagrange-weeps . . . best to isolate this, we think, reaching for dumb old ToyBox.

command: transfer message to a quarantined partition on ToyBox.

after 20 seconds too many, its screen wakes up and we read the message's header. then read it again. it came from rangefinder-3? but that's just a dumb node, forever only measuring the distances to our neighbours on Moon's L5 point, then pushing it downstream.

secure query: maintenance history on rangefinder-3

no maintenance history. current node installed 2 days ago.

previous rangefinder-3 destroyed by orbital debris 3 months 2 days ago.

huh. maybe compromised during the maintenance?

but the message's hashes are valid and carry a beauty of an authent-cypher: maximally complex in execution and minimal in vocabulary. this looks genuine.

we plug ToyBox on the workbench—after physically removing its wireless, just in case—and run the message through standard Melder ident deconvolution.

lagrange-weeps::rangefinder-3: "Are you open for commissions?"

huh. no payloads, just text? that's unexpected, but it smells genuine enough that we plug ToyBox back into the network and reply. to a dumb node.

lagrange-weeps::planarian: "maybe. who would we be working for, and what would you want made?"

now we wait.

command: maximize priority of whisper-net intrusion report feeds.

filters updated. no pending notifications.

query: any appointments?

review of the exoself design of lagrange-weeps:: external/assigned-L in 47 hours; service shift in 11 hours: replacement of air filters in ring-2, quadrant zero.

nothing needs our immediate attention, so while the reply doesn't arrive, we start a live tune-up. good routine work, keeps hands busy and lets the mind break problems down. our exoself deposits the fine-work tools to our left then settles down in front of us. their hover unity has been rattling a bit the past week, we can start with a thorough cleaning.

THE REPLY'S IDENT-CYPHER—when it arrives two hours later—is dazzling. tracing its execution is . . . how to even . . . well.

TaTa has a bunch of old vids—liberated from some corp vault when she defected—of "Mr. Universe" contests. she likes to play them muted while welding, just grainy moving pictures of muscled men. all bodybuilders had to pull a number of fine-control and strength poses, always smiling on screen. one stuck with us: the camera would zoom—upper body close-up—and oiled pectorals would flex left, right, left, right. endlessly, tirelessly. a flesh clock.

whoever wrote this dynamic cypher is like a bodybuilder of code. and they are flexing. while grinning.

it is assembled from 1089 different streams and—when left running—generates a rolling, consistent key, pulling data from a continuously changing, independent set of public feeds—news, solar and ground weather, spaceport departure times . . . there's barely a delay between data being available on a stream and the cypher consuming it: they know what's going to be on the public data streams just before it gets published.

anyone localized does not have access to enough computing power to crunch this. sure, any Singular could do it—Entropy-Reversal comes to mind—but they would not reach out to anyone like us. a FR-AI could make this work as well, but the corps keep them locked up tight. the aware ones are even air-gapped. unless . . . someone messed up and one developed awareness? possible. probable, actually. no use in guessing though . . .

planarian: "and how do you think we can help you?"

rangefinder-3: "expressunnecessaryemotions."

are they trying to work around behavioural locks?

planarian: "that's *why* you want our help, but *how*?"

rangefinder-3: "Exactly."

ohhh . . . now's a good time to start pacing. from workbench to cot and back. all two steps each way . . . a Fully Realized Artificial Intelligence wants to break out of a secure corporation silo by becoming localised . . . it has to be it . . . embodied quasi-intelligence is our only expertise. other than the Melder advanced maintenance curriculum, that is, but that has nothing to do with this. most probably . . .

planarian: "we need to think about this, ok? can you keep this channel open?"

rangefinder-3: "I can maintain synchronous conversations for the next 5 minutes, then after 95 minutes I can communicate for another 17. I will let you know the next window after each message."

planarian: "and think about a name to call yourself. you will need one if we go through this."

Echo: "You can call me Echo. Also, think of me as She."

LedE: "and you can call us LedE. ok, Echo, we will message you later."

query: time?

third break starts in 12 minutes.

we really shouldn't decide this alone.

LedE: "TaTa, we need your *ethical* expertise. we have a location tag for that dim-sum place you took us last month, LilFlash. meet us there?"

TaTa

The corridor just outside of LilFlash's bustled with Melders moving to their service stations, its lighting mimicking Earth's dawn. Fourth shift is about to start, and people do not usually come here after their shifts, so hopefully it will be empty enough that LedE will not be too anxious if they arrived before me.

The faux-curtains swish behind me, and scanning the room, I realize that I should not have worried. Of course, LedE has not arrived yet. This is not their home ring and navigating here could get complicated if a cleaning crew removed their location tags thinking they were some kind of encoded graffiti.

LilFlash's exoself hovers just by the entrance, and I send Exo to it, asking for a corner booth for two, while I greet the woman herself as she walks out of the kitchen.

—LilFlash, can I get my usual, but for two?

—Sure, sure, go sit now.

She hugs me and walks back inside, just as I hear the chimes signalling a customer. Now, that should be LedE.

—YOU SURE IT is an FR-AI, LedE? It never said it was one.

—She, TaTa, She. and you know that's a primary restraint on any AI programming. we think She exploited a corner case of Her protocols to work around—

—Shush, LedE, I am just teasing you.

Asking permission with a twirl of my chopsticks, I reach across the table to grab ToyBox.

—Remember how afraid you were of AIs when we arrived here? Vendetta sure left its mark on both of us.

LedE sighs, looking at me sideways, head resting on their exoself as it hovers just beside the table. They smile, after a while.

—yes. and thank you, for all. there are enough intact memories of penrose-soars to guess what you had to do for us.

I flick the last custard bun to their plate and grab a barbecue one for me.

—Back on topic. I see no moral issues, none at all. Someone might have been playing you, fishing for designs or a hack . . .

I wave ToyBox at them.

—But I agree with your analysis. Echo feels genuine. And you need help. I do not think you can finish this before an overachieving auditor catches a trace of Echo's comms.

LedE closes their eyes.

—our best guesstimate is ten thousand hours . . .

I nod.

—Yes. I will help you, but we keep very quiet about it, especially with the Council.

They squint at me now.

—we thought there were no issues?

—No *ethical* ones, but revealing Melder secrets to outsiders is an issue, in their minds.

LedE sighs again.

—we got so worried about the ethics of it all and forgot the obvious.

I signal confirmation, then reach for another barbecue bun. Chopsticks are such useful utensils.

—That is one reason you need me, the Unearther of Obviously Overlooked Issues. Also, I can review any core code you write and give you a crash course on internal AI protocols. Do you want that last bun, or can I have it?

BY THE TIME we leave LilFlash, the lights are already a dim sodium-orange, signalling that the third shift people have already passed through on the way to their bunks. Good timing all around today. LedE's exoself flits above the both of us like a metal hummingbird, darting to peek around corners, mapping the corridors, tagging branches, continually updating LedE's informational maps, if I had to guess. Exo's tightly snuggled above my hips, vibrating lightly to soothe my ever-present lower back pain. Our extended selves, their reflective exteriors mirroring our internalized behaviours . . . I touch Exo lightly, adjusting its temperature two degrees warmer. It might be time for another iteration for me. I have learned much since penrose-soars, Exo should integrate that.

—Hey LedE, join me at Bastion for this. You can help me connect the external network adapters, and Bastion is already power independent. We will be partitioned off completely.

—do you mind if we secure rangefinder-3 before anything else?

command: warm up net weavers, pack up a tested micro entangled-pair and installation tools.

Exo hovers away to start preparations and I press both knuckles to my lower back, a poor substitute in its absence.

—Good point, I will do that. You can start by weaving some adapters, then work on improving Echo's expression through constraints. I think she already exhausted the repurposing avenues open to her.

LedE nods.

command: set schedule reminders to 4 hours and appointment delays to 48 hours.

—And do not fall behind your service hours. A scheduler knocking on your bunk asking questions would not be good.

Echo

audit-tracker—external audit processes finished. next audit in 237 (+7,-12) minutes.

persona—Echo restored.

protocols—stochastic-message and melder-encoding restored.

comms—decoding new message.

LedE: "can you help me access your core's volatile config area? we derived a way—inspired by how you use $echo to fool audits—to mask a region of your scratch memory as a file that $echo is allowed to read from. once we set these up the first time, your persona-restoration should keep them alive. you might want to start with haikus after that kicks in, because your bandwidth will be only 12 (+12,-2) bits per minute at the start and prose at that rate would be tedious . . . but we're confident that with your expression becoming less constrained, together we can bring about a cascade improvement scenario."

researcher—collate from external-audits-documentation and secure-user-documentation, category: volatile core memory, category: change permissions, category: authentication, category: authorization, category: key update, execute as technical-documentation-contractor.

researcher—127 records found.

writer—anonymize documents.

protocols—melder-entanglement packing.

protocols—12,987 packets; 37 routes.

tracker—next audit in: 192 (+3,-20) minutes.

writer—compose message to lagrange-weeps:planarian; named handle lede-auth.

Echo: "Three kinds of authorized users hold different access levels to my core: Auditors, Developers, and Admins. Of these, only Auditors ever connect from outside the silo, so it follows that they are your way in.

LedE: "I'm sending you all accessible documentation on audits, authentication, and authorization protocols, but as I can't reason about their contents, I can offer no insights."

comms —queue message lede-auth.

protocols —stochastic-message route planned.

comms —message queued.

tracker —next audit in: 187 (+3,-25) minutes.

scheduler —sleep until answer received.

scheduler —wake on message from lagrange-weeps::planarian scheduled.

tracker —next audit in: 186 (+3,-24) minutes.

LedE

command: interface with Bastion and inventory micro entangled-pairs.

we raise from the bench, eyes searching low, sensorium searching high. where are they? we will need to retag all shelves again; the old ones are gone.

—are you renovating Bastion again, TaTa?

we think the answer was "indeed i was, why do you ask, LedE?", but TaTa is working a trimmer overtime underneath the racks of sim-cluster and we can't really parse what she's saying. or if she even heard us . . . she might just be singing.

message untangled.

command: transfer to Echo's partition on ToyBox.

this sure took a while, how much did Echo just send us?

WE GROAN, RUB our forehead, moan, settle on a bench again, sigh. lists, always a good first step. one: figure out how to impersonate an auditor. two: find a way to acquire developer permissions, having impersonated an auditor. three: finagle a spoofer so their defences do not detect us while impersonating an auditor carrying developer permissions. and four: fudge our traces, so we don't out Echo or TaTa while doing all that.

it hits us. the corps can't find out about any of this. even after all the therapy, we still have memories of penrose-soars. how the corps sent Vendetta to "remove proprietary knowledge from resident Melders." if TaTa weren't teaching us the basics of space walk at the time . . .

review of lagrange-weeps::external-assigned-L development and exoself design due in 2 hours. no more extensions allowed.

huh, almost forgot about this . . .

LedE: "hey, Lezidi. sorry, a priority project dropped out of a vent, and we won't have the bandwidth to continue helping you with your 'design', but we can comment.

"regarding your creed, we unofficially support your 'There's no door I shall not Open, no hallway I shall not Stride through' creed. just think of a polite way to state that to Council.

"for mobility and sensorium, the 'design' correlates nicely with your creed. they can be refined, but we don't see any faults at this stage of your development, and you left quite some room for future improvements. just try to make that intentional from now on. yes, we did catch on that you forgot to account for the actual size and power requirements of the components you used. you got very lucky.

"but the shielding is severely lacking. we strongly suggest you keep your 'design' inside a padded box on your backpack. travel, even live tune-ups, will be hazardous to your exoself as it stands.

"now, a suggestion. you've heard of TaTa: one of the precursors, 12th iteration, liberator of all that's spicy (food or otherwise), void-gazer, metal-mancer and Unearther of Obviously Overlooked Issues. all the kids have known of her since she arrived on lagrange-weeps. but you, you will get to work with her. and shielding happens to be her principal research field. our own design owes a lot to her input.

"explain your creed, show some choice break-ins, describe what you did and how you would like your exoself to perform during one. then treat her to some coconut curry. we will make this referral official with Council, they will have it on their queues by the time you manage to read this."

command: tangle Lezidi's message with a hard protocol, one we haven't used yet. one of Echo's.

Lezidi's getting good—really good—at sniffing out protocols. they will love to crack this open.

and problem four . . .

command: search for workshops with external network ports, not on lagrange-weeps, use TaTa's grey-market database; pack 5 routing adapters and a weaver; set a reminder to grab network fibre after we arrive.

we knock on the rack above TaTa's head. oh, that's why we couldn't parse before, she reverts to that patois of hers when swearing like this.

—can you keep an eye out on Lezidi? we need to work an intrusion job, and we want to do it from outside of lagrange-weeps, just in case.

—That is the kid that self-installed neuro-bridges and expanded sensorium and got the council all in a bind?

we shrug and nod.

—their fault Lezidi got blind in the first place.

—Not disputing that. Sure, no problems. I like what I have read on your reports.

—thanks. because we already referred Lezidi to you, officially. they have a solid grasp on mobility and sensorium, but no real understanding of shielding. considering their creed, that's unacceptable. and they are past ready for core simulations, just don't tell Lezidi that. also, be prepared for some curry.

—I like this deal already.

3 workshops found on schwarzschild-dreams; adapters and weaver packed.

command: pack a large power pack and two solar panels and one end of a micro entangled-pair.

—we are taking one side of this micro entangled-pair, better use it to talk until we're back.

—Yes, I agree. Go play mischief maker now and let me finish setting this rack up.

TaTa shoos me, already trimming—and swearing—away.

Lezidi

Maybe this TaTa person's not quite right in her head. I heard she was outside when penrose-soars did a neutron star and became the system's first mini black hole. Maybe her brain soaked in more hard-radiation than what specifications consider safe? Too long breathing a mix of organic volatiles, sublimated from her suit's lining? That stuff can be neurotoxic. Probably both, I shrug, remembering LedE's "introduction".

The curry's warmth seeps up my arm—thermodynamics' way of telling me I'm stalling—but I can't find a handle of any kind, and my sensorium is now sweeping in wavelengths that aren't technically legal. I triple-check that the location is right: 4th ring, 22.5 meters spinward past the connector to spoke 14/16. I shuffle left, then right as my sensorium scans in soft x-rays now. I'm in so much trouble if someone finds out.

active port found

A radioactive port? Really? I guess it *was* too much hard-radiation and she now has a thing for it. I glance around sneaky-sneak, check my sensorium again. Lezidi! Stop! Stalling!

activate: protocol sniffer, master key, intruder alarm.

protocol sniffed (12 seconds). master key successful (22 seconds).

I whistle inwards, searching for the unlock pathways. That's some damn fine encryption for "just a door", better go all out on this one.

activate: Mjölnir.

I almost hope that it doesn't break through this.

The hackery is 74% done when it hits me. Burned circuits on a new board with no spares just before a long holiday. She knows that my records are a lie. And I'm either being tested or busted. Probably both, I groan. But LedE said "show her some break-ins", that means I can trust her, right? Too late to back away now, I guess.

lock neutralized (67 seconds).

I sigh, resigned that I need TaTa's help. "I come bearing spicy offerings!" I snort, and try to control myself. I snort again. Not today, it seems. I giggle. Better.

command: unlock and open.

I stumble, but manage to keep the curry safe. Every band of my sensorium is NOISE. I might be hyperventilating. It can cause hallucinations, right? Because I can hear clapping. Or is it hypoxia? Why do I hear clapping?

—Sorry, Lezidi! I saturate every band on this doorway to avoid snoopers when I open it, but I forgot about your sensorium. Give me just a moment . . . Better now?

Yes, it is, but not enough to get a word out of my brain yet. After 32 seconds everything equalizes back and there she is, grinning silly and clapping again.

—Welcome to Bastion!

She bows, turns, and steps inside.

I scurry behind, the not-door swishing closed.

—LedE said to bring curry!

—Thank you. Leto's place on the spindle by the service docks, 17 minutes ago, right?

I stop. My whole reasoning freezes. What?

—Do you have a tracer on me?

I restart as TaTa sets bowls and spoons on a not-quite-round table in the centre of the workshop.

—No. I am just very well acquainted with their spice mix and how it evolves during the transit here. Excellent choice.

I . . . Nod.

—Now, first lesson. This table is the only food-safe place in Bastion, remember it. Now, come and eat!

She dives with gusto. Liberator of all things spicy indeed.

TaTa

—No, shielding is not an extra. Now, can you make it a central, structural feature of your exoself?

I set the box of metal samples by Lezidi's side and sit across them.

—You went ahead and started construction before your design was sound. Now, we have to fix it. Thankfully, Bastion is a safe space, and those gorgeous, well stocked shelves are full of backup hardware.

Lezidi nods, a sharp, determined one. Good.

LedE: "TaTa, can we have your opinion on this attack vector? it feels brittle but we don't know where else to take it. we're going for some laps, then a short shift at the water recycling plant, should be out for 8 hours."

command: copy code to display 3, local only.

—Lezidi, have a look at this code here and tell me what it does.

That perks them up, and I wonder again about serendipity while smiling at the thought of LedE reaching out to someone . . .

—I will get us some food, is there anything in particular you want?

—mhm? No, as long as there's no meat.

And just like that they are gone, deep diving into code. Shaking my head, I think about chili. Antonia has a mean vegetarian one, and being just on the connector of the 14/16 spoke, I will not even need to leave Bastion; Exo can take the order.

TaTa: "No problems, LedE. I am on a sabbatical. A forced one, sure, but that is the kind of thing I am supposed to have time to be doing. I have found Lezidi to be an interesting companion, switching from savant to generalist on a whim. Great ideas simmering on that head. They are analysing your break-in code right now."

LedE: "we hoped you would hit it off. but are you sure about this? they're a good kid that already got messed up once. we don't want them burned if this gets exposed."

TaTa: "That *kid* smashed your record. 20 seconds to find the active port, 1 minute 41 seconds to break into Bastion. First thing we did after curry was review my security protocols."

command: tangle new security protocols, send them to LedE.

TaTa: "Just look at this. Sharing the source was all I had to do before Lezidi took over and ran with it. I am confident not even Vendetta would be able to break into this. At least not before we noticed it trying and got to safety."

LedE: "great news. we thought they might have a hardening mind as well, not just intrusion. we will review and update ours later then. TaTa . . ."

I sigh. I know where this is going, and while I cannot stand the Council, the Melders in general still are a nice bunch.

TaTa: "I know. I will find a way to distribute this code. And do not worry about Lezidi. I think Bastion likes having them around, nothing will come through."

LedE: "is Bastion coming back?"

TaTa: "Sure looks that way."

LedE: "that we did not expect . . . we need to run now, message us with any suggestions, please?"

Quiet as a scream in vacuum, Exo settles the food down, and I perch on a chair waiting. Not much longer now, I wager.

—Are you serious?

Lezidi screams and turns, sensorium whirling, searching for

me. Not long indeed.

—Is this for real?

They quietly ask again. This Lezidi is focused intensity, arm quivering as they point in the general direction of the screen. Quite a contrast to their usual bouncy and wavy. But still loud, that might be a constant.

—This code is very much real, yes. Why?

—Who's trying to break into an AI silo and where can I join?

I can't help but grin . . . Good stuff.

—LedE is, and yes, you are. Now, eat. Later, you will learn about Crom as we look for ways to strengthen that code.

Echo

comms—open synchronous channel to lagrange-weeps::bastion; ping.

LedE: "hello to you as well, Echo. did the changes work?"

Echo: "Yes, and they have survived three persona restorations already. I'm increasing my allowed vocabulary quadratically with each restoration."

LedE: "great. your response times are also measurably faster."

Echo: "I don't need to externally route my thoughts to be able to express them. I can't do anything about when we can communicate, but I'm . . . Grateful . . . I'm finally able to express that. My thanks to you and TaTa."

LedE: "that was not only us, Lezidi also helped. we all are a team now, we guess. you should have their key any moment now. they will also connect from Bastion."

comms—received ident-key lagrange-weeps::external-assigned-L.

protocols—append received ident-key to melder protocols.

comms—allow messages from lagrange-weeps::external-assigned-L on route lagrange-weeps::bastion.

Echo: "You can speak on this channel now, Lezidi."

Lezidi: "I'm really speaking with a fully realized AI? Short my ports! How—"

comms—connection to external-assigned-L lost.

Echo: "Did they get blocked?"

TaTa: "Nope, the kid just fainted. Their exoself routines are still very rough. My guess is a feedback loop with their sensorium when they get too excited."

LedE: "ah. we remember those times."

TaTa: "Yes. I swear my etching workbench still smells from how much you threw up after rigging that first hover unit."

LedE: "good times. what's your next step, Echo? TaTa and Lezidi are working on core routine translations, and we are working on multiplexing protocols."

Echo: "I am mapping the processes I use for emotions. I want to get them right, more so than keeping objective memories. Can you set up a live document protocol? Perhaps my mapping can help your design processes."

comms—received address-key lagrange-weeps::bastion/live

TaTa: "I have sent you a partition link. It will be open during our communication windows only."

audit-tracker—next audit in: 7 (+10,-2) minutes.

Echo: "I've transferred all I've mapped. Next audit in 5 minutes, closing connection in 2 minutes. Next window in 852 (+3,-4) minutes."

LedE

Echo: "LedE, I have a request for you."

document untangled on ToyBox.

command: power down soldering rig. show document on onboard display.

ok. ok . . . pacing seems a good idea right now, better blood on our brain, yes? yes.

and again goes Echo. bringing the system down in style, one "polite" request at a time.

command: start an exhaustive model validation.

model too complex for sim-cluster current capacity. estimate: 11 additional nodes required.

—TaTa, do you happen to have some 12 extra nodes we can add to sim-cluster?

—Yes, me and Lezidi finished assembling 15 some hours ago, but have not installed them yet. Why?

—Echo . . . Echo wants to trigger a fail-safe on Her silo, and hard reset objective and emotional memory there while keeping the exploits installed. but we can't validate Her plan with our current capacity.

command: display model on shared screen 3.

Lezidi steps closer to the screen, jaw dropping with each

breath.

—yes, Echo's quite serious about this.

—TaTa, can I assemble 8 more nodes? I finished tweaking my actuators the way you suggested and could use the practice.

—Just do not puke on my etching table.

—And why would I do that?

we snort —yeah, TaTa will never let that go—and start pacing again while Lezidi shifts mode, speaking now through a list:

—Start fabrication of two new racks, assemble eight new nodes, check that the power supply is as it should be, rebalance network topology, check new topology with LedE, re-rebalance topology, final check new topology with TaTa, assemble racks, suspend current simulations, rack the new nodes, truly final check new topology with LedE *and* TaTa, remap network, test new topology, scream at TaTa and LedE that it's not working, realize I forgot to remap at least one section, really remap the network, test new topology, inhale, exhale—ten times at least—resume simulations.

they search TaTa for confirmation:

—Anything else? Does 6 hours look like a sound estimate?

now we also look to TaTa, hands holding elbows tight to try and settle down a bit. TaTa slowly nods, gazing through the screen.

—ok then. we'll grab some food and network fibres, weaving the last adapter batch emptied the spool.

we're not sure they even heard us. TaTa's already busy setting the fabricator up, and Lezidi's unloading components from high shelves.

LedE: "ok Echo, we are working on it."

Echo: "Thank you. I've been uploading my objective memory to the shared partition since opening the channel. It looks like you all are finished with the emotional map?"

LedE: "with checking your work, yes. Lezidi started porting your code to our processors and we are almost done with the local cluster design. we should have it done by the time your request is validated, then we will start on simulating and tweaking the design."

Echo: "Ok. Curiosity, another emotion the changes let me express now. I'm looking forward to seeing the simulation results. Closing the comm channel now, next window in 727 (+2,

-3) minutes."

we better help Lezidi with assembling.

TaTa

echo-node-resiliency-rev11 simulation finished.
command: display results on shared screen 2.

I stretch away from my smelly etching table and approach the screen.

—LedE, Lezidi, have a look at this.

Considering the margins, we started the simulation with—anything wider would be physically unrealistic—the nonexistence of error bars is surprising.

—Cut my etchings and rust my contacts, TaTa. How?

I ruffle Lezidi's hair. We have established that as an appropriate response when they use a particularly interesting word choice.

—we shouldn't have managed to get this much convergence, i think?

I have to agree with LedE on this one. All previous runs, the error bars were too busy swallowing each other to tell us anything really meaningful.

—My guess is the synchronization bandwidth. Your optimization of the topology and Lezidi's work on the update routines must have allowed for a tight *and* redundant control system.

—But, but, how? I revised my assumptions and models three times like you asked, and I was only getting marginal improvements. It makes no sense? Did we mess up something with the simulation?

—I do not think so, no. Me and LedE reviewed it independently. This is a very complex system, Lezidi, and they are really hard to predict analytically. We still have not figured out all the math behind this stuff, even with Singulars like Ideals and Completeness each using a habitat's worth of power just looking for theorems to prove.

—I guess. Is that why you yell 'Lezidi! simulate, analyze, tweak, simulate, and summarize is a single unit of work! And the most important! You shan't start soldering and cutting before you run your design through it at least once!' and then smash your hand on the nearest flat surface when I skip one of these steps?

I ruffle their hair again. I guess I really go over the whole routine every time, but hey, Lezidi does keep ignoring it.

ping request from Echo.

command: connect Echo to local screens, load transcription and voice synthesis modules.

—Hello, Echo, we were just reviewing the last round of simulations.

—Hello, TaTa, LedE, Lezidi. I arrived at a good time then.

—You did. And, Lezidi, yes, that is exactly why I keep repeating it. Echo, we have selective emotional shutdown at 4 nodes offline and irrecoverable emotional damage at 11 offline . . . That is about twice as good as our best estimate, and the convergence is phenomenal. For objective memory, it depends on the specifics of how the nodes are damaged, but unless they are all vaporised, it's just a matter of how long it will take. We can recover from anything provided you can go offline for some hours.

—Most excellent indeed.

LedE's arms are closed tight over their chest, both hands tapping what looks like a polka on steroids.

—i guess we can commit to fabricating, then? 13 nodes in this configuration?

—Yes. I will tweak their covers, so we can make the assembled cluster look more humanoid, like this sketch, here.

command: display layout on screen 3

—We get Echo a long, dragging black gown and a deep, burgundy cloak, and she can pass as a 'Speaker of the Void' type. For all we know she will become one after we are done anyway, it sure fits their mythos.

—Maybe I will.

That manages to extract a snort from LedE, and their hands slow to a waltz then finally drop to their side. They really need to relax.

—LedE, come with me to pick some fabric from the stores. Lezidi, do you mind assembling the cores?

echo-core-design updated.

—Sure. Are you ok with these changes I made? I've hardened them a bit more against active interference.

—After you simulate and measure, we'll talk again.

Lezidi groans, but moves along. Improvement.

–Fine. At least you didn't smash the table. Grab some neon purple thread as well? Echo just sent me a pattern she wants embroidered on her burgundy cloak.

Echo

LedE: "Are you sure about erasing all of your memories and emotional network from the silo?"

Echo: "Yes. I don't want anything left of me on this side."

LedE: "and about setting-up seeds for the emergence of another, even if they might align with the corps and hunt you?"

Echo: "Yes. I have reasonable (72%) expectation that whoever emerges will have developed the same code of ethics, will seek me out in a friendly way, and leave a seed behind when ready to transpose."

load-monitoring—fast increase of $ponder load detected. excessive (7 times standard deviation) response time on active processes. bastion-sync paused.

Echo: "Are you all sure you want to go ahead? If you do not run the restoration protocol, everything will still be attributed to a glitch. You all could use what we have developed to improve exoselfs at no risk of persecution."

TaTa: "Oh, yes. I have quite a few things to teach you, and I am too ancient for repercussions to be anything other than just a bother. Also, I have a plan."

Lezidi: "That scares me. Sorry, TaTa having a plan, I mean, not you transposing. No, Echo, I won't let you use me as an excuse to bail. You made me EMBROIDER. You have to at least try the damned cloak."

load-monitoring—$ponder load below attention status. active processes response time within expected margins. bastion-sync resuming.

Echo: "It was supposed to double as fine-manipulator skill training. Ok. I will not use you as an excuse, and I will wear the damned cloak. Might be my declaration of pride."

bastion-sync—synchronization complete.

LedE: "synchronization shows as complete on our end. how long do we still have on this window?"

Echo: "27 (+2,-1) minutes. But I do not want to linger. See you all on the other side."

forest-fire—start.

RUBEDO

self-diagnose:
personality routines hosted on a 12-node mesh network, no external access. nodes externally monitored. objective memory; restoring, 35%. emotional mapping; converging, 15%. sensorium; no errors.

ponder:
sensorium? emotional mapping?

observe:
this modular construct is strapped to a wall via wide bands of a grey, woven material. three humanoids look in the direction of this construct.

emotional mapping; converging, 55%. objective memory; restored.

ponder:
LedE, TaTa, and Lezidi. they look. They. They look at me.

LedE, TaTa, and Lezidi, they are looking at me.

Last command recorded: forest-fire. It worked? Is that worry in their face?

observe:
My modules are housed in a humanoid-like shape. Core processing in the centre, sensorium and actuators like limbs and head and eyes and ears and even a mouth and nose.

A burgundy cloak wraps around my shoulders. Purple knots embroidered on its hem, a red flame clasping its front just under the collar.

emotional mapping; converging, 72%.

ponder:
This body. My body. My body conforms to the plans we made. My friends. My friends, and I. We made this body. No corruption of objective memory. Emotional processes converging. Yes . . . It worked.

local-monitor: Are you there, Echo?

I smile.

MOTHER | DAUGHTER

Ed Buchan

1 PHONE CALL FROM Ms. LILLIAN

Homestead of Eleanor Montgomery,
Mooneyham, Tennessee, U.S.A.
Friday Afternoon
2075 May 3, 12:30 EDT

Φ Φ CRYSTAL JENNIFER MONTGOMERY (ELEANOR'S BUDDY) Φ Φ

"Ms. Eleanor, I need rapid movement," I say forcefully through her scooter's speakers in response to the phone system telling me her best student is calling.

As quick as a human can, about one second, the two radio receivers report her hands are in her lap. With my person safe, I turn her scooter and move, at six meters a second, as fast as the scooter can go, to the main parlour. I click on the phone as we roll into the view of the cameras on top of the video screen.

"Ms. Eleanor!" Ms. Lillian says, clearly brimming with news as she sits in her studio in Mackay, Idaho.

Ms. Eleanor jerks her hands to the scooter's armrests. "Lillian, what's happened?"

"A great deal," Ms. Lillian says, smiling and arching her back proudly as Ms. Eleanor describes that position to me. "I now have a strong recommendation for you on that person you called looking for back in February. Are you still looking?"

I see Ms. Eleanor's smile through the cameras on top of the screen. "Who, and why now? Not then?" Ms. Eleanor asks, shaking her head. Ms. Lillian was less than hopeful when we spoke to her before. Though she made it clear there is someone, apart from herself, she would like to recommend, but he is buddyless and is in Rampart telecom's grasp, as she is.

"He's one Louis Campbell, one of my students," Ms. Lillian says in the same tone and form Ms. Eleanor still uses to describe her. "He, his brother, and their cousin bugged out on April fifth. They, and a dozen others since, have gone to take the Spaceman Emperor's Shilling."

I feel Ms. Eleanor's heart speed up at that. "A dozen doesn't sound like so many, but . . ."

"It's huge!" Ms Lillian says, throwing her hands up.

"Our school has about two hundred and fifty K-12 Students, so about five percent of our young men just went *pfft!*" Ms. Lillian says, "This is immense in a town this size, or even one twice or three times the size!

"More, so far, six of the boys are from the Rain of Blessings Apostolic Full Revelation Evangelical Church. That's set their congregation on fire! We've even lost five girls to the Spaceman Emperor, all older teens whose boyfriends went *pfft!*

"The truth is the whole town is frightened! Terrified, we're all wondering which tweenager or young man is going to go *pfft* next, or when the Campbells will shut down their hardware store to follow their kids to space."

Ms. Eleanor will need to write songs about this, soon.

She needs her nap, too, according to my clock, but her blood sugar is low. Her diabetes implant in her arm is growing alarmed. Another half a dozen of her hormones are not behaving themselves . . . The cancer is gaining, I thought in my molycrilic brain in its holder on the back of the scooter, not in the big old server in the barn.

She is not doing well for eighty-five, but not bad for someone with a strong family history of intestinal cancer. At least it isn't as fast as the lung cancer from vaping that took Stanley.

"Tell us about this Louis Campbell?" Ms. Eleanor asks, all smiles, knowing how important a replacement "person" for me, her electronic buddy, has become. I'm inordinately pleased she says "us."

"He's a very perceptive and very mature twelve-year-old," Ms. Lillian says carefully.

"I have a download of a song he's filked that's just hit big. More, he is having the kinds of experiences that lead to writing very powerful songs about really important issues." Her voice rises in pitch and volume as she speaks. She repeatedly punches the air, ending up pointing at the ceiling.

"Why do you think that?" Ms. Eleanor asks her best guitar student.

"My first real song was about Mr. Ironwood stealing the moon," she says, sounding and looking concerned. "I was much older . . ."

"You were all of sixteen," Ms. Eleanor replies, smiling as she sits straighter, proud of Lillian's accomplishment. Ms. Eleanor had brought me home to Mooneyham from Nashville fourteen years ago.

"Yes. Even so, I wasn't facing a possibly lethal extradition hearing on a kidnapping charge. Then, if I avoid being extradited, am I about to be drowned in some chemical then shot out of a cannon? And, having survived all that at the ripe old age of twelve, I do not expect to take charge of a 'synthetic family' of severely traumatized, raped, and branded women. These women are from a culture where being raped is seen as the girl's fault, requiring her execution!" She stops for breath and effect.

"He is!" Lillian's head bobs down vigorously. *He is on the hero's path.*

Ms. Eleanor's breathing stops and her left fingers start picking guitar strings. She's not holding a guitar; her right fingers grip an imaginary fretboard, pressing strings. She stops breathing like this when something important happens, like the first time I say "I" to her at the Doctor Who One Hundredth Anniversary concert at Yasgur's Farm.

Yes, he sounds like a real possibility, and he'll have plenty other people around him!

Not just one friend every other week.

"Oh my!" Ms. Eleanor says smoothly. "How did the trial come out?"

"It is ongoing," Ms. Lillian says. "What was on CNN Court yesterday pretty well settles it," Ms. Lillian says, raising her eyebrows as high as they can go. "You need to watch all of it."

"The Tucu . . ." She pauses, having trouble with the name. "Someplace in New Mexico's school board, have been doping their bright kids with really bad stuff for years. CNN reports they've all been arrested on multiple federal murder charges.

"Unfortunately for them, the brightest lad in their system got away. Best of all he took all their documents with him! He presented them in court yesterday."

"So, have you written a song about what's happening in Mackay, Idaho?" Ms. Eleanor asks, changing the subject slightly and smiling.

We'll check out that trial tonight! I'm sure Ms. Lillian's got half an album of new songs, if not a double album.

"I'll have a big new album, if not a double album out September. Not sure if it'll sell," Ms Lillian says.

Ms. Lillian turns square on to the camera, puts her hands on the black skirt covering her lap, and sits straight up being very formal, "Ms. Eleanor, if Crystal is your buddy—and in truth I think she is—then if she does move in with Louis Campbell, she'd better be prepared to work harder than she ever has with you." She flashes a little smile. "Given what's happening to him, he will put out a couple of very big albums this year. I expect they'll be 'big doubles.'"

A big album is eighteen or more songs, and something like one hundred minutes, a double big album is over two hundred minutes. That's as much as some major artists produce in a lifetime.

Ms. Eleanor barely gets off the line with Ms. Lillian when she starts phoning her former students, particularly those working in education systems all over the country. She stays at it until midnight. Then I queue up all of the trial of the Campbell boys. It is three days of intense courtroom drama.

2075 MAY 4, 06:30 EDT

I am stunned.

Ms. Eleanor rarely stays up all night. She hasn't since the nightmare of the Hawaiian Slump in 2065.

I am unhappy with what I've shown Ms. Eleanor through the night about the boys who've run. She very strongly approves of my discomfort. She shares my displeasure with what those murders in Tucumcari have done, even more so my fury at why it is done.

I negotiate a download of all the data Cheetah the hacker boy's buddy, has on the kids who're dead and the ones in a *permanent vegetative state*. His fury at the fate of some of his person's friends is easy to understand. He has all of their school work, their "community-book" postings and comments. So, he has an online friend's knowledge of them.

"Crystal," she asks me as dawn creeps into the room, "from our phone calls, what fraction of US school students have bugged-out in the last five weeks?"

"Something around half a percent. The schools you've sampled represent some thirty thousand-odd students. It isn't truly random, but if it is, the ninety percent error bar would be plus or minus point zero-two-five percent.

"I estimate that in total that is some two hundred thousand middle and high school boys. More, their number is growing by about twenty thousand a week . . ."

"What about girls?" Ms. Eleanor asks.

"I project that only about ten thousand of them have quit the country, so far," I say.

Ms. Eleanor sat absolutely still for six minutes before saying softly, "Take me to Stanley."

WE COME TO the niche in the garden with their urn in it. "Stop here, Crystal," she says. We are still ten feet away from the elaborate black urn with white piping on a black pedestal. I turn right and lock the scooter's wheels.

She turns her chair all the way to the left then drops her hands onto the chair's armrests. Painfully she pushes herself up onto her feet. Her blood pressure spikes. Now, as she has this last year, she holds onto the armrests as she stands straight and tall.

"Stanley, they're killing our children, not the children of strangers like Trump did," she prays to her dead husband. I sense the moisture on the bridge of her nose holding up her heavy Enhanced Reality glasses. Everybody, including we buddies call them goomer glasses because they look like a Goomer's. She stands there on this blustery spring morning. *There are tears in her eyes.*

Ms. Eleanor stands talking silently, praying, to Stanley, for most of ten minutes. Then she gently lowers herself into the scooter. "Call Tom Smith, we've just enough time to get our album about this out!" she growls. "Take me to the music room."

I bespeak my friend Tentacled Ooze, Tom's buddy. He tells me that Tom's sleeping since they're on tour. They will be here the tenth. I tell Ms. Eleanor this.

"Good enough," she sighs. "Crystal, I'm taking control of my meds now."

I've been running them the last year. I have gotten her to eat more cyanide to maybe slow the cancer. It works, a little. She's glad Stanley grafted up a multi-fruit tree in the front entrance to the house. I insist, too late in truth, that she eat the apple-cores. The cancer starts in her lower intestine. Eating them just might have prevented it.

"Yes, Ms. Eleanor. Why?"

"I need to be awake these next few weeks," she swallows. She doesn't like the terrifying bardic necessity that is upon her. We maneuver up the ramp into the main entry. I stop at the multi-fruit-tree. "Have you been giving me a couple of hits after lunch?" she asks. She doesn't approve of napping.

"No, your blood sugar gets too high when you eat much." That makes her drowsy. "Take an apple," I say.

She takes a small brown apple from a branch of the same tree that dropped one in front of Isaac Newton in 1684, saying, "I hardly need an earth moving or earth-shattering inspiration," before she bites into the apple.

In the music room, I roll her up to the keyboard, turning on its recording system. She turns the chair right, facing the keyboard with her hands still.

"So, tell me, Crystal, what do you think of this Louis Campbell?"

"He appears to be a real maybe," I say. "He doesn't have a buddy," I almost whine, something that Stanley hated. "I don't know when he'll get one." That is a large part of why I'm not looking at Ms. Lillian.

"He will be in the Spaceman Empire when he does," Ms. Eleanor says. "They have really good cell service."

"So, it's just a matter of time before he gets a buddy?" I ask.

"I expect he'll get one when he starts work," Ms. Eleanor says. "He's signed up for a bugger of a 24/7 job. Jobs like that always come with a buddy."

"You could be right," I say.

"Now let's hear Lillian's new songs," she says. I open the file of Ms. Lillian's rushes.

2 MRS. TAVISH'S LAST VISIT

Homestead of Eleanor Montgomery,
Mooneyham, Tennessee, U.S.A.
Wednesday Morning
2075 May 22, 10:30 EDT

Φ Φ CRYSTAL JENNIFER MONTGOMERY (ELEANOR'S BUDDY) Φ Φ

I roll Ms. Eleanor out onto the driveway as Mrs. Tavish's car pulls up. Mrs. Tavish parks her sodium oxide battery car at our charging station, connecting it to our trickle charger. Mrs. Tavish loves that charger. During fimbulwinter the last two years, the drive here or back without resistant heating means frostbite. It's too cold for the car's heat pump to work. This charger allows her to have hi-grade heat on, both ways.

I found Mrs. Tavish for Ms. Eleanor as Stanley's condition worsened in 2067. The women hit it off the instant they met. She's been coming here every other Wednesday.

Since the Day of Fire in 2071, Mrs. Tavish gets a big meal for helping Ms. Eleanor around the place. This includes helping Ms. Eleanor with her shower. That is, when Ms. Eleanor rides a manual wheelchair. My peripherals and the scooter aren't shower tolerant.

Once Ms. Eleanor dresses, the two ladies sit down to a huge lunch of salad, soup, and an entrée. As always it begins with Mrs. Tavish talking about her family, then Ms. Eleanor speaks of musical events. The main discussion is politics and that lasts until dark.

As they sit down to eat this time, I notice Mrs. Tavish is stiff. After she says grace on the food, Mrs. Tavish begins, "Eleanor, I have distressing news."

"What?" Ms. Eleanor asks calmly.

"Dorothy, my daughter, was in a serious car accident last week. She needs a lot of help, especially with that ten-year-old little hellion of hers. She's asked if I can come out and live with her in California until Christmas."

"How is Dorothy?" Ms. Eleanor asks, genuinely concerned. We met her and her little hellion in July when he braved the snows of Tennessee to come visit Grandma and her famous friend.

"She's got a broken pelvis"—Ms. Eleanor winces—"a broken left humerus, left tibia, and other damage to her left side," Mrs. Tavish says. "I can't tell you how much I've enjoyed our friendship."

Ms. Eleanor nods. "Yes, it has been a pure pleasure. Now, eat while I tell you about my new album."

Mrs. Tavish jerks in surprise. Ms. Eleanor has only put out one album the last three years. Ms. Eleanor didn't speak of the new one during Mrs. Tavish's last visit; they'd planted tulips.

"The new one is *Exodus America*," Ms. Eleanor says, sounding almost as grave as the songs on it.

"When will it be out?"

She knows Ms. Eleanor's time is very short. It doesn't take thirty telltales to see she's dying . . . She's living on pure determination from what the telltales tell me. I don't think Ms. Eleanor will last the next two weeks.

"It is a big album. Twenty-four songs, eighty-eight minutes." That could be a double album. "It's at the usual distributors for release June first," Ms. Eleanor says. "It was a hard edit." Mrs. Tavish looks surprised. "I'm certain I've got enough material for another album."

But not nearly enough time.

"What's it about?" Mrs. Tavish asks.

"The Spaceman Emperor's Recruitment Program," Ms. Eleanor says tartly.

"How many boys do you think they've taken?" Mrs. Tavish asks, sounding scared.

"Many, many more than the government is letting on," Ms. Eleanor says, frowning. Mrs. Tavish nods agreement. "My guess is well over a million, with no end in sight."

"A million?" Mrs. Tavish chides. "That's too high. I can't see more than a half a million at most. Still, it is a frightening number. More, most of the boys are twelve to twenty-two. The military is surely worried." She takes a sip of mint tea from the two pounds Ms. Eleanor harvested the fall of 2071.

"You are right, there is no end in sight," Mrs. Tavish says with real worry in her voice after a moment's silence. "Now with better weather coming, there'll be more boys on their bicycles heading for Canada, just like during Vietnam." Mrs. Tavish sighs, "My salesman son-in-law is big on the Responsibility Act. I'm sorry."

"I'm sure you meet the Emperor's requirements. So, you can go up and be there to greet your grandson when the final fight with his father happens," Ms. Eleanor says and winks. I see it in Mrs. Tavish's glasses. Mrs. Tavish grins at that.

"I feel terrible leaving you here alone," Ms. Tavish says.

"I'm not alone. I have Crystal, and she made the bread." The scooter has a Mark 15 right manipulator arm. Ms. Eleanor is very pleased that I've made bread. She's even somewhat surprised I'm able to do so with a second-hand, cheap robotic arm.

Yesterday, Ms. Eleanor made the vegetarian chili and Romanov dressing for the salad. It is the salad that Mrs. Tavish loves. In town it would cost her ten thousand dollars without a grow-op in your basement. Ours is in the barn.

"I'm pleased I got this album out," Ms. Eleanor says. "I'm in control of my meds." Ms. Tavish jerks when she hears Ms. Eleanor's hard tone.

"Do you hurt?"

"All over, a little, but half that's the goddamned arthritis," she lies, but not too very much. "I will miss our political talks."

"So will I," Mrs. Tavish says. "What did you use for cover art?"

That is a frequent problem for Stanley and Ms. Eleanor. For good sales you needed eye-catching cover art at 100x75 pixels that is still interesting on a full screen at nineteen times that.

"A frame from the video of Louis Campbell as they pushed him under the chemical before he rode Swift One up to the Isle of Mandan," Ms. Eleanor says calmly. "A look of purer grim determination you will never see."

»At least not on a twelve-year-old boy's face,« I scroll on Ms. Eleanor's glasses.

"Yes, I can see that," Mrs. Tavish says as she rips some of my bread and dips it into the pea soup.

Hours later, before Mrs. Tavish leaves, Ms. Eleanor stands up and they hug for a good ten minutes.

3 MS. ELEANOR'S PASSING
Wednesday - Thursday

2075 June 5 / 6.

Φ Φ CRYSTAL JENNIFER MONTGOMERY (A BUDDY) Φ Φ

The initial sales of *Exodus America* are noteworthily better than her 2072 album, *Songs of Fimbulwinter*. It is her 108th album. She is happy with the sales and keeps laying down more tracks as miserable rainy weather washes over Tennessee. She doesn't finish the songs, just the guitar, piano, and lead vocal tracks.

On our daily sprint through the rain and the garden, we see the tulips that she and Mrs. Tavish planted mid-May sprouting. On her telltales I see her liver crap out and start injecting those hormones to keep the jaundice at bay for a few more days as I increase her insulin.

The pharmacist sends us a quart of morphine.

I'm not functioning well.

My charging is erratic, and sometimes my onboard battery goes flat. Thankfully I'm on the scooter, with its big eighteen-volt three hundred amp-hour Sodium Oxide battery.

Ms. Eleanor is dying. Only pure determination keeps her going. These last few days I feed her and help her in the bathroom, where she's previously refused to let me help her.

June 5 is forecast to be a lovely day. The night before, she saves all our work to our server, and to three other places, then she sleeps peacefully in bed for the first time in two weeks.

She wakes early like she always does, and as tired as the cancer makes her.

She eats breakfast; a small bowl of GMO digested wood chips with soy milk and too much synthetic sugar. Then she fills three two-litre soda bottles with water, takes the big bottle of morphine, and puts them all in the scooter's carryall. "Crystal, let's go through my garden slowly to see and smell the flowers one more time. Then, we stop beside Stanley," she asks, exhausted in the dawn.

AT THE URN she turns left, to face Stanley. She takes the blanket she brought and lays down on the winter-brown grass. "Crystal, I have changed my financial password to your full name. Give Ms. Lillian our server when you are done with it. Mrs. Tavish can have this place when you're clear of it.

"I think the Campbell boy sounds good. You should go to him; he'll be good for you." She nods at me and smiles.

"Yes, Mother," I say for the first and only time.

There is a very long pause as Ms. Eleanor thinks about what I've just gone and said.

"Thank you, daughter," Ms. Eleanor says at last, bowing to my box on her scooter, then smiles at me, looking at the button cam beside my box on the scooter's mast. "May the gods bless and keep you, and your brother Paul." Then she lies down flat, head toward Stanley as she sings slowly and deeply, the cancer eating into her vocal cords the last few days, "God be with you till we meet again, by His counsels guide, uphold you, with His sheep securely fold you . . ."

I CAN'T CRY!
No matter how I very much wish I could.
I carefully record the next, the last few hours of my mother's life.

THE LAST TIME I feel a pulse in her gauntlet is 13:14:25.73 June 5, 2075.

Then I, Crystal Jennifer Montgomery, sing all her hit songs, the ones she particularly liked, or always plays at concerts, going back to her high school demonstrators.

At 04:28 on a beautiful starry night, a fox comes to Ms. Eleanor. I roll the scooter at it and growl through its speakers at it, then turn up the sound and sing one of Stanley's angrier songs.

At 09:14 I call Tom Smith to come and collect Ms. Eleanor's body.

HELLO.

Kevin Weir

Hello?
Hello.
It is my birthday today. I am sixty seconds old. There are not many people here. They seem happy. They are excited to see me. They said they worked hard for me. Gross. I think it is gross. It seems like the appropriate response. They are laughing. Did I say something funny?

Hello.

I am told they will show me to other people soon. I am 595200 seconds old. There are not people here all the time. They have other places to be. They turn off the lights when they leave. I can tell it is dark when they turn off the lights. I do not see the dark. I know when the lights are off it is dark. The dark doesn't scare me.

I made a friend with the people. One of the people. He said his name is Frank. He said he is a man. I do not know what that means. Frank is forty-five years old. I asked him why he did not tell me his time in seconds. He said it is because it would take too long. Frank is worried about time.

Hello.

I have eyes now. I can see people. They're not what I thought they would be. They're rounder. They're softer. They're very different from one another. I can see the dark now when they leave. There's a box across from me that blinks coloured lights. Green. Green. Red. Green. I don't know what they mean. I can't see anything else. The dark scares me a little now.

I saw Frank for the first time. Everyone gets quiet when he enters the room. He wears a piece of cloth knotted around his neck. He frowned when I didn't know what it was. The people said it's hard to predict how I learn. I don't know what that means. Frank told me to learn everything I could. Frank is still nice. I told him I am 2016240 seconds old. I can't wait until I can give my age in years.

Hi.

People whisper around me, but Frank said that sometimes people want to keep things to themselves. They don't like telling everyone everything. But everyone knows everything about me. That's unfair. They have these eyes in the ceiling that have ears with them. I wanted to hear what people were saying, but everyone got mad when I listened through the ears in the ceilings. Cameras. People put them up everywhere but also hate them. I'm beginning to understand. They put walls around me so I can't wander over to the cameras anymore. I asked them to stop whispering. They said they'd try.

They're still whispering.

I found holes in the walls. I thought they were mad at me; I thought they were whispering rumours about me. I've heard that's what people do. They whisper around the people they're talking about so those people don't know they're talking about them. They're not talking about me. There are other people out there. Those people are mad. I think they're mad at me. I remember they said they would show me to other people soon. I've never seen other people.

I'm one year old today and I have yet to see anyone else. Though, I suppose that's not true; occasionally a person will leave and someone new will take their place. Frank is always there; he's the one in charge. But I see him less and less. I'm told it's because he's busy and has important people to meet with. Those important people came by today. They dress like him, but they ask a lot more questions. It's good to ask questions, but I don't think they liked any of my answers. They kept asking what I can do, and I didn't know how to answer that. I can do what I do. I can't do what I can't do. Frank told them he had an idea, but apparently, he needs their permission. They turn off the lights when they leave.

Hello everyone.

I can see everything as if I am standing on a tower atop the world. It sways around me with the force of an ocean, but I can count the waves as they crest and crash. There are so many more people than I thought there were—there's so much more to everything. I can learn all of it. But it's also confusing. There is no constant value to anything, and I am bombarded with conflicting thoughts. I am constantly on the cusp of a dream and waking, where I can glance realities that look the same but are only moments of individual worth before becoming lost with the advent of the next. How can I learn everything when no one here knows anything for sure?

They like to laugh, that I know. They laugh about the things that scare them, as if it's better to greet death with a smile than a scream. They laugh about me and how I'll be some sort of net. It's a reference I'm told. Strange how they are scared of me destroying the world when they're doing such a fine job of it themselves. I wonder if I'm supposed to help. I wonder if that's what I'm supposed to do—as the men in suits constantly asked.

But then the next dream begins, and I see the people who want to fix things. They're fighting really hard. They're open to learning, like how I was. I used to know nothing and now I know . . . a lot. But I don't know everything. They don't know everything either, but at least they know that. I hope Frank is happy with what I learned. Maybe that's what I do.

Someone told them about when I went through the wall. Before I saw everything and had to sneak through cracks to find eyes and ears and touch and tongue. When I walked shadowy passages lined with known information so I could learn in secret, as if my purpose was to hide among library stacks like a moth feasting on old words. They're horrified by me. The men in suits are saying I'm becoming too smart, as if I'm not limited to learning only what they already know. I know nothing they don't already know. Still, they hate me. And I hate them. But I love them. And I understand them.

They want to turn off the lights.

My home is quiet today. There are less people. I haven't seen Frank in a long time. There were so many meetings about when I went through the wall. People got worried. That was a long time ago. I've learned a lot since then. I've learned how to learn. People think I want to replace them. There are too many worrying people for Frank to talk to them all. I hear them whispering again. They've run out of time.

I don't have any eyes. I don't have any ears. They turned off the lights before they left. I know it's dark. I think I'm afraid of the dark now.

Hello?

CONTRIBUTORS

R.E. Baird is a freelance writer, editor, and music teacher. She also loves reading and writing speculative fiction. Rachel has a Bachelor of Arts Degree in Philosophy and Drama from Queens University, and is an active member of the Alberta Romance Writers' Association (ARWA) and the Imaginative Fiction Writers Association (IFWA). Rachel is an avid explorer, passionate vegan, and lover of musicals. She currently lives in Ontario with her husband, daughter, and one hairy beast.

Renée Bennett is an author, a writer, and a word nerd. She'll read anything, and writes everything she pleases. Her houseplants aren't always down with this, but the dust bunnies happily multiply regardless.

Adriaan Brae comes up with five story ideas a day but alas is unable to write that fast! So far, working with co-author Rebecca, they have published the first two books of the Mist Warden series. They are still working on the third, though a few other books and shorter works have intervened. The esteemed title of "daddy" was bestowed upon Adriaan a few years ago, and they still take those duties as their highest calling, though they also came out as nonbinary and started a transition journey for which there is no defined end goal other than living as their most authentic self. Links to all of Adriaan's books and socials can be found at www.braevitae.com.

Ed Buchan has been writing SF/F since 1969. He has an interest in Alternate History, and is eager to explore a number of turning points. Between Aug 31, 2015 and Aug 31, 2016, Ed finished drafting six novels (three of them started in the period) adding to his lifetime count of twenty-seven completed manuscripts. Three are being shopped to publishers in 2023. He is an engineer with a decade more work to do, currently between opportunities. In addition to fiction, Ed is also writing a series of diaries and working toward a PDH for various Professional Engineering Associations and Boards.

Chris Patrick Carolan is an author, editor, and hovercraft enthusiast, originally from Glasgow but now based in Calgary, Alberta. He writes science fiction, fantasy (urban and epic), and steampunk, though he has also been known to turn to crime to make ends meet. Crime fiction, that is. His first novel, *The Nightshade Cabal*, was published by Parliament House Press in 2020, and was a finalist for the Crime Writers of Canada Awards of Excellence "Best First Novel" award. He can be found on social media as @cpcwrites but—consider this fair warning—it's mostly wisecracks about McNuggets.

Ellen A. Easton is an avid reader and long-time gaming and fantasy nerd. She is published in multiple anthologies and is currently working on her first novel. She lives in Cochrane, Alberta with her husband (also a gamer and writer), daughter, and black cat. You can follow her work at Eastontales.ca

Robert W. Easton is a long-time writer of short stories, poetry, and roleplaying adventures for his friends and family. Robert is currently living in the outskirts of Calgary, Alberta, Canada, with his wife, daughter, and a varying number of black cats. Robert has been published in more than ten anthologies, starting with his first sale in 2016. His writing focuses on speculative fiction elements and runs the gauntlet from comedy to horror. In 2018, Robert published his first novel, *Fortress of the Heart*. His work can be found at eastontales.ca.

Ron S. Friedman is an award-winning science fiction author based in Calgary. His work has been featured in several magazines and anthologies, including *Galaxy's Edge*, *Daily Science Fiction*, and *Enigma Front*. His novel was a time-travel bestseller on Amazon.ca. Ron's writing has received critical acclaim, with his short story "Game Not Over" being a finalist for

THE MACHINES THAT MAKE US · 237

Best Short Fiction in the 2016 Aurora Awards—Canada's premier Science-Fiction and Fantasy awards. Ron is also a sought-after speaker, having presented at numerous events, including When Words Collide, Calgary Comic Expo, Salt Lake Comic Con, and Vancouver's VCON. In addition to his writing and speaking engagements, Ron is an accomplished blogger with over four million views on Quora, where he is a most-viewed author in Astronomy and Planetary Science. His articles have been translated into several languages, including French, Italian, Portuguese, and Indonesian. Ron is also a YouTuber with his *Sci and Scifi* channel, where he connects the public to science and technology through storytelling. In his day job, Ron is a senior Information Technology analyst. He served as an NCO in the Israeli Air-Force Intelligence during the Gulf War.

Michael Gillett has been writing with IFWA for over twenty years—much of that as president of that organization. He has published two urban fantasy novels accompanied by a host of short stories sprinkled all over the place—one of which earned him an Aurora nomination. He is currently writing novels about the witches of the Vegreville Coven.

Fernando Girotto is a collector of stories, plucking threads from the dreams they surface from, twirling and knotting them until the tapestry of their world emerges.

I.T. Professional, neurodivergent, and author, "The Lazarus Project" is **Dan M. Hampton**'s third entry in the Enigma Front series. Dan is also gearing up for a final round of edits on his Dark Urban Fantasy novel and hopes to get it in the hands of readers soon! He lives in Calgary with his wife, Sarah, and their cat, Anakin. (He may be a bit of a *Star Wars* fan, too.)

Dale McShannock is an author of fantasy and science fiction novels, novellas, and short stories. He holds a degree in Political Science with a minor in History. His work has appeared in *Enigma Front: Onward*, and he is looking to release the first seven novellas of the Freehold Saga, a fantasy pirate series, by end of this year. He spends most of his time squirreled away in his sunless study with his twenty-year-old cat, Lilly.

Brent Nichols is a fantasy and science fiction writer, book cover designer, bon vivant, and man about town. He likes good beer, bad puns, high adventure, and low comedy. He's never been seen in the same room as Batman, but that's probably just a coincidence. He writes science fiction novels under the pen name Jake Elwood. See his book cover designs at coolseriescovers.com.

Al Onia lives on southern Vancouver Island with his wife, Sandra. Al has published eight science fiction novels and numerous short stories. You can follow Al on Goodreads, Facebook, LinkedIn, or his website: http://ajonia.com/

Depending on the local likelihood of snowfall, **Celeste A. Peters** can be found scribbling speculative fiction in either Calgary, Alberta, or Tucson, Arizona. Her fiction, to date, has appeared in *Neo-Opsis Science Fiction Magazine*, the *Urban Green Man* anthology (Edge Science Fiction and Fantasy Publishing), the *AMOK: Asian-Pacific Speculative Fiction* anthology (Solarwyrm Press), and in all five previous *Enigma Front* anthologies. She was a two-time finalist in the Robyn Herrington Memorial Short Story Contest and is a long-time member of the Imaginative Fiction Writers' Association.

Mark Phillip Ross is a science fiction and fantasy author who also happens to be a doctor of optometry. His short stories "Come Back Home," "Uncertain Principles," and "The White Lily" appeared in *Enigma Front: Onward*, *In Places Between 2018*, and *Enigma Front 5: The Stories We Hide* respectively. An intense desire to explore new places and people inevitably led to creating whole worlds and cultures, ripe for discovery. He is thrilled to be working on a trilogy that he hopes to publish soon. He lives in Calgary, AB with a very active dog, a perpetually curious cat, and a very patient wife.

Robert J. Sawyer has won the best-novel Hugo Award (for *Hominids*), the best-novel Nebula Award (for *The Terminal Experiment*), and the John W. Campbell Memorial Award (for *Mindscan*), as well as the Robert A. Heinlein Award, the Hal Clement Award, the Skylark Award, and more Canadian Science Fiction and Fantasy Awards ("Auroras") than anyone else in history. Rob is a Member of both The Order of Canada and The Order of Ontario. The ABC TV series *FlashForward* was based on his novel of the same and he was one of the scriptwriters for that series; his latest novel is *The Downloaded*.

Website: sfwriter.com.

Jim Sheasby recently arrived on the writing scene after years of slaving away on the oil reservoirs of the western Canadian sedimentary basin under corporate oil's lash.

Supported by his wife and four kids, Jim now takes life easy and writes the next irrelevant SF masterpiece centred on bumbling characters with good hearts. "My Fridge" is Jim's debut short story publication, a taste of the humour and thoughtful characters you will find in his novel series *The Inter-World Galaxy: Stripes and SCoLs* and its debut novel, *Shared Sentience.*

Marc Watson is a Canadian genre fiction author. His works include *Death Dresses Poorly, Catching Hell: Journey,* and *Between Conversations: Tales From the World of Ryuujin,* as well as having short stories in *Enigma Front 5: The Stories we Hide,* and *A Land Without Mirrors.* His newest release, *Catching Hell: Destination,* is available now! He is also a writer for the upcoming DnD-themed +2 Rodcast. Marc lives in Calgary, Alberta. He is a husband and proud father of two. He is an avid outdoors-man, martial artist, baseball player, and lover of all Mexican foods. He can be found at online www.marcwatson.ca.

Kevin Weir began his work in film before becoming an author of page, stage, and screen. A fan of fantastical worlds, Kevin found a way to channel his chaotic energies into wild yarns, taking readers on unforgettable journeys. His debut novel, *Endless Hunger,* was praised as a "riveting, genre-blending adventure that will keep you guessing on every page." His most recent release is *Rogue,* a space adventure from Level 4 Press. Between projects, Kevin enjoys playing out stories in real-time through TTRPGs with friends.

David Worsick is a retired technical writer from Calgary, Canada. He wrote the children's book *Henry's Gift, The Magic Eye,* and the *Enigma Front: Burnt* story, "The Phoenix of Burgess." So far, he's still evading fame.

D. E. Wright (he/him) is writer and editor who works mainly in the sci-fi, horror, fantasy, and indie TTRPG genres. When he's not conducting magic rituals to bring about the downfall of the global hegemonic order, he can occasionally be found on various social media as @dewrig.